Stage Blood

A Sean Maston Mystery

by

Bret Jones

For information, email **Cozy Cat Press**, cozycatpress@aol.com or visit our website at: www.cozycatpress.com

COZY CAT
P R E S S

ISBN: 978-1-946063-26-7

Printed in the United States of America

Cover design by Paula Ellenberger
www.paulaellenberger.com

1 2 3 4 5 6 7 8 9 10

To Dilley and Robert

Chapter One

The thunderous applause exploded and rippled from the back of the auditorium up to the front. People sprang to their feet and pounded their hands together in one bombastic rhythm of sound. A few of the overwhelmed audience members whistled and some even hollered as the cast came to the lip of the stage and took their bows. The leading actress got the final bow and dipped low in the bright spotlight. Another wave of hand clapping shot through the audience and anyone remaining in their seats stood and saluted the lead. She took three deep bows by herself and blew kisses to the crowd.

When the applause finally subsided and the lights came up, the cast split into two groups and left the stage.

"What a piece of crap!" Tony Tarver yelled at the top of his lungs. He jerked hard on his fake nose and threw it across the dressing room area at the rear of the theatre.

"Calm down," Sean Maston said. "It's only community theatre, dude." He pulled a velvet hat off of his head and threw it in the dressing room that he shared with Tony.

"I didn't come back here, Sean, to do crap night after night!" Tony shouted. He grabbed a baby wipe and handed one to Sean. He scrubbed the make up on his face until it disappeared. Sean followed suit.

"I'm just saying that there are other places to talk about this, that's all," Sean added.

The rest of the cast funneled through the backstage area and most were congratulating each other. The leading actress, Marie Winters—called Taffy behind her back—swept into the make up room and grabbed some cream to clean her face.

"Great show again, Marie," a young girl said. She grabbed for the cream and Marie pulled it away from her.

"I'm not finished yet," she said. "There's some more around here somewhere."

"Oh. All right." And the girl left in search of more cold cream.

Other faces popped in and told Marie how great the show had been. She thanked them all and said it had indeed been a good show. The director flew into the room and hugged Marie and kissed her on the cheek.

"You were marvelous," he said.

"Thanks, Mike," she said. "It was a great night out there."

"They loved you! Absolutely loved you!" he said. Mike Shaw had directed community theatre shows for over twenty years and had eighty plays under his directorial belt.

"They loved what you did with it, Mike, really," Marie purred. She hugged him again and kissed him lightly on the mouth. He blushed visibly and left the room.

Just outside, Tony and Sean peeled costumes off and threw them on the floor. Mike walked over to them and snarled.

"Costumes don't go on the floor, guys," he said. "Pick them up and get them to Jo Ann so we can get them washed.

"The show's over, Mike," Tony said. "They'll get there and get washed. Don't worry about it."

Mike punched his hands on his hips and glared at Tony. "Why is it that every time I said or did something on this show you contradicted me, Tony? Can you tell me that?"

Sean stepped back out of the line of fire and pulled his tunic off.

Wiping some make up from his brow, Tony flung another piece of his costume on the floor. "I haven't, Mike. Not every time."

"They gave a standing ovation out there."

"They don't know any better," Tony retorted.

"Remember I've been doing this longer than you have, Tony. This is the eightieth show that I've directed."

"For community theatre," Tony reminded him.

"Then what are you doing here? I thought you were out in Hollywood," Mike said, knowing Tony hated to have his failures of not making it out west brought to his attention.

"I came back here to do good theatre, Mike. That's why I'm here."

"And you did."

"Okay," Tony said reluctantly. "I have an M.F.A. in directing and I have a pretty good idea what makes a good show, Mike."

"I'm sure you do. You tell everyone when you get the chance." Mike walked away in a huff. "Just get those costumes to Jo Ann," he said over his shoulder.

"Jerk," Tony whispered.

Sean put a hand on his shoulder. "You two need to quit doing that, you know."

"He's an idiot."

"Everyone knows that. Everybody knows how you feel about it, too," Sean chided. "The show's over. Let's just get cleaned up and get out of here and get ready for the next one."

Tony took off his shoes and piled them up with the rest of his costume. He kicked the mound playfully as if to mock Mike. "I'm Mike Shaw and I've directed eighty shows. I'm the king of community theatre!" Tony yelled.

Marie stuck her head out of the make up room. "That's not funny, Tony. Show some respect."

"I will to those who deserve it, Marie." She flicked her fingers under her chin at him and disappeared back into the make up room. "Taffy," he said quietly.

"We've got to get you out of here, man. This place is getting to you," Sean said.

"I can't wait 'til *Death of a Salesman* tryouts. I am so Willy Loman," Tony bragged.

"Are you sure about that? Aren't you a bit young?" Sean asked. He wanted to tryout for the play, too, but didn't count on a major role. It didn't matter, though. He liked being a part of the community theatre in Lyle and on its board of directors. He would do whatever needed to be done for the shows that they produced.

"Young? Are you kidding me? It's called make up if I have to use any. I can scrunch my face if I have to," Tony joked. "And, really, who else here can play the role?"

Sean ignored his arrogance and shrugged his shoulders. "Oh, I don't know; how about Lynn?"

"You're kidding me, right? He's a good character actor, but Willy Loman? No way. And he's the assistant director."

"Since when has that stopped anyone around here?" Sean reminded him.

"And you think you can play him?" Marie said, having overheard the conversation.

"Private discussion over here, Marie," Tony said. "Not for your ears."

Marie stepped up into his face. "Then maybe you shouldn't broadcast it for the entire cast to hear." She spun on her heels and walked away.

"Somebody ought to run her over with a truck," Tony mumbled to himself.

"She's not that bad," Sean said.

Tony dropped his pants and piled them up with the other clothes. Some of the younger people in the cast blushed and ran for their own dressing rooms as he did so. He laughed hysterically and pulled his undershirt off. Sean frowned at him, but he ignored it.

"None of these runts would've lasted at grad school," Tony said.

"It's community theatre, Tony, in the little town of Lyle," Sean reminded him.

"I know that. In the piney woods of Oklahoma, to boot, too," Tony added. "Back east in school they would've left this piece of crap at intermission. Before intermission."

"What piece of crap?" a new voice said from one of the dressing rooms.

"This piece of crap," Tony repeated. "The one we just got a standing-o for."

"Yeah. Pretty wild, huh?" the voice said.

"That's right, Lynn. This town wouldn't know the difference between good and bad theatre if it came and bit them on the butt. And they wouldn't know that Taffy was up there milking it for all it was worth. And they also wouldn't know that she wouldn't make it anywhere else but here in nowhere-ville."

Lynn stuck his head out of his dressing room and smiled big. "Yet you're here."

"Not you, too. Oh, man!" Tony flung a shoe at Lynn playfully and they shared a laugh.

Sean put on his pants and laced up his shoes. The show tired him out and he thanked his lucky stars above that it was now finally over. The strain on everyone had been overwhelming. There had been fights and arguments over the littlest things and Sean had tried his best to keep the peace with everyone involved. Tony had returned back to Lyle only a few months before and had been a thorn in the side of the community theatre in the town. He had tried his very best to flex his theatrical muscles that had been ignored out in Hollywood.

Years ago Sean and Tony and some other folks involved in the community theatre in town had been at school together at the local college. They had gotten degrees in theatre and had done some pretty good work in those days. Sean had stayed in the area and gotten work at the local radio station and then later at a computer company doing PR work. Tony left to pursue his dream out west via a grad school out east. He got his M.F.A. in drama and flew to the coast and immediately planned to be the next Spielberg.

It didn't work out that way so he returned back to Lyle to find the happiness that had been denied him.

Sean took a deep breath and finished tying his shoes. He counted Tony as a close friend, but knew that he chafed others with his abrasive personality. Sean usually played the peacemaker for Tony and tried to keep everyone else from knocking his teeth out.

Lynn poked his head out again. "Listen, T.T., the show was a big hit with the audience and the theatre made some money. That's what counts."

Tony scoffed at that. "Now you're sounding like Taffy and Mike at the board meetings. There is a difference between doing a good show and doing crap."

"And yet they stood up when they applauded," Lynn said as he pulled his shirt over his head. "Let it go and get ready for the next one."

"Consider it done." Tony pulled on a pair of jeans and buttoned the fly. He slapped Sean on the back and exited into the dressing room.

"He's so critical of Mike and Marie," Lynn said.

"He refuses to understand how a community theatre works. Or, at least around here, anyway," Sean said. He grabbed his mug of soda and slurped through the straw. The ice had melted and had watered it down, but at least it was wet. Doing the show made him parched.

"Maybe he'll get along better with Darin on *Death*," Lynn said. He pulled his shoes on quickly and pulled the Velcro tight across the tongue. "Some of the others are beginning to wonder if he'll fit in around here."

"They aren't the only ones," muttered Sean. He drank again from his cup. "It'll all be fine around here. It always is."

"True enough, I guess. You guys going anywhere?"

"I think Darin and some of the others wanted to grab something to eat down at MoMo's."

"Good. I'll meet you down there," Lynn said. He grabbed a bag stuffed to the brim, and exited through the back door of the theatre.

"Mr. Maston, darling, you were ravishing out there this evening," a mocking voice rang from the back of the stage. Sean recognized Darin's signature growl even when he tried to disguise it.

"Thank you, love," Sean threw back.

"I love you, I love you, have my children, you swine!" exclaimed Tony from his dressing room.

"Oh, is that T.T. in there?" Darin asked.

"Yeah. Hey, Darin, when are tryouts next Tuesday again?" Sean asked, needing to be reminded. He could lock away trivial facts and figures, but couldn't recall dates and times of events too well.

"Eight o'clock. You going to be there?" Darin asked.

Tony pranced out of the dressing room and took a bow. "Of course he is. As will I. I'm going to show you a Willy Loman that will boggle the mind."

Darin laughed at Tony and punched him playfully on the arm. "I'm sure. But isn't that called brown-nosing the director."

"Not at all. Just being honest. As director for the next show, you need to know what kind of talent will be there," Tony added. "And you will be amazed." He bowed again and exited through the back door.

"I'm sure he'll do just jim-dandy," Darin said with a wink to Sean. "Ready?"

"Let's go. I'm ready for one of MoMo's chicken-fried steaks with extra gravy." He rubbed his tummy and followed Darin out the back door into the cool Oklahoma night.

MoMo's stayed open late, especially on show nights because it brought in much-needed business and the owner, Sara Black, was on the theater's board of directors.

"Hey, you," she said as Darin entered. She kissed him on the mouth and gave him a hug. "I heard it went great tonight."

"From who?" Tony asked.

Sara pointed to a table filled with theatre folk in the back of the restaurant. "Marie and the gang."

"She's here?" Darin asked.

"Oh, great," Tony mumbled.

"Of course, she is, guys. She likes to follow you wherever you go," Sara joked. She kissed Darin again with Tony staring at them. Darin broke away and walked around back where the others were.

"Hi, there," Tony said and reached for a hug. Sara returned it reluctantly and gave Sean a high-five.

"It's okay. I won't bite," Tony said, "not anymore, anyway."

"I know that," Sara said. "I just don't want things to be uncomfortable for any of us."

Tony smirked and mockingly placed a hand to his chest. "I shudder at the thought. Just because we were dating for a while and now you and Darin are dating doesn't mean things will be uncomfortable. Promise." He grabbed her and kissed her on the cheek and then departed for the rear of the restaurant.

Sean shrugged his shoulders and patted her on the back. "Life in the community theatre, huh?" he said. "Never a dull moment."

"You got that right," she said. "Chicken-fried steak, Sean?"

He pressed his fingertips to his forehead. "You read my mind. How do you do that?" She playfully pulled at his nose and left for the kitchen.

"Be out in a minute," she said.

Sean thanked her and wove through the tangle of chairs and tables to the back of the restaurant. A crowd of community theatre folk had gathered. Word had spread like a wild forest fire. Lynn, Marie, Darin, Tony, and Mike sat in a row against the wall with a half dozen or so of the others from the cast scattered around the banquet table. Lynn and Tony were in a heated discussion about all things theatre and Darin and Mike whispered in low tones about the budget for Darin's production of *Death*. Marie sipped from some kind of spritzer and waved for Sean to sit down.

"And what part do you think you'll get in this extravaganza?" she asked him as he sat in his seat across from her.

"Any that I can get," he said. He grabbed for a straw and tore the top off of the paper wrapping.

"How do you think I'd do as Linda Loman?" she asked. "I've really been thinking about trying out."

Sean dodged the bullet by saying: "You better talk to the director about that."

"I don't have to worry about him," she purred. She threaded her arm through Darin's and blew in his ear. "Isn't that right?" she asked.

Darin turned his attention away from Mike and glared at her. "What do you want, Marie?" The words were simple enough but the acid in them stung even Sean across the table.

Marie pouted and stuck out her lower lip. "Nothing. Never mind."

"Okay," Darin said and went back to his discussion with Mike.

"That's the way we did it back at Cordova, anyway," Tony said loud enough for everyone in the restaurant to hear him.

"Applied cubism to Oscar Wilde? Are you kidding?" Lynn asked.

"Yeah. Think about it. It's really a stroke of genius," Tony said.

"And you thought of it?" Mike asked nonchalantly.

"Me and another directing grad there did," Tony replied. "It was really very cool."

"I'm sure," Marie said, the words biting. Tony gave her a mock smile and continued his deep discussion with Lynn.

Sean blew the paper off the straw at Darin and it bounced off of his forehead. Darin grabbed a piece of ice out of Marie's cup and playfully flung it across the table. It hit Sean in the chest and fell to the floor.

"Hey!" Marie complained. "That's my cup, thank you very much."

"Yes it was. And thank you very much!" Darin said.

She said something under her breath and grabbed a piece of ice and stuck it down his shirt. He instinctively grabbed her wrists and pushed her arms back behind her head. He held them with one hand and poured her drink on her blouse with the other. She screamed and slapped him in the face.

"Jerk!" she yelled.

"Prima donna!" he yelled back and slapped her back across the jaw.

"Hey, hey, hey!" Sean said. He stood up and tried to pull Marie out of there to stop the fight. Darin scooted away from her as she kicked out at him with her boots.

"You better not, Marie!" he warned.

"Make me!"

"Come on, Marie," Sean said. He gently tugged at her sleeve and pulled her from behind the table.

"There's no reason to be juvenile," Mike said. He pushed some of his gray hair out of his eyes with authority in his tone. "Just sit down and quit making a scene."

"Me?" Marie yelped as if she'd been bit by something. "What about him?"

"Both of you!"

"Shut up, Mike. She stuffed ice down my shirt," Darin said.

"And what are you calling people juvenile for, anyway, Mike? That's pot and kettle if you ask me," Marie said.

"Just drop it," Mike warned.

"This isn't the show anymore, Mike. You can turn the directing off," she said. By this time the rest of the cast had turned their full attention to the argument.

"You wouldn't take direction, anyway, Marie," Mike said with a wry smile.

"Okay, now," Lynn said, getting into the fray. "Let's just sit down and try to enjoy the evening here."

"Shove it, Lynn!" Marie yelled at him. "Just because you're some hoity-toity professor at the college doesn't mean you have a clue."

"I just asked you to sit down, Marie. That's all." He said it quite gently to her and tried to get her to sit down. He put a reassuring arm around her for support.

"Oh, bull!" She spun on Tony. "And you can shut up, too, T.T!"

"I don't like being called that. And especially from you, Taffy!"

Sean cleared his throat trying to get their attention, but to no avail. He sat back down and grabbed another straw and tore the top off the paper wrapper.

This is ridiculous, he thought.

If this bunch hangs around with each other much longer, someone's going to die.

And, sadly enough, he was right.

Chapter Two

Tryouts came too soon for Sean. The weekend flew and he wanted a couple more days of off time before he did another community play. But the others depended on him and he really did love it. He gathered up his two dogs, Titan and Weejo, hopped in his Volkswagen bug, and sped off into town for the tryouts.

He knew that the others would be there already. Sara said she would be trying out for this one. She'd stayed out of the musical because of her work at the restaurant, but had eagerly helped out with the PR and selling tickets. Tony would be prepared with acting sides clenched in his fist. Mike, he knew, would stay away and tend to his job as president for the community theatre. Darin and Lynn would breathe a sigh of relief and get down to work on *Death*. Lynn acted as Darin's assistant director on the show and would help corral all the actors during the tryout process.

Sean took the exit off the highway that led into town and turned off on Constance Street. The community theatre had a building at the end of the street across from the Methodist Church.

He parked the bug and let the dogs out to run around the parking lot.

"Stay close, gang," he ordered as he entered the theatre.

Inside, all of his predictions turned out to be true. Sara and Tony were working hard on a scene by themselves getting ready for the tryouts, Darin and Lynn contemplated set changes as they examined the script, and Mike was nowhere to be seen. He also caught a glimpse of Marie primping and preening in front of a mirror in the lobby. He waved at her, but she ignored him.

"Hey, guys," he said as he stepped into the auditorium.

"Ah, our Charlie!" exclaimed Tony from the stage.

"Is he pre-casting this thing?" Sean asked Darin.

Darin nodded and rolled his eyes heavenward. "He's been doing that for the past thirty minutes, man."

"Trying to intimidate everyone else trying out," Lynn remarked.

"That's just Tony," Sean mumbled and grabbed a tryout sheet.

Tony jumped from the stage and gave him a bear hug and slapped him on the back.

"Nice to see you, too," Sean said.

"What's been going on?" Tony asked.

"Work and the rent," Sean stated flatly. "And a dozen other things that keep me busy." He studied the lines in one of the cuttings and took a seat on the front row. A young man named Ron sat next to him. Ron had done a couple of community theatre shows and had turned out some pretty good performances. Sean said hello and got to work on the cuttings from the play.

"Are you going to work on Willy?" Tony asked, looking over his shoulder.

"I'll do whatever at this point. It doesn't really matter to me."

"Ah, sure it does, man," Tony said. He leaned back in his seat and stuck his feet on the back of Sean's chair. "You know it does."

"No, it really doesn't matter, Tony," Sean repeated. It drove him crazy when Tony got smarmy and so self-assured that he knew all there was to know about him. But he could be longsuffering with him knowing that deep down he could be very vulnerable and sensitive to anything someone said or did to him.

"I see our prima donna made it," Tony tried to whisper, but didn't succeed.

"Shut up, T.T.," Marie shot back as she grabbed an acting side and sat down.

Tony huffed hard and blew out a stream of silent obscenities. "I don't like being called that, Marie," he said, reminding her for the thousandth time in recent memory.

Marie giggled childishly and dug into the cutting sheet. Lynn and Darin came down front next to the stage and prepared themselves for the long night of tryouts.

"Okay, gang," Darin began in all seriousness, "most of you know the routine and know how it works."

"And for the rest of you who are new, don't bother," Tony added with cheerful glee. He didn't exactly mean it, but it was his way of intimidating anyone new who might stand in his way of a primo part.

Darin ignored him, but smiled to let him know he'd heard. Darin and Tony fed each other's egos on occasion and everyone knew it. They had made a not-so-secret pact that the following season at the community theatre they would choose a show they wanted to star in and have the other direct them in it. Recently, some of the board members—Darin primarily—chose shows they wanted to play the lead in and directed themselves in it. The people who showed up for tryouts could only hope for a secondary role because the lead had already been taken by its director. There had been some grumbling so the board of directors were encouraged by Mike to not do this anymore. Darin and Tony reluctantly agreed, but had found a convenient way around it for next season.

"Pick a scene and get a partner to read with," Darin instructed, "and state your name and the part you're reading. That way Lynn and I can keep up with what everyone is reading for. Any questions?"

There were none and he left the stage and found a seat near the front. Tony bonded with Sara, dragging her behind him to the lip of the stage. He stepped into the lights they'd turned on for the tryouts and cleared his throat dramatically.

"Anthony Tarver, as you well know, and I'll be reading the part of Willy Loman."

The night flew by for everyone as scene after scene of the tryouts was performed on the stage. A variety of approaches were tried by everyone there, especially the "old guard," which included Marie, Sara, Tony, and Sean. Sean had loved the play since college and felt a strange kinship with the character of Willy. He bellowed and bullied in the cuttings with Linda Loman and shifted to a lost and quiet loner in other scenes from the play. Most of the others took note of his tryout and secretly admired his silent strength as he performed the cuttings.

At the end of the night, the crowd gathered outside for conversation and speculation about the casting. Marie lit up a cigarette and blew smoke rings in front of her face.

"That went pretty well, I think," she said.

"Should be pretty easy casting," Tony remarked. His confidence exuded out of him in waves. "I figure they'll have it done before we leave tonight."

"Boy, I don't know," Sara whispered to herself. "There was a pretty good group in there tonight."

"Agreed," Sean said.

"Where was Heather?" Sara asked. "I thought she was going to be here tonight."

Tony clicked his tongue and rolled his eyes. "Who cares?"

"She had to work tonight. I think she was going to try and set up a special time to try out for the two of them," Marie said.

Tony's face turned red. "Are you kidding? That's not right or even fair."

"For whom?" Sean asked. "Just because you don't get along with her doesn't mean she can't try out for the show, Tony."

"Correction, my friend, I don't like her. There's a big difference between not getting along with someone and not liking them," Tony said.

Marie blew more smoke rings above her head and mumbled something unintelligible under breath.

"What's that, Marie?" Tony asked.

"Nothing."

"It would be."

She flicked her cigarette in his face and he jumped back and tripped over an ashtray canister near the outer wall of the building. He fell flat on his face and groaned. He cursed Marie and pushed himself up off the ground for revenge and restitution.

Marie laughed hysterically and doubled up. "Sorry about that, Tony," she said through chuckles.

Tony cussed ferociously and stepped toward her. Sean grabbed him by the arm and pulled him back. Tony jerked against him, but Sean held him against the wall to calm him down.

"Don't. She didn't mean to make you fall," Sean said.

"She flicked a cigarette in my face!" he yelled.

"Hey, just cool it, Tony," Sara said. She walked over to Marie and whispered something to her.

"Just shut up, Sara!" Tony said.

Sara whirled around and pointed a finger at him. "I'm not around to be bossed, Tony. Not anymore."

Sean pushed Tony away over to his car and ordered him to sit down on the hood and not move. Tony agreed and Sean left him there to stew. Marie and Sara were in a heated discussion over the event and Sean asked for a truce. He begged for one.

"This isn't going to make this theatre work if you guys can't put your differences aside and try to get along," Sean said. He hated conflict and the butterflies were popping up in his stomach.

"What differences? I flicked a cigarette at him, Sean," Marie said, not relenting.

"Did you think of the consequences?" he asked.

She laughed and slapped her hip. "Of course I did!"

"Of course you did," Sara said. "You always do, don't you, Marie?"

"What's that supposed to mean, Sara?"

"Guys," Sean said, trying to interrupt them and failing.

"Just what I said, Taff," Sara spit out. "You try to make everyone around here ticked off about something. You never think of the consequences."

Marie smiled wickedly and stepped closer to Sara. "And you do?" She winked at her and blew a kiss with her lips. "Or should we ask some of the guys around here about that?"

Sara screamed as loud as her lungs would let her and threw a punch at Marie's head. Marie ducked out of the way and ran around the other side of her car. Sean reached for Sara and got her by her shirt as she tried to chase Marie.

"Let it go, Sara," he said to her. Tony came back around with new anger on his lips.

"What'd she do now?" he asked.

"Nothing!" Sara yelled.

"Nothing? He'd be the one to ask, wouldn't he?" Marie said viciously.

Sara fell apart and folded into Sean's arms and cried so hard she gasped for air. He had no idea what had just happened but he held her tight. The tears soaked through his shirt. Whatever nerve Marie had struck hit very deep.

"One day, Marie," Tony said with his fists tightening until his knuckles turned white.

Marie looked on what she'd done in revulsion. She had no idea that Sara would react that way and tried to say so. Sara cried louder and Sean asked for Marie to go somewhere else. She walked away a bit in embarrassment with Tony slinging more curses her way.

The door flung open with Lynn and Darin coming out for a breath of air.

"What's going on?" Darin asked. Sara fell into his arms and let the tears flow. "What is it, baby?"

"Taffy, yet again," Tony said.

Marie shrugged and tried to apologize.

"Oh, just stop it, Taffy," Tony spat at her.

"Quit calling me that, Tony! I've had it with that!" Marie yelled, her own tears starting to flow.

Lynn touched her on the shoulder to reassure her, but it didn't help. She pulled away from him and leaned against the building. He followed closely trying to hold her, but she wouldn't let him.

"Sometimes we just step in it, don't we?" Sean asked to no one in particular. "I think we're all just a bit anxious about casting. That's all." But it wasn't and he knew it. Marie had triggered something in Sara that lay dormant—and with very good reason. Sara continued to cry in Darin's arms.

"And us with good news and bad news," Lynn said. He put his hand on Marie's shoulder and she shrugged it off. "Good news is everybody did a great job. Bad news is we need call backs tomorrow."

"You're kidding?" Tony asked in a huff. "Tomorrow?"

"Yeah," Darin said, "it shouldn't take long."

The others from tryouts had funneled out and received the news. They stood bewildered by Sara and the rest of them with pinched faces and sour attitudes.

"Man, have we been around each other too long, or what?" Sean said quietly and walked around the building to find Titan and Weejo. Tony followed him and helped him whistle for the dogs. They came barreling full speed at Sean and he dug some doggy treats from his pocket and tossed them in the air. Titan snatched it in his jaws and crunched it. Weejo licked hers off the ground and munched it until it was gone.

"I think she's the only person I actually hate," Tony murmured.

"I thought Mike was the thorn in your side," Sean remarked.

Tony nodded vehemently. "Him, too."

Sean petted his dogs and whistled for them to follow him back to his vehicle. Tony followed him, sour at the universe. Sara and Darin stood in front of the theatre in deep discussion. Sara wiped tears away and pointed at where Marie had stood when she'd made her comments. Lynn had disappeared back inside to shut the place up for the evening and some of the others were still milling about the place.

"I take it you know what Marie was jabbing Sara about?" Sean asked. He opened the door to his bug and the dogs piled into the back seat.

"All too well," Tony said. "You got anything to smoke?"

"No, I quit a couple months back."

"Oh, yeah."

"That bad, huh?" Sean asked, sensing his friend's dark mood rising.

"Very much so. I really don't want to talk about it, man. I'll see ya tomorrow night."

"You did a good job tonight, by the way," Sean said in hopes of bringing his spirits up.

"Thanks. I'm not worried about it. The best I can hope for is probably Happy." Tony walked away and entered the theatre. Lynn passed him on his way out and walked over to Darin and Sara. She waved him away so he sauntered over to Sean.

"Man, what a night," Lynn said. "This place is turning into one big soap opera."

"*Waiting for Guffman* on acid, I call it," Sean said. They both laughed at the reference to the Christopher Guest movie that lampooned life in a community theatre.

"I suppose it's something that we're not privy to," Lynn observed. He glanced back over at Darin and Sara. They had walked to her car and he opened the door for her. She got in, started the engine, and drove away. "And probably something we don't want to know."

"Where's Marie?" Darin asked. His face flushed with anger as he stormed over to them at Sean's car. "Where is she?"

"I think she's inside making a phone call," Lynn said. Darin spun on his heel and entered the theatre. "This place," muttered Lynn.

"Maybe we should stick around and make sure nothing happens," Sean said. He shut the dogs in the car and walked back inside the theatre. He heard voices shouting from the theatre's office. "Too late." He and Lynn made sure all the lights were out in the theatre before they went back to the office.

"It's none of your business!" Tony yelled from inside. Darin's voice mumbled. "Or, yours, either, Darin," Tony replied. Darin said something else that they couldn't understand outside the door and then Marie bolted out and left the theatre. Before they could catch up with her, she had hopped in her car and left.

"Just leave me alone about it, man," Tony said as he left the office. "I'll see you guys tomorrow night." He rushed out of the theatre and was gone.

Darin slumped against the wall and bowed his head to the floor. Sean put a hand on his shoulder. "This place is a nuthouse sometimes, you know that?" Darin said.

Sean repeated his *Guffman* joke and they had another laugh. Lynn shut the office up and they left the building. Sean bit his tongue trying not to push too hard as to what had transpired tonight although he really wanted to know. Lynn didn't show the same courtesy.

"What was it all about?" he asked Darin, who only shrugged his shoulders.

"I don't have a clue. Sara won't tell me and Marie certainly wouldn't say anything to me about whatever it is that she claims she knows," Darin said.

"Personal business?" Sean found himself asking.

"I don't know, man," Darin answered back. "All I know is that the girl I care about is very upset. And the person responsible is someone I loathe and would like to see hanging from the nearest tree."

Lynn turned on the outside light and then locked the theatre up for the evening. "Yeah, she can get on your nerves sometimes," he said.

Darin cursed under his breath. "She's the worst thing that's happened to this place." He opened the door to his car and sat down in the driver's seat. He started it and turned the radio onto the local rock station. "The absolute worst," he added.

Some of the other people who had tried out for the play were still congregated at someone's truck so Lynn walked over to talk to them for a while. Sean leaned against Darin's car and tapped his foot to the beat of the song playing on the radio.

"And this play," Darin mumbled.

"Pretty tough to cast, huh?" Sean asked.

"Yeah. I hate callbacks, but Lynn thinks we need them. Too many folks did a good job and we need to see everyone in different scenes before we cast it."

"Hopefully we won't have a repeat of what happened tonight."

"If we could be so lucky," Darin said. "I'll just not cast her, that's all. The more she opens her big fat mouth, the more we'll work to keep her out of shows down here."

"Blackball her?" Sean asked.

"I will," Darin said.

Sean wanted to counter with something about fairness and it being a *community* theatre, but he thought better of it. Darin needed to vent and that's all he was doing. His anger got the best of him and he had to let it out somehow.

"You know, why can't people like her die in a brutal car crash?" He laughed bitterly and spat on the ground.

"You don't mean that," Sean said quietly.

"Yeah, I do. Maybe tomorrow I won't mean it, but right now, yeah, Sean, I really do." He shut the door to his car and rolled the window down. "See ya tomorrow night. You did a good job tonight, by the way."

"Thanks."

Darin put his vehicle into drive and sped away from the theatre. He gunned it as he drove out onto Constance Street and roared off into the night.

"The joys of community theatre," Sean mumbled to himself.

Sean joined Lynn and the others hoping for more entertaining conversation.

Chapter Three

Sean arrived for callbacks and let the dogs out of his bug. They roamed around the parking lot barking at each other and a few passing birds that flew overhead. He played with them some and pitched a few doggy treats at them. Marie and Mike were already there. Sean let himself through the front door of the theatre and heard them talking in the office.

"I just want to see the receipts, Mike, that's all," he heard Marie say. He would feel like an intruder if he walked in, so he did the lesser of two evils and eavesdropped instead.

"Marie, it's all in the books," Mike replied matter-of-factly.

"That's just it, Mike, they're not. None of the board has seen any of the credit card receipts in months, maybe even a year or two. All I'm asking is to see them."

"That shouldn't be too big of a problem," he answered back. Sean knew that wasn't true because he'd been one of the board members who'd been asking to see those receipts.

"Then where are they? Are they here?" Marie asked.

"No," Mike said and laughed quietly. "I think I've got them at home."

"Why?"

"What's that?"

"I asked why, Mike. That seems a pretty odd thing to do, don't you think?"

Mike cleared his throat and shuffled papers around on the desk. "As president of the community theatre, Marie, I do have an obligation to take care of the finances."

"Along with the treasurer and the board," she said.

"Of course them," he said quickly. "I'm not suggesting that I'm doing this solo."

Marie laughed at that. "You could've fooled me, Mike. This place is run by the board and not by one person, but folks in town are getting other ideas."

"I don't see why."

She laughed again. "You know perfectly well why, Mike. And don't get me wrong, either. I appreciate what you do around here. I'm thankful you cast me in the lead of the musical we just did. I even appreciate the glowing review you wrote for us in the paper."

"Wait a minute!" he said, anger building in his voice. "Who said anything about me writing the review in the paper?"

"Oh, come on, you don't think we know? Forget the ethics behind it. We could care less, but some of them are upset about you writing that you were a 'genius' of musical theatre." She laughed again, which made him slam his fist into the table.

"I did not! I don't know who's been saying that about me, but it's not true."

"Everyone's been saying it, Mike. We all know. Too many of those reviews of yours print personal information that only cast members or officers would know. Clara Ann Hillway? Come on, Mike, that's a pretty poor pen name and everyone knows it."

He hit the table again and Sean heard him shove his chair back against the wall. "Shut up about it, Marie. It's not true and you can tell all the wagging tongues that it's not. And you can forget the receipts, too."

"Then we'll present it to the board and see what they do about it," she replied. The room got quiet and Sean heard footsteps slowly move from back behind the desk toward the door where Marie stood.

"I wouldn't if I were you, Marie," Mike said. "That's all I'm saying. Just don't. You'll regret it if you do."

She stood her ground and whispered back to him: "Or, what? What could you possibly do to me? Nothing. And we'll see what the board says. We meet this Saturday morning. We'll find out all about it then."

Sean quickly exited into the darkness of the theatre auditorium and found a place to sit. He heard footsteps rush from the office and out the front door. The theatre rattled as the door slammed in its frame.

Lynn and Darin arrived shortly thereafter and set up the stage for the callbacks. They had prepared other scenes from the play to use and were laying out the play scripts up on the apron of the stage. Sean said hello and grabbed a script. They told him to look over a couple of scenes and get ready. Marie joined them and received her assigned scene.

"I hope this doesn't take long," she said.

"It'll take as long as it takes," Darin answered.

"That's pretty profound, Darin," she said and laughed. She thought the others would join in, but she was mistaken.

"Just study the scene and get ready," Lynn said.

She thumbed through the script and found the right page number. "This one?"

Lynn leaned over her shoulder and pointed at the script. "Yeah, that's the one."

"This is the one with Willy and the slut that he's seeing on the sly," she complained.

"That's the one," Darin said. "Perfect for you."

"Very funny," she threw back at him.

"I wasn't trying to be funny."

"It's a good scene for you to do, Marie," Lynn said in all seriousness. "It's a very good role and an important one." He meant every word, but Marie would hear none of it.

"You're just the assistant on this, Lynn," she said. "And you know as well as I do that the only reason it's done is to insure that you'll get to direct next season."

"Do we always have to fuss and fight around here?" Sean asked, breaking into the conversation. "I mean, come on."

"I'm just tired of us always avoiding the truth about things around here, that's all," she said.

"I wanted you called back for that role because I thought you'd be good in it. And that's all there is to it," Lynn said.

She touched his face and squeezed it until his lips pushed out. "I believe you, Lynn. I really do. And I do appreciate it. It's just that I really doubt your directing abilities on this thing. You need Darin to hold your hand so you'll know what to do next year." She patted him on the face and found a seat to study her lines. Sean thought Lynn would explode, but he merely sighed and sat down on the front row. A sad expression washed over Lynn's face as he stared back at Marie.

The doors opened in the back and Tony swept in through the back of the auditorium. All faces fell a mile as he entered and made his way to the front of the stage. He had come in full costume as Willy Loman, complete with fedora hat, raggedy jacket and tie, and two suitcases. Tony shuffled slowly and stopped in front of Darin and Lynn. He recited Willy's first lines from the play and took a bow after he was finished.

"I have the first scene completely memorized for your enjoyment, gentlemen," he bragged. "I know Willy inside and out."

Marie made a gagging noise, to which Tony responded by flipping her the bird. She said something about it being in his dreams and he retorted with something just as inane.

Sean buried his face into his script and wondered why he enjoyed doing community theatre so much.

The callbacks flew by and the directors hid themselves in the office to cast the show. Mike had stayed to see what was going on and removed himself when the directors needed the office space. He wished everyone luck on the show and that he'd see them on Saturday for the board meeting. Marie reminded him that they would definitely see him and it ought to be an interesting meeting.

Sara, Tony, and Sean went outside to wait for the outcome. Another member of the group, Dora Floyd, had been called as well, even though she hadn't been there the night before for the original tryouts. She flopped on the hood of her car and lit up a cigarette and offered the others one.

"Who'd you mooch those off of, Dora?" Marie asked as she joined them. They didn't want her to, but there she was just the same.

"Up yours, Marie," Dora said.

"Actually that was what I was going to ask," Tony said. "I'm still missing groceries from the last time you came for a visit."

"Up yours, too, Tony," Dora said. She flicked ash at him and he stuck out his tongue as if to catch it in his mouth.

"And I'd like my Shakespeare back, too, if you don't mind, Dora," Marie said. "I've been wondering if I'd ever get it back."

Dora angrily sucked smoke from her cig. "You'll get it back. Just quit asking about it. I'm not through with it."

"Do you even know where it is?" Sara asked. "Surely it's not in your car. You'd lose a person in all that junk." She pointed to the inside where Dora had let months of trash pile up from the back seat into the front.

"You shut up, too," she said. "In fact, everyone shut up!" She turned the conversation playful, but Marie would not be deterred.

"I want it back, Dora. I may decide to do *Romeo and Juliet* next year."

Tony burst out laughing and held his sides. "Not in a million years. No way."

"You can't do it. You can't find the people to do it," Dora said.

"That will be a problem," Sara said. Sean noticed the strain for her to talk to Marie, but admired the effort.

"If I have people like you to cast, Dora, then yeah, I'll have trouble," Marie said.

"What's that supposed to mean?" Dora shot back. She hopped off her car and squashed the butt of her cigarette into the ground.

"I didn't get fired from a show around here. Someone around here did," Marie snapped.

"I did not!" Dora said.

"Well, yeah, you were, too, Dora," Tony said. "I should know. I'm the one who fired you."

"So I didn't have a few lines down," Dora complained.

"How about a lot of them," Tony countered.

Lynn flipped open the door and smiled at everyone. Everyone waited in eager anticipation for him to open his mouth and say something, anything.

"I think we've got it."

Death of a Salesman Casting:

Letta.....................................Diane Cameron
Miss Forsythe...........................Heather Reeves
Stanley....................................Lynn Adkins
Jenny......................................Dora Floyd
Howard Wagner.........................Tony Tarver
Uncle Ben...............................Darin Peters
Charley....................................Don Kennedy
The Woman.............................Marie Winters
Bernard...................................Alex Sampson
Biff..Tom Hewitt
Happy.....................................Alan Cushing
Linda......................................Sara Black
Willy Loman.............................Sean Maston

Needless to say there was some fallout over the casting decisions that Darin and Lynn had made for the play. They both broke the unspoken rule that stated that the directors shouldn't cast themselves in the play. Darin's reasoning was that there wasn't anyone else who could play the roles, especially that of Uncle Ben, which he viewed (with all meekness) as one of the key characters to the whole story. Lynn had been cast because they just didn't have the time or inclination to find someone else for the part of Stanley.

Marie griped and complained to no end about being cast as the woman in the hotel room that Willy had the fling with, but it didn't matter, she took the part, anyway. Sean knew she really wanted the part, but she complained for sport. She also whined about the director's girlfriend getting cast as the female lead and how that didn't seem fair. No one paid her much heed and she shut up after a while.

Tony sat on the curb of the sidewalk for a long time in muted silence, keeping his distance from the others. Sean thought how strange it was to see him pouting in full Willy Loman regalia in front of the theatre. Tony never did say congrats to Sean for his efforts or casting, but did promise that he would make a wonderful Howard. He also vowed to sweep up, clean, paint, construct, sew, or do anything else that needed doing for the production. He wanted everyone to know how much of a team player he was.

The other members of the Lyle Community Theatre rogue's gallery were satisfied (overall) with their parts and were anxious to begin rehearsal, which would start the following Monday. The newcomers to the theatre were overjoyed to actually be cast and set to memorizing their lines.

The board members promised they'd be there that Saturday with bells on to discuss many things that were important to the future of the theatre. Everyone was encouraged to be there. Everyone promised to be there.

Chapter Four

Sean lounged in his recliner with Titan and Weejo at his feet early Friday morning. He had taken the day off to do some things around the house, one of them being watching a little tube. He scratched absently at his knee as he flipped through the channels at light speed. He found a game show that appealed to him and settled back to exercise his trivia knowledge as the show got underway. The first question had to do with classic movies, which just happened to be one of his areas of expertise.

His cordless coughed to life at his hip. He punched the "Talk" button. "What is it?" he asked, knowing it was his buddy, Ric Steinman, police officer for the Ardmore PD.

"Got the news on?" Ric asked.

"No. Game show. Why?"

"Try Channel Six and call me back." The line clicked dead. He grabbed the remote and turned the channel.

A perky girl with even perkier hair droned on about a special report coming out of Lyle. She turned it over to a reporter live on the scene. The reporter hunched behind her microphone on a residential street that Sean immediately recognized. He hit the volume button and leaned forward in his chair. The woman turned so the viewers could get a better look at the house that had police tape wrapped around it like a bow on a present. Sean glazed over as he heard the words, but they refused to compute in his brain. He stood up from his recliner and walked over to the TV.

"Can't be," he mumbled. Titan came up and licked him on the foot. He ignored the attention and squatted directly in front of the screen.

"The police indicate that the incident was reported just a few hours ago by a neighbor who heard the car running in the garage," the reporter said. "It appears that the victim had been there in the garage for hours before being discovered this morning." She turned again to face the camera. "Police have concluded an apparent suicide in this case and are making further inquiries of neighbors and friends and family who knew the woman. We do know that the woman's name was Marie Winters and was a prominent citizen in this small town of Lyle."

Sean hit the mute button on the remote and grabbed the phone. He punched Ric's work number stored in memory and waited while it rang.

"Okay. Talk," he said.

"I don't know much. It's not exactly in my jurisdiction. But I have a couple of friends on the force down there in Lyle and can call them later when things quiet down some."

"Suicide?"

"That's what they say. Walked into her garage early in the morning, got in her car, and took a carbon monoxide overdose," Ric said. Sean wasn't offended by his wording. He had become accustomed to Ric's unique descriptions of things over the years.

"It's hard to believe. I just saw her the other day," Sean said.

"Yeah. I thought you'd want to know before hearing from someone else."

"Thanks. Was there a note found?"

"No idea. All I know is what you know. Did she seem distraught?" Ric asked.

Sean rubbed a throbbing place at his temple and thought about it. "Not really. She never really was, come to think of it. She got down sometimes, but not any more than the rest of us."

"The rest of us meaning the community theatre folks down there?" Ric asked.

"Yeah. I can't believe she took her own life."

"It's strange what some people will do. I know."

"No," Sean said, "that's not what I mean. I *can't* believe she took her own life."

The phone rang off the hook at his house after that. So much for taking the day off and catching up on some much needed R-and-R. He hadn't found out much more from any of the news stories on the television. Lynn had heard rumors floating around town about Marie being upset and seen in her front yard yelling and screaming at what the neighbors didn't know because they didn't see anyone talking to her. Darin and Tony hadn't heard a thing, but were concerned about how it would affect everyone in the show and on the board. Darin was especially worried about who he could find to replace her in the show.

Sean ate a hastily thrown together lunch and met Sara down at the park later in the afternoon. She called him and wanted to meet for a walk. They did this about once a week and enjoyed the time stretching their legs and letting Sean's dogs roam around and frolic. They counted on each other for their weekly ritual and for the friendly conversation it brought them both.

"It's beyond understanding, you know," Sara said. She absently reached down and picked up a stick and threw it ahead of the dogs. They took off like a shot to retrieve the branch.

"Death usually is," Sean said, agreeing with her. "And Marie, too. I would never have thought in a million years."

Sara wiped at a tear on her face. "You think you know someone and then you find out that you really didn't. It's really sad. I feel guilty."

"About what?" he asked.

Sara shrugged and stuffed her hands in her pockets. Titan brought the stick to her obediently and she threw it again. "She made me so upset the other night and I wished every bad thing in the world to happen to her."

"Wishing it didn't make it happen," Sean reminded her.

"I know that, but as much as we didn't get along, she was still one of us."

Sean decided to tread on ground he knew was sensitive. "What happened the other night, anyway?"

She stopped on the pathway and grabbed him by the arm. "Don't ask. Okay? Just don't. It's over now and I'd rather not talk about it."

"Okay."

She started walking again and he followed after her. The dogs brought the stick back and ran off into the woods after some invisible creature. Sean whistled after them, but they ignored him and vanished from view in the thick overgrowth of trees and brush.

"Did you hear from Mike yet?" Sara asked him.

"No. Why?"

"He called and cancelled the board meeting for tomorrow. He said it was the best thing to do in a situation like this."

"I suppose so," he said.

"Why do you sound so skeptical about everything?" she asked suddenly.

"What?" He stopped at the edge of the pond set dead center in the park. He picked up a couple of rocks and skipped them across the water. Did he sound skeptical, as she put it? Could he not accept the fact that someone he knew had died in a horrible way?

"Hello in there," Sara said, breaking his train of thought. She let a rock sail through the air and bounce across the surface of the water.

"Sorry. It's just...well, I don't know, really. It all seems so surreal somehow. You know what I mean?"

"Not really, no."

He threw another rock and watched it fall into the water and disappear from sight. He watched the waters ripple out from the point of impact and fade out. *Just like our lives*, he thought.

Just like everything we do in life.

He pointed to a ripple and told her of his analogy.

"Yeah, you're right. And we just don't see it unless someone close to us dies," she said.

"And for some not even then."

"What about the show?" she asked.

"You know Darin. Probably better than the rest of us. The show must go on, right?"

She threw another stone and waited for it to stop its journey and sink before she said anything. "The show will definitely go on. I think he may have cast her in that role as some form of revenge."

"For what she said the other night?" Sean asked.

"Yeah. And other things."

"What other things?"

Another rock flew out of her hand and hit the water. "You know, just not liking her in general and all the trouble she causes wherever she goes."

"Who doesn't in our merry bunch?"

She laughed at that and high-fived him. "You're so right. What a crew of trouble makers, huh?"

"Sometimes. Yeah." He whistled for the dogs and they came bolting out of the woods.

"I need to get ready to run the restaurant. Let's go," Sara said. She grabbed Weejo by the ears and took off down the trail.

Sean threw his last rock into the water and watched it ripple and fade.

Just like our lives.

"I didn't want Willy, anyway," Tony proclaimed over dinner that evening. "I think Howard is one of the key roles in the entire show. Without his firing Willy, there's no reason for him to commit suicide later on in the play."

Sean smiled and took a bite of his spaghetti—Tony's creation, and a pretty good one, too. "You came dressed in full costume," Sean reminded him.

"So? That's what all good actors in the profession do," Tony countered. He wiped some sauce from his face and took a drink of his water. "Just my training, man."

"It's like we threw a party and said it was casual and you suddenly decided at the last minute to show up in a tux," Sean observed.

"No, it's not. You guys could've done the same thing."

"Why?" He knew it was a moot point with Tony and a waste of breath to even argue about, but he found his friend's behavior curious and strange from time to time.

Tony pontificated for fifteen minutes over the professional actor's courage and bravery in tackling any given role at any time. That meant he would go to great lengths in an audition or tryout or callback to catch the attention of the director. He explained that since he had his M.F.A. and had gone to Hollywood for a few years, he had a viewpoint that the others in the community theatre just didn't possess. They could learn a lot from him if they would just listen to him. He didn't brag about it. He just stated it as simple fact to Sean, who had heard the argument before. Sean tuned him out as he finished up his meal. He had come over to watch a movie, not debate the experience and resume of his friend.

Sean stuck in the DVD he'd rented in the machine and grabbed for the remote. Tony grabbed it away from him and hit a couple of buttons.

"It's my house, after all," he said with a smirk. "Let me play the proper host," he grumbled in an English accent that needed lots of work. He found the menu for the DVD and pressed play.

"And you're sure this is a good movie?" Sean asked.

"Absolutely. A classic of the genre. The cinematography is amazing. And I think it's one of the best movies he's ever directed."

"Sounds good." Sean settled back onto the couch and put his feet on the coffee table.

Tony raided the fridge and pitched a soda to Sean. He tore open a bag of chips and settled in his rocker next to the couch.

"You haven't said anything about Marie yet," mused Tony.

"I didn't think you'd want to talk about it."

"I think it's a shame."

"You do?" Sean asked, not believing it.

Tony looked hurt and hit the pause button. "She was one of our own, Sean."

"You hated her guts."

"What's that got to do with it? We had our differences."

"You were hoping for her death the other night!"

Tony smirked. "Merely words. *Words, words, words*. Right? I mean, come on, I didn't really mean that."

"Could've fooled me," Sean said.

"Listen, Sherlock, quit acting like this is a cross-examination. I'm thinking that we should do something in the program for her or some other kind of dedication during the next show. It would be a nice tribute."

"Isn't that a bit two-faced?"

"Not at all. So we didn't get along. And so what if she opened her fat mouth too much and too often? She's dead now and I'm sorry for whatever misery she was experiencing that caused her to take her life."

Sean sat forward on the couch and looked at his friend. "You really mean that."

"Of course I do. I wish everyone would quit having this bad image of me. I'm not an ogre."

"Well, not all of the time, at least," Sean said.

Tony hit the pause button again and settled back in his chair. "But you know, the good thing is that business should run a lot smoother down at the theatre now. There's a silver lining in everything, I guess," he said.

Sean opened his mouth to say something in refutation, but thought better of it. He leaned back into the couch and drank from his can of soda. Some things couldn't and wouldn't be changed. Better to watch the movie and wait for the credits to roll.

Chapter Five

On Saturday afternoon a few of the community theatre regulars met at the building to start work on the complicated set. Darin had scratched it out on a scrap piece of paper. He reassured everyone there that he "had it all up in his head" and that construction shouldn't be any big problem. He declared that design hadn't been a good class for him when he was in college getting his theatre degree. Along with Tony and Sean, he was the only other person who worked at the community theatre who had any educational theatre background. The others just did if for fun and trusted Darin and Tony with their knowledge and expertise that they said they had in all things theatrical.

Sean arrived early that afternoon to do whatever the director and his assistant dictated. He liked getting there early and letting the dogs run around and get some sun.

He parked the bug on the front row next to the building and let the dogs out. They galloped at full speed and began chasing a couple of quail in a ditch bank by the theatre. He ordered them to behave and went indoors.

The hammering and sawing echoed with earnest throughout the building. Sean found the others in the work area behind the stage putting together a couple of bed frames. Lynn and Darin were working on something else at one of the chop saws. Tony had his hands full with cleaning up the make up room.

"I thought someone was supposed to clean this up after the musical?" Tony yelled so everyone on stage could hear him.

"They were," Darin answered. He peeked through the door and growled. "Who was supposed to do this?"

"That would've have been Marie," Heather, another community theatre regular, said from her place near one of the beds. The others mumbled things Sean couldn't make out. He volunteered to assist Tony with the clean up.

"She should've cleaned it up," Darin declared.

"Darin!" Sara said. She bolted part of one of the bed frames in place. "That's a bit cold, don't you think?"

"She could've cleaned it up before she kicked off," he said, hoping to elicit some laughter for his efforts. None came.

"We'll clean it up. It's no big deal," Sean said. He joined Tony and they got started cleaning up the mess of make up, used baby wipes, and other bits and pieces.

The work progressed as it usually did on work days like this. There were the jokes and anecdotes passed around. Gossip and hearsay followed concerning what had happened to Marie. Everyone speculated on why she would take her own life. It didn't seem like her and most expressed their confusion over her actions. Sean drank it all in and let the discussion absorb into his mind. He found the gossiping and bantering somehow refreshing after receiving such sad news.

Dora and Darin took a smoke break after a half hour and Sara soon followed. Heather wandered out onto the stage with part of the bed frame, leaving Sean and Lynn examining the plans that had hastily been drawn by Darin.

"I can't make heads or tails out of this," Lynn complained.

"I think it goes this way," Sean remarked and flipped the piece of notebook paper around. "See? The audience is here and there's the kitchen area and the boys' bedroom up here."

"Oh. Okay. It shouldn't be too hard."

"I hope not. You never know with our sets, huh?" Sean quickly remembered a loose staircase railing that had come off in the musical and nearly sent Marie tumbling over the side and falling onto the stage. He mentioned it to Lynn, recalling how everyone had been horrified at Marie almost falling and hurting herself.

"She was a strange person in a lot of ways," Lynn mused. He grabbed a two-by-four and put it in the chop saw. He made sure it was plugged in properly and hit the red button that brought the saw blade to life. He cut through the wood and shut the machine off.

"How's that?" Sean asked.

"You know."

"I'm not sure what you mean."

Lynn stacked the piece of wood on a couple of others that were cut to identical lengths and grabbed another two-by-four from a pile underneath the table the saw rested on. "She barely got along with anyone around here," Lynn said quietly.

"Who does?"

"You know what I mean. Darin and Tony have been trying to chase her away for months and Sara obviously didn't like her, especially after the other night."

"It was a rough couple of weeks, I guess. The musical wasn't exactly the best experience in the world. There was a lot of resentment built up against her and Mike," Sean said.

Lynn frowned as he framed the two-by-four under the blade of the saw. "I know that Marie acted the prima donna around here and ticked some folks off, but Mike?"

"The 'genius' bit printed in the paper, supposedly by our mysterious reviewer."

"We don't know for sure that it's Mike, do we?"

Sean shook his head. "Too many things have been planted his way on purpose just to see if he would bite. He did and it got printed in one of the reviews. Everyone knows he's the one."

"Reviewing his own shows. How gauche," Lynn said. He stuck out his teeth over his lower lip and put on a false English accent. "I say, I do think that my show was superb and glorious and all that, what?"

Sean laughed and helped him put the board where he wanted it. Lynn cut on the line and then stacked it with the growing pile he had accumulated.

"I still don't see why you think she was so strange. I mean, not any more than the rest of us," Sean said.

"I don't know, Sean. The musical was her second big role and she suddenly thought she knew everything about this place. She thought she could run it better than Mike and told me so a couple of times. She also criticized everyone else's acting around here and complained about the financial records being kept secret from the rest of us."

Sean leaned against the table and hooked an arm over the saw. "Sounds like the rest of us around here."

Lynn thought about it and agreed. "I guess you're right. I don't know. Maybe it's just me. I just can't imagine her killing herself."

"Believe it," Tony said from the back door. "She couldn't stand looking at herself any more in the mirror."

"That's right," Darin added. "Can you imagine?"

"Is it suddenly cold in here?" Heather asked as she reappeared back from the stage.

"We know you liked her, Heather. We're just playing," Darin said. "It's very sad that she's gone."

"It is. I lost a good friend," Heather said. Tears sprang in her eyes and rolled quickly down her face. She wiped at them and asked if there was anything else she could do. Darin and Tony took her back onto the stage and got her to start painting the floor black. During the musical, the crew had painted bits of scenery to blend in with the flats that were brought onto the stage.

"It's karma, I think," Dora said after a time. "It comes back to bite you in the butt sometimes."

"What are you talking about?" Lynn asked.

"Marie."

"Karma?"

"Well, yeah. Fate, baby. She reaped what she sewed," Dora said.

"She took her own life, Dora," Sean reminded her. "What does karma have to do with that?"

"And isn't karma about transmigration or some nonsense?" Lynn asked.

"It's not nonsense, Lynn," defended Dora. "And all I'm saying is that Marie set herself up for the forces in her life to tear her apart."

Sean rubbed his temples with his fingertips and rolled his eyes toward the ceiling. "So what you're saying, Dora, is that it was her destiny to end up like she did."

"Yeah."

"When's your turn coming then, Dora?" Lynn asked before Sean could.

"Very funny," she said and grabbed a paintbrush and exited for the stage.

"I think this whole thing is getting to us," Sara said as she walked over to join them at the saw table.

Sean grabbed a two-by-four and placed it on the table. Lynn measured and marked it and put it underneath the blade. She grabbed the board before Lynn kicked the saw on.

"Have you noticed that none of us has said anything nice about her?" Sara asked.

"I thought you'd be the last person on earth who would do that," Lynn said.

She thought about that for a minute. "Yeah. I am, but I thought someone around here would."

"Heather was her friend," Sean said. "She's pretty torn up about it, too."

"Yeah, but Marie couldn't have cared less about Heather, no matter what she says."

"I don't think so, Sara," Sean said. "They were a lot closer than you might think."

Lynn fired up the saw and cut the board and stacked it. He pulled off his gloves and popped open a soda out of a cooler that he'd brought. He offered Sean and Sara one and they each grabbed a can out of the ice chest. Sean sat down in a chair and brought the cold can to his lips and took a sip.

"Whatever the case," Lynn said, "it's sad that she died. Very sad. It takes a lot of grief for someone to end their own life. I would never have thought she would do something like that, but apparently she did. It won't be long before we're not talking about it anymore and things will move on around here. They always do."

"That's kinda sad, don't you think?" Sean asked. Okay, so maybe she wasn't well-liked, but she died in a terrible way. Didn't that deserve something more than them scorning and forgetting her? Maybe he was sensitive to the fact that they were being honest about their feelings, which wasn't a bad thing. The timing was bad, that's all.

"Of course, it is," Lynn said, breaking Sean out of his trance. "But isn't that the way of it?" He prepared another board for cutting and Sean got out of the way.

Heather re-entered from the stage area with her cell phone clutched in her fist. She had it pressed hard to her face and listened intently to someone on the other end. Sean smiled at her, which she ignored. He was about to walk over and pick up a can of paint when she grabbed him by the arm and dragged him out the back door into the back alley behind the theatre. She stayed on the line and kept nodding her head up and down. Whatever it was, it had her complete attention.

"Okay, okay, Mike," she said at last. She hung up the phone and stuffed it into her pants' pocket.

"What do you need, Heather?" Sean asked. "I thought we were trying to get some work done." He wasn't being critical, but he knew how quickly Heather got distracted by other things.

"I think we may have a problem here," she said. She paced around and stared down at the ground like she was looking for loose change.

"Who has a problem?" Sean asked.

She wrung her hands nervously and waved around in the air. "We do, us. The theatre, Sean."

"What now? Who was that on the phone? The landlord?" he asked playfully. She didn't bite.

"It was Mike. Let me ask you something."

Sean leaned against a trash barrel and folded his arms across his chest. "Fire away."

"Did you know that Tony keeps an online journal?"

"Yeah. He's mentioned it a couple of times. He's kept one out online for years. He says it gives him some place to vent."

Heather laughed at that and waved her arms around again. "Well, Mike found it."

"He what?"

"He heard Tony talking about it the other day and so he went out there and looked for it online. And he found it. And he's pretty hurt and upset by what's out there."

"What's out there?" Sean asked.

"He went off about Mike's lack of directing ability for the musical and a thousand other things that went wrong with the show," Heather complained.

"Okay. It's his diary, Heather. He's going to put things out there like that."

"There's stuff about me out there that Mike said I needed to read."

"It's no big deal, Heather," Sean said.

She disagreed. "It could be. That's public access and he's blackening our eye down here. Folks in town can go on there and hit it and read his garbage about us."

"As long as it's online, they can do that, no matter how horrible it may be."

"Mike's ticked off about it. You should've heard him on the phone," she said.

Sean chuckled to himself and headed back for the door. "Because it's out there on the web, or because he got called on some things that have been coming for a long time?"

"Does it matter, Sean? He's upset."

Sean grabbed the door handle and pulled it open. "I would say that with Marie's death that's the least of our worries."

She grabbed him and shut the door. "That's just it. Mike said that there's some stuff on there about Marie."

"What? That she's a bad actress? Was a bad actress. We've all said that around here."

Her voice dropped to a whisper and turned sinister. "Mike said something about Tony saying he was glad she was gone and that the world was now a much better place without her."

Sean leaned against the wall and gritted his teeth. He knew Tony could be heartless, but this—if it were true—could cause really bad problems for everyone at the theatre. He watched Heather as she paced in the alleyway. It infuriated her. He could see that, but there was something else, too. It enlivened her. She enjoyed the drama no matter where it came from.

"And a lot of it was written before she died, too," she said. She sounded like a spy in the middle of a conspiracy.

"Like threats?" Sean asked, suddenly nervous.

"That's what Mike said."

Sean opened the back door again and swung it wide. "Let's not jump to any conclusions just yet, Heather."

"I'm going out there and read it," she said, excited suddenly by the prospect of finding out dirt on the theatre troublemaker.

"Why don't I talk to him first?" Sean offered.

"No. I'm going to get online as soon as I get home," she said and walked past him into the building. "I just thought you needed to know."

Sean followed behind her and let the door slam shut. If what she said was true, then he knew that Tony had buried himself. He knew Mike well enough to know that he could be one vindictive individual. He also understood all too well that Mike could and would stir up enough trouble about this to cause difficulty for their member from Hollywood. He rubbed the throbbing in his temples and found the can of paint he had been searching for earlier.

Lynn and Darin were working with the saw. It had apparently shorted out again, which was nothing new and they were banging on it with a hammer. Darin threw it down in anger, almost tagging Sean on the foot.

"Sorry, sorry, man," he said. "Sorry."

"It's okay. The saw again?" He leaned down to pick up the hammer and handed it back to Darin. On the butt of the handle someone had burned in LCT to mark it as the theatre's property.

"Yeah, the saw again. You ready to paint?" Darin said, seeing the can Sean carried.

"Thought I might help with the floor," Sean said.

"Sounds good. Sorry, man."

"Don't worry about it." They high-fived and Sean shuffled off toward the stage where he found Dora slapping black paint onto the boards of the stage.

"Hey, you," she said, "you've come to assist! I love you forever!" She laughed and flung a dab of paint at his pant leg and hit her target.

"Not cool," Sean groaned and dipped his own brush into her can and slapped some paint on her arm. They had a good laugh and then set to painting the stage. Tony joined them for a few minutes and Sean took him aside to pass on the information that Heather had funneled to him.

"Oh, you've got to be kidding me," Tony said, looking around the back stage area to make sure they were alone. "I've had that thing for a long time."

"I know that." He wiped at the spot of paint on his leg and smeared even more than it was. "I'm just passing along what Mike told Heather."

"This is great. Have you gone on there?"

Sean shook his head that he hadn't. "Even if I had, it's still your own site."

"Yeah, but it's not private," Tony admitted.

"Heather said Mike is really hurt by what you wrote on there."

Tony stuck his face in his hands and pushed his cheeks together. He yelled something unintelligible and kicked the wall with his foot. He then yelled because he hurt himself on the wall and slumped to the floor cursing and mumbling to himself. He took off his shoe and examined the toe he had smashed. Sean waited for his tantrum to run its course. He had seen his friend do this before and it was best to stand back and let him just get it out of his system.

"Are you done?" Sean asked after a time.

Tony rubbed his toe and grumbled something.

"What was that?"

"I'm done. I suppose I need to apologize."

Sean agreed that might be a good plan. "And put it out there on your site, too."

"You think so?" Tony asked.

"If Mike has read it, how many other people do you think know about it?"

"Good point."

Sean decided now was the time to tread on dangerous ground. "Heather also said that there's some stuff on there that you wrote about Marie."

Tony froze suddenly and then pulled his shoe back on. "Man, I have stuff on there about everyone here, including you."

"I hope it's only good things," Sean said.

"You can go on there and read for yourself." He pushed himself off the floor and tested his foot by putting weight on it. He stumbled a couple of steps and then limped around the back stage area.

"What about Marie?" Sean asked.

"The usual stuff, you know," he said, ready to change the subject.

"No. That's why I'm asking."

"Listen, Kojak, it's just what everyone else around here has said about her."

"Wishing her dead? Is that what everyone around here said about her?" Sean asked, suddenly very serious.

"Did she say that?" Tony thundered. He stormed over to the back wall of the building and raised his fist to hit it. Remembering his recent encounter between the wall and his foot, he thought better of it and slammed it instead into a prop table. He yelped in agony and stuck the injured hand under his arm.

"Feel better?" Sean asked. "Listen, I'm only asking. That's all. This isn't an interrogation. I'm your friend, remember? Not everyone in the world is trying to tear down your castle."

"Tell that to Mike," he grumbled.

"Look at me a minute," Sean ordered him. Tony did so. "Did you write what she said you did about Marie?"

"Sean, it's just another attempt around here to keep me down," he whined.

"Did you?"

"I may have."

"May?"

"Yes, I did. But now I'm going to go out there and delete every bit of it." He spun on his heel to take off, but Sean grabbed him.

"Better not," Sean warned.

"Watch me."

"They all know it's out there, man. Just print your apology and leave it up for a couple of days and then make the site private. The server site will let you do that, right?"

"Yes, but I've never had to before," Tony said.

"You've never popped off about the Lyle Community Theatre before," Sean joked. He knew it wasn't something to laugh about, but he knew he had to keep Tony calm before more damage could be done.

"Okay. You're right. I'll put the apology out there and then I'll make it private with a user name and password."

"Good."

"Now, where's Heather?" Tony asked with new fury rising in him. Sean jerked him by the arm and sat him down on the props table.

"Don't."

"Why not?"

"Just don't. That's all. There's enough drama around here as it is. We don't need any more for a while. And besides, one of our own is dead. And maybe that's what we need to be thinking about right now."

That sobered Tony up and he quickly agreed that Sean knew best. Sean left him there to stew and meditate on it and rejoined Dora on the stage. He retrieved his paint brush and got back to work. Dora playfully slapped some on his work shirt and he returned the favor.

"It's karma coming back to bite you," he said as he dabbed paint on her nose.

"That's right!" she screeched. "Bad karma!"

But as for Marie, he had an itching feeling that bad karma didn't have a part to play in her departure from this world.

Chapter Six

"Get up, man. Are you awake?" the faraway voice echoed from the phone. Something warm and wet washed over his face and he pushed out in the darkness to get it away from him. Titan whined and jumped off the bed and vanished into another part of his house. Weejo ran after him leaving Sean alone in his bed.

"We need to talk."

"What is it, Ric?" The recognition finally kicked in and he rolled over onto his back. "What's wrong?"

"Could be plenty. How 'bout some breakfast at Mama's Café?" Ric asked.

"What does this have to do with?"

"You'll see," he said and hung up the phone.

Sean rammed the receiver back into the holder. "Not cool. Not very cool at all." He pounded his pillow and stuck it under his head.

What's going on that Ric needs to call me about in the middle of the night?

He set his mind to work on it, but the dogs raced back into the room and wrestled on top of him until he ordered them to stop and go back to sleep.

And then he did the same.

"Eggs, scrambled. Sausage, hash browns, biscuits and gravy, and OJ with some java," Sean said to the perky waitress who had pen eagerly poised over her ticket pad.

"The same," Ric said and shut his menu. The waitress grinned widely, gathered the menus up in her arms as if they were her children, and hustled off with their order.

"I'm starved," Sean mused.

"Do you eat like that every day?" Ric asked.

"My appetite is fine. What about yours?" Sean fired back.

"I thought you were buying," Ric said with an evil grin.

"Uh, no, think again, *compadre.*"

Ric grabbed a sugar packet and tore the top off of it. He tilted his head back and poured the sugar into his mouth. Sean had seen him do this a thousand times and each time it made him wonder about Ric's sanity.

"That's pure lunacy, pal," he said.

"It gets me going in the morning."

"It's called coffee."

Ric laughed and tore into another sugar packet. "A bad habit I got into back in college."

"I remember," Sean said. The waitress brought them both cups of coffee and then zipped off back into kitchen. "She's too happy for me," Sean remarked. "Doesn't she know it's morning outside?"

Ric blew on his coffee cup as he laughed and pushed the paper he had with him over to Sean. He tapped on the front page and waited for Sean to absorb the info.

"What's this?" Sean asked as he began reading.

"The Oklahoma City paper about Marie."

Sean scanned through the opening paragraph about the apparent suicide of one Marie Winters in the sleepy hovel of Lyle. *Since when was her death an "apparent suicide?* he thought as he read through the rest of it. The article explained Marie's work background and about her being a long-time resident of the Lyle community. It was the last paragraph that raised eyebrows.

"Say what?" Sean asked as he re-read the last couple of sentences.

"I thought that might interest you."

"What does this mean? 'Investigators aren't ruling out the possibility of foul play.' Can you explain that?"

Ric tipped his coffee cup to him and drank from it. "The reason I called you for breakfast."

"Why would investigators think something like that?" Sean asked, very agitated all of the sudden, which didn't go unnoticed by Ric.

"Why do you think?"

Sean shrugged his shoulders and read the article again. Ric let him as he put a packet of sugar into his coffee. He reached for the creamer and added a teaspoon in the mug.

"What's been found?" Sean asked.

"You assume something's been found?" Ric asked, sounding almost amused with his friend's behavior. "You're the problem solver. You tell me."

"Hey, just because I told you to look for that car-jacker in that hotel a few months back doesn't mean I have a clue here."

Ric tipped his cup to him again. "You have a nose for this type of thing. An apparent suicide means that there's some kind of evidence at the scene or on the body that leads investigators to think something's amiss."

"On the body?" Sean asked. "Wait a minute. Did someone request a postmortem?"

"Bingo."

"Who? Her family?"

"Nope. A Detective Stiles got suspicious. And there was also a spot of blood beside the car on the concrete."

Sean stirred creamer into his own mug and took a deep breath. A postmortem meant the family didn't for one minute believe the idea of suicide. It couldn't be as

simple as shutting the door to her car, starting it up with
the window down, and letting her life ebb away. They
must have suspected from the first things that had been
scratching at the back of his own mind. And the spot of
blood also pointed to something sinister.

"What was found at the scene? Anything?" Sean
asked.

"Don't you want to know about the body?"

"What about it?"

Ric drank the last of his coffee. The waitress
appeared from nowhere and refilled it. She called him
"honey" twice and then disappeared again.

"What do you think?" Ric asked.

"Why are we asking each other so many questions?"

"I don't know. Why?"

"Are you going to tell me?"

"Will you answer my question?"

"Why?"

"Why not?"

"Because."

Sean gently slapped the table and pointed his index
finger up into the air. "I won that one," he said.

"The question game maybe, but not the answer about
your friend."

Sean finished his cup and waited for the refill. It
came and went in a flash before he could blink. "I
assume that something had been done to her prior to the
asphyxiation. Or was that the way she died?"

"What did the paper say?" Ric asked.

"That she asphyxiated."

"Then it had to be prior then."

"She was forced to stay in the car? I don't know,
what?" He leaned back in his chair and gazed at his
friend, who had his best poker face on. "Couldn't be at
gun point, the guy would've have died, too."

"You assume it was a guy," Ric said.

"True. Sorry."

"Come on, you're the man for deduction. What do you think?"

"If she wasn't forced that way, then it had to be completely without her knowledge."

"What does that mean?"

"I don't know. I'm just feeling my way through this while you sit over there watching me sweat," Sean said.

"I like to see your mind work."

Sean snapped his fingers. "Without her knowledge means she was out. Am I right?"

"Very. Try a blow to back of the head."

They finished the rest of breakfast in silence. They both committed wholeheartedly to their food. Ric covered his eggs in a layer in ketchup, which Sean sneered at, but kept his opinions to himself. He used the pepper liberally on his biscuits and gravy and tasted to make sure he had the right amount. The waitress appeared from nowhere again with coffee pot at the ready. If it weren't for the news about Marie, it would have been one of the better breakfasts Sean had ever eaten.

Ric paid as arranged and the waitress made them promise to come back again. They walked through the parking lot to Ric's car parked by the post office. Sean leaned on the hood, still contemplating the implications of his friend's information. Marie committing suicide had been bad enough to think about, but now the thought of murder came to mind and it scared him.

Someone he knew had been killed. The life taken from her by someone else. The thought unsettled him and he knew Ric could sense it.

"It's never easy. Especially when it's someone we know. I see that look you have from time to time and it's always the same. Bewilderment and confusion and then trying to figure out who did it," Ric said.

"Who did?"

"They don't know. The postmortem revealed that she had been cracked with a blunt instrument on the back of the head. Just about here." Ric reached up behind Sean's ear and pressed the spot of the wound.

"And she didn't do it in the car?" Sean asked, knowing the answer already.

"Not possible. Whoever popped her, cracked the back of her skull, but not enough to kill her. He let the car fumes do that."

"What did it?"

"They don't know yet. A bar, or a wrench of some kind. They don't know."

"Why didn't they find the wound sooner?" Sean asked.

Ric smiled deviously. "Who said they didn't? There were traces of blood in her hair. Not in the car. She had enough hair to absorb any from the wound. They were probably sitting on it until the family arrived in town."

Sean sat on the hood and rubbed the sides of his head. "What's the assumption? The killer bring it with him and knock her out with it and then drags her in the garage?"

"There's lots of speculation, but you've got to remember I'm getting this from the chief when he's got a minute. And he doesn't have many to spare. Lyle isn't a Mecca for death and destruction. They have their hands full."

"Will the O.S.B.I. move in and give them a hand?" Sean asked.

"Not sure about that one. But who's to say on something like this?" Ric took the keys from his pocket and spun them on his finger. He jingled them in a steady rhythm and it distracted Sean.

"Why?"

"That's motive, my friend," Ric said, "and that may take some digging. They're right at the start of it. They just found out it wasn't a suicide."

"And by this afternoon it will have spread through the town."

"That's exactly right. Sunday or not, folks will know by supper time." He unlocked the door and opened it.

"Man, I wish you were up here on this thing," Sean said.

"I'm Ardmore, dude; I'm just in the loop because the chief is a pal. And I knew you'd want to know all about it."

"Will they go back to the house to check it out?" Sean asked.

"Absolutely. They're going to go over that car with a fine-toothed comb."

Sean stood up and stuffed his hands in his pockets. "And her poor family. How they must feel. What a mess."

"Will you guys call off the play with this bit of news?"

Sean laughed bitterly at that. "The show must go on and all that, you know," he said. "They'll say something trite like, 'she would've wanted it that way,' but it won't really matter one way or the other. We have patrons that have paid for a season of theatre and we have an obligation to provide them one."

Ric shrugged his shoulders and sat in his car. "But, really, maybe that's not such a bad thing. Keep things going and don't get bogged down in the nightmare of all this."

"You've done a show or two with us. You know how dramatic everyone is down there. We'll wallow in this for a while."

Ric slid the key into the slot and turned the motor over. It fired up and purred quietly. "Well, whoever did this was very calculated and slick about it. The chief said there were no signs of struggle in the house and nothing appeared to be missing. At least that's what her family is saying," Ric said.

"Hate then."

"Very likely, my friend. It looks like someone out there hated Marie's guts enough to end her life."

"In a very vicious way."

"To say the very least."

"Where will they start looking do you think?" Sean asked.

"Everywhere. Anywhere they can sniff a motive. The how is always important, Sean, but the why leads to the source every single time. Mark my words on that one."

"Will you keep me in the loop?"

"Are you that interested?"

"You know I am."

"I'll do what I can."

With that, Ric put the car in drive and eased out of the parking lot. Sean watched him go and dreaded everything he had said.

Chapter Seven

Sean hustled his bug to church and found a pew in the back. He sat with the Williams clan and enjoyed seeing everyone at services. The preacher droned on about forgiveness and how precious it is to receive, but also how important it is to give to others. Sean found a simple comfort in his words and his thoughts continued to drift back to Marie and the news Ric had delivered.

A hate that drove someone out there to kill.

Could it have been something like that? Something so ugly?

Why couldn't it have been a burglary gone awry, or a random act of violence? And who knew, maybe it was, but the evidence hadn't been found yet.

But why did he hear that little voice in the back of his mind saying that it could only be an act of horrible murder?

The preacher gave the invitation and asked if anyone was pricked by God's words and wanted to have their sins remitted by being baptized. No one came forward as they sung the invitation song and everyone sat back down and prepared for the communion. Sean shut his hymnal and put it back into its slot.

Did God offer redemption to the murderer? He mulled it over. Did He give forgiveness to those so driven by hatred that they would rob someone else of their life?

He knew the word said that He worked in mysterious ways and offered salvation to anyone needing it and searching for it through Him.

But what about Marie's death? His mind kept turning back to that. He imagined a faceless person kicking in the door of her house and jerking her out of bed. He saw the wicked hand bring the instrument down on her head. This faceless creature then dragged her limp body to the garage and put her in the front seat of her car and started the engine. Having completed his murderous task, he left, content that his work was done.

Did it happen that way?

Could it have happened that way?

So many questions and he had let his mind wander too much for one morning. He turned his attention to the passing of the emblems and tried to focus his attention on other things.

The wind whipped through the cab of his car as he drove down the stretch of highway outside the Lyle city limits. He turned up a song on the radio and began singing it at the top of his lungs. Anything to keep his mind off of Marie. He found the exit he needed and spun the bug off the main road and onto a dirt path that wound lazily through a row of pear trees.

Most of the others were already there. He counted four other cars besides Mike's parked in front of his garage. Sean found a spot behind Lynn's Buick and killed the engine.

"Hey, there he is," Darin said, waving his hands up in the air. He put an arm around Sean and led him to the front door. "You know what this is about?" he asked.

"I assume the deed of the web log," Sean said.

Darin rolled his eyes and patted Sean on the back. "I think so. I get the feeling it's going to get ugly in there."

"There won't be any blackballing, that's all I have to say about it," Sean said, meaning it.

"I agree. I think this whole thing is a farce, anyway. We all thought that Tony had guts to write what he did in his diary."

"Did you read it?" Sean asked.

"I did. This morning. And it's no big deal. Mike thinks otherwise and as president of the community theatre he wants to flex."

"I can't believe he cancels the meeting yesterday because of Marie's death, but then calls an emergency meeting because of Tony's blog."

"Believe it," Darin said.

"He can get enough votes for whatever he wants to do. You know that as well as I do. The other members of the board will back him on whatever he throws down."

"Except for you, me, Lynn, Dora, and Sara," Darin reminded him. He grabbed the doorknob and twisted it.

"Not enough to block anything he may want to do. But all I'm saying is that I don't want to see Tony banned from the theatre. Heather tried that crap before and I don't want to be party to it," Sean said, making his stance clear.

"Okay." Darin sucked in a deep breath of air and let it out. "Let's go in there and do this thing."

The meeting didn't start off well in Sean's opinion. For one thing, Tony hadn't been asked to attend, which he considered to be in poor taste. The condemned man should at least face his accusers, but he knew Mike well enough to know that wasn't going to happen. Mike's style was to fire at the guy from the shadows, blindsiding him.

Mike opened the meeting and he and Heather read from printed pages they'd gathered from Tony's website. The other members sat horrified as they read all of the hateful things that he'd written about Mike and his job directing the musical. Sean took in all of the faces of the board members. All of them were members of the Lyle community and committed to keeping the theatre afloat. A pharmacist, a florist, a mechanic, a CPA, and a score of other faces that made up the board sat around Mike in a semi-circle and drank in every word that he said.

Heather then read from Tony's most recent blog and his retraction of everything hateful he'd ever said about anyone associated with the community theatre. She went on to read long passages that Tony had written, confessing his error and how he regretted writing anything hateful about anyone. She also read a sentence that said that he would never let this happen again. He would never get caught like that again, the blog read. In one week he would make his online journal private and for his eyes only.

Heather and Mike put the pages down on his coffee table and Mike addressed the board in all seriousness about the severity of what Tony had done. Heather added that the blog had given the theatre a black eye and a message needed to be sent to this "upstart from Hollywood."

"It's his journal, Mike," Darin countered. "It's a bit unscrupulous for you to go out on the web and try to find his online diary."

"Not at all. It's public domain and so I went out there and looked. He should've thought before he wrote anything like this out there," Mike said.

Sean watched a sea of bobbing heads shake in full agreement. It didn't bode well for his friend Tony. He stuck a hand up in the air. "I think his apology is sincere and it should be taken as such," he offered.

"And I do, Sean, very much so," Mike said. "But it doesn't take anything back."

Sean immediately thought of the preacher's lesson in church that morning and how they all could learn something about doling out forgiveness, but he knew it was not to be that afternoon. Tony would have to pay somehow.

"So what are you proposing?" Lynn asked. "Kick him out of the play that's in production?"

"No way," Darin said. "We already have to find another woman to replace Marie."

The room got quiet and a heavy stillness settled on each of them. Looks were exchanged and they all waited for Mike to say something—anything—to break the silence.

Heather said: "We lost one of our own and I lost a good friend." Darin muttered something under his breath that Sean couldn't make out. He could also tell from Heather's tone that she didn't know about the revelation concerning Marie. He made a point of watching for reactions from the others in the room. Heather continued: "She'll be missed and I really think we should do something nice for her and her memory on this show."

More bobbing heads readily agreed with her suggestion. Even Darin found himself agreeing, begrudgingly, but still agreeing. Sean found some small comfort in that.

"First thing's first," Mike said, interrupting their moment of remembrance. "We need to make a decision about Tony."

"He needs to be banned from the theatre," Heather said.

"No way," Sean shot back. "That's been tried before and it isn't right, us being a community theatre and all, kicking members of the community out of it."

That brought a round of discussion, but Mike—surprisingly enough—agreed with him. Other arguments were offered, but Mike held up his hands to silence everyone.

"He's sorry for what he did and I believe him. And Sean's right. We don't ban anyone from the theatre. That's not the spirit of community theatre." Sean wondered if Mike knew what that spirit might actually be. "I suggest we not permit him to direct next season."

Darin raised an objection, but then thought better of it. Too many bobbing heads were against him. Sara and Dora had remained silent throughout the meeting thus far and they did so for the rest of it as well.

Final vote: 8-5. Tony would be prohibited from directing in next year's season of plays at the Lyle Community Theatre.

As the meeting broke up and people milled around the food that Mike had set out, Sean cornered Heather and asked if he could have the printed sheets from Tony's website. She handed them over and he tucked them away to examine later.

"Real crappy if you ask me," Darin said as he joined Sean by the cheese and crackers.

"You knew he would do something about it," Sean said. He sliced a piece of cheese and put it on a cracker. "It's his way of saving face."

"Something like that, I guess," Darin said quietly as he scooped up a tuna sandwich from a tray.

"He'll take it pretty hard, but he'll get over it," Sean added.

"Who's going to tell him?"

"I guess I will. I'm supposed to go over there anyway this afternoon and watch a movie with him." He stuffed the cracker into his mouth and munched away. He grabbed another and went through the same routine.

"Well, the ax has fallen," Lynn said as he meandered over to them. "One of our own on the chopping block."

"If you don't count Marie," Sean said before he could stop himself. Lynn bowed his head to the floor and said something they both couldn't hear.

"What's that?" Darin asked.

"It's a bitter thing, that's all," he said.

"What is?" Sean asked.

"Losing someone in your life that way," Lynn said.

Darin laughed and grabbed another sandwich. "I thought you were talking about what happened to Tony."

"That was coming no matter what anybody did today," Lynn answered back. "He and Mike have locked horns too many times and this was Mike's way of leveling the playing field."

Darin rolled his eyes as he ate his sandwich. Sean found another cracker and pushed it into his mouth. Lynn grabbed a cup full of punch and plopped himself down in a seat by the living room window. Sean followed, feeling like a conspirator from *Julius Caesar*. Sean commented on it to Darin.

"Yeah, I hear ya," Darin said. "Ever since I joined this outfit I've felt that way."

Lynn remarked: "You know if Marie were still alive I don't know if she would've tried to stop Mike from doing this to Tony or not."

"Definitely not," Darin muttered. "She wouldn't have lifted a finger."

"Probably not," Sean agreed. He sat back against the couch and watched the other members of the board as they conversed and ate their food. So many of them hadn't been down to the theatre in months. Some didn't even make it to see the last show. But here they all were with voting rights ready to exercise to punish one of their own. And Tony's actions were ignorant, to that he readily agreed. But this pomp and circumstance set by the others who rarely graced the theatre with their presence angered him. Tony struck every set whether he performed in the show or not. Many times he was the last to leave a production's strike. And yet, these monarchs of artistic taste and very little elbow grease held power over one who tried to do what he could for the theatre.

"Yeah, but he's a pain in the butt," Sean mumbled to himself.

"What's that?" Lynn asked.

"Sean's going to tell him later today," Darin threw in. "I don't envy him."

"He'll throw a fit," Lynn said. "Can't say as I blame him. He'll go ballistic."

Sean ran his fingers through his hair and felt the warmth of the sun sink to his scalp. "He'll be all right. Maybe not at first, but he'll get over it."

"I hope so," Lynn whispered as Heather came over to the couch. She sat down next to Lynn and looped her arm through his. "What's up?" Lynn asked her.

"You guys are off by yourselves," she observed.

"With good reason, Heather," Darin said none too kindly.

"The things we have to do, huh?" she asked. No one responded to her and she felt the heaviness in the air. "I know you guys didn't approve, but I think it needed to be done."

"Let's just not talk about it, okay? He's reprimanded and that's all there is to it," Darin said. He thought about getting up and "making an exit," but changed his mind and sulked on the couch.

"Mike was really hurt, Darin," Heather said.

"So what?" Darin spat back at her. "Everyone in this lovely bunch gets hurt about something. It goes with the territory."

"And I wouldn't say that Mike's all that innocent," Sean added. "We're still going to have to do something about him writing his own reviews for the paper."

Heather opened her mouth to say something, but thought better of it. An uneasiness about the subject hung in the air. They all knew the seriousness of the allegations, but they also knew they needed some kind of proof.

"The problem is we still don't know for sure," Lynn said.

"He is. There's no way anyone in their right mind would call him a 'genius' of anything," Darin said. "It's him. And if that isn't unethical, I don't know what is."

"It's just a lousy review," Heather countered.

"No. No, it's not, Heather. If it was a lousy review, we wouldn't suspect anything," Darin said. He leaned across Lynn and pointed at her face. "And if you guys are going to sit on Tony for what he did, what do you think should happen to Mike for doing something like that?"

Heather refused to answer. She leaned against Lynn and Sean noticed the cozy friendliness that each of them showed for each other at that moment. Was something brewing that he didn't know about? He gave Darin a look, but Darin didn't catch on to his intimations.

"Marie knew, I think," Lynn said out of the blue.

"About Mike's review policy?" Darin inquired, not hiding his bitterness.

"I think so. She hinted anyway."

"What about her confronting Mike about the finances?" Sean asked. Heather hadn't heard this yet and she reacted sharply. "And it's funny, you know. I think Marie wanted to bring it up at our regular meeting, but Mike cancelled it when she died. But we have an emergency gathering for Tony? Something's not right in Denmark."

"Denmark?" Heather asked completely dumbfounded by the reference.

"Never mind," Darin said through laughter.

"Marie thought there was something fishy with the books?" Lynn asked, suddenly very interested. "I've wondered that myself for quite some time."

Sean decided to let the conversation roll for a bit and see what came of it. He didn't want to give away that he'd overheard Marie and Mike's conversation, but he did want to stir things up some.

"If we don't get somebody else as president, he's going to drive this sucker into the ground," Darin moaned. "He's been president for nine years, which is five too many. The by-laws state very clearly that you can't hold that office for more that four at a time."

"Do you want it?" Heather asked offhandedly.

Darin snorted at the suggestion. Apparently he had no intention of taking the office.

"Then who's going to take it if you want him out so bad?" she asked, prodding him for some kind of answer.

"Definitely not him," Darin said. "I don't know who, but not him. I don't want the job."

Heather grinned from ear to ear as she leaned back against the couch. "Well, until someone's willing to take it, then maybe we should all keep our mouths shut."

"Maybe," Darin said. He left to go back to the table of food. He got into a conversation with two of the other board members and didn't return.

"The books are a problem, I think," Lynn said, testing the waters with Heather.

"I'm not saying they're not, Lynn. I haven't seen them," she answered back.

"Maybe we push for it at the next board meeting," Sean suggested.

"He'll just put it off like he always does," Lynn said. "That's classic Mike strategy."

Sean checked his watch. "I guess I need to go and be the bearer of bad news." He got up from the couch and said goodbye to everyone else in the kitchen and dining room areas.

"Good luck on the show, Sean," Mike said as he followed him to the door.

"Thanks, Mike."

Mike shut the door behind them and squeezed Sean's arm until it hurt. "I know Tony's your friend, and all, but I hope you understand why we did what we did today."

"I know why, Mike. It's just I hope that we're all willing to play fair with everyone else on the board if anything else happens."

"I'm sure we will."

"One can only hope, huh?"

Mike stared at him not fully understanding what he referred to. Sean said his goodbyes and thanked Mike for the food.

He walked off the porch, got into his car, and left for Tony's.

Chapter Eight

Things didn't go exactly as Sean planned at Tony's place. He received his customary hug and they chatted about everything under the sun except what he had to deliver. He could tell that Tony suspected the worst and he put it off as long as he could. The time came, however, when Sean had run out of things to say on every other subject they discussed and he made his revelation. Tony reacted as if he expected at first, but then his coldness erupted into a string of obscenities and raging about how unprofessional and idiotic the whole bunch was down at the theatre.

Sean gave him some space and played some video games in the other room. Tony fumed and pouted for a while and then joined him. He sat beside him and watched as Tony conquered some unnamed foe with a very big sword. Tears came to Tony's eyes as he sat there.

"It isn't the end of the world," Sean encouraged.

"I just don't know how to react."

"It could be worse, I guess."

"Yeah. That's true. Someone could kill Mike. That'd be bad, wouldn't it?"

With the news Sean had about Marie, Tony's remarks didn't set well with him. "Don't say that."

"I'm just talking."

"Just don't talk that way."

"Why not? He's a jerk," Tony said as more tears flowed down his face.

"Just don't."

"I'm just blowing off steam."

Sean threw the control pad down on the floor. "No, you're not. It's bad form to talk that way so soon after Marie."

"And I thought I was the sensitive one."

Sean bit his tongue. He wanted to tell what he knew, but he had to keep quiet. He had to let them find out in their own time. The last thing he needed to be doing was spouting off about the postmortem report.

"Let's just watch that movie, okay?" Sean suggested.

"Fine."

The film had its usual explosions and inane dialogue that Sean had come to loathe with modern movies. He'd take *Casablanca* any day over the garbage pumped out today, but Tony liked that sort of thing so he acquiesced. His attention wandered as he sat transfixed to the flashing sequences of death and murder and some alien planet where the vegetation had taken on its own life force and gobbled every person within fifty miles.

Marie had been murdered.

The thought echoed over and over in the back of his mind. He tried to refocus his attention on some plotline in the movie, but couldn't.

Marie had been murdered.

The words were harsh and angry somehow. Someone he knew had been killed. The thought refused to compute in his already befuddled mind. The same questions crept back and wouldn't go away.

He watched Tony sit glazed over with every new scene that rolled in front of him. His reaction to his punishment had been so typical. How many tears had he shed for Marie? The possible answer to that made Sean depressed. He didn't shed any. How could he when it had nothing to do with him?

Or, did it?

Sean watched Tony's reactions as a funny line was said or some new plot twist revealed itself. How could someone so enclosed within himself and not able to see two feet in front of his own face reach out and take another life?

Wait a minute. Wait just a minute. Let's not start suspecting everyone that knew her. The police will handle it. It couldn't possibly be anyone he knew. It had to be a stranger.

Didn't it?

He found his thoughts imagining different scenes with a faceless figure chasing Marie into her garage and hitting her on the back of the head. But the faceless shape would change and alter into the face of friends he knew. And every scenario he created in his mind's eye brought a sharp retort. It's just not possible for anyone to have harmed her—not anyone he knew, anyway. Of course, someone hurt her and took her life. But someone he knew?

It's just not possible.

He kept telling himself that as he sat there in front of Tony's television trying and re-trying to engage into this horrible movie. But the suspicious part of his mind continued to creep up on him and remind him that anything was possible.

Not everyone's a saint, he thought bitterly. He remembered the preacher's lesson from the morning. He looked at his watch. It was almost time for evening church services and for this terrible flick to be over.

The credits rolled a half hour later and he endured Tony as he pontificated about the intricacies of the writer's intentions of the director's vision. Sean wanted to argue every point, and would have on any other day, but Sean's thoughts had carried him away to a silent and lonely place.

Marie had been murdered.

Sean made his excuses about the time and needing to go to church and left.

Services were over in an hour, so Sean spent extra time staying afterward and visiting with some of the other members. He caught up on the latest news from a couple that lived down the street from him. They were both retired and Sean liked to keep an eye on them as they got up in years. He said hello to a couple of the ladies who ran their annual food drive and promised to bring cans of something the next time he saw them. He shook hands with the preacher on his way out the door and thanked him for the lesson. It had been about the good Samaritan and Sean loved reading along with the story every time it was talked about from the pulpit.

He sped through the drive-through at Candy's and ordered a couple of burgers and fries with their special "suicide drink" of a half dozen or so sodas all mixed together with a lime on the rim. He got his change and raced out onto the deserted streets of the town.

Since he was single, he liked cruising the streets of Lyle after church on Sundays. He had nowhere special to go and the dogs could wait for him. He eased back in his seat and opened up the bag of burgers. A honk here and there caught his attention and he waved absently at the passersby he knew and recognized. The townsfolk had always been a friendly bunch and he cherished that. It was one of the things that convinced him to move here all those years ago.

He devoured the burgers in a matter of minutes and had slurped most of his "suicide" down when the thought of Marie hit him again. During the evening services, he had shut all thoughts of her demise out of his head. The images of her death at the hands of someone she might have known horrified him. He could see the hard and heavy instrument cracked repeatedly against the back of her skull, sending her down to her knees. The shadowy figure with intentioned malice dragged her limp body to the car and started the engine.

The image kept replaying as if he had a remote control punching for rewind. He shook the pictures from his mind and finished his drink.

The twilight settled lightly on the quiet town as he wove in and out of its streets and byways. He liked the town at night with all its shadows and streetlamps sending out delicate fingers of light onto the ground. The businesses littered the landscape and made him nostalgic for long gone days of his youth when he cruised main street with friends in a far away town in a far away place.

And tonight one citizen wouldn't share the joys with the rest of the tiny village. Off in the funeral home somewhere in the heart of town rested the body of someone he knew.

He couldn't shake the feeling in his gut. The images popped into view again.

He saw in his mind's eye people passing on the other side of the street and not paying attention to a broken man crying out in pain. The sermon of the Samaritan nearly always filled him with guilt for not doing enough to help those who needed it. In the movie, he remembered a bloody hand raised up, reaching out for someone, anyone, to assist.

He braked and spun his car down a side street off of main. He knew the way instinctively and a fresh wave of energy and anxiety filled him.

What did he think he was doing?

It felt like a dare as he turned down another street on the south end of town. Wasn't there someone who could help her? Couldn't any of them do something for Marie?

He heard Ric's voice chiding him from the recesses of his mind. Obviously, he wouldn't approve, but something had moved him that evening. A clear, sharp dagger of regret sliced him open, making him realize that he hadn't taken more time to get to really know Marie. Like the others, he held grudges which kept him at a bitter distance.

Granted, she got on his nerves, but she didn't deserve to die and she didn't deserve to be lost and forgotten.

He had gauged her reactions to him and to life to determine how he should treat her. Instead of treating her based on who he was, he allowed her actions to control his reactions. A twinge of guilt crept to life and spread in his heart.

Ric's agitation came at him again from the depths of his mind. He knew the precautions and even knew the law, but he also understood something else that drove his curiosity forward. He understood a sense of justice and not allowing the worst to happen to those around you by asking why.

I'm going to ask why.

Sean pulled his car down a darkened alleyway and killed his lights. He instantly shook with the sensation of growing tension and nerve. The yellow police tape glowed in the early twilight and drifted gently in the soft breeze easing through the town. He slowed his vehicle down as he rolled up behind Marie's house. Shutting the engine off, he sat there in the inky blackness and planned his next move.

The yellow tape sent a message loud and clear: stay out. He knew that and even appreciated it. This was a live murder case now with the postmortem revelation, but he decided to ignore all that for now. He had eyes and he would use them. Ric would chide him for it, but maybe he wouldn't have to know.

Sean stepped out of his car with care and quiet, easing his way up to the backyard fence that encompassed Marie's property. He slipped underneath the tape, through the back gate, and onto the back porch of the house. Marie had let him stay over when he'd had some major plumbing work done on his house and she'd shown him her secret hiding place for her key.

Although he had stayed there for a couple of days, he rarely saw Marie, which prohibited them from getting to know each other better. But she'd let him stay and that meant a lot. And although they'd never been close after that, he appreciated her moment of uncharacteristic kindness. He regretted never thanking her properly with nothing more than a kind word.

He reached underneath a pottery lily pad and found what he was looking for. The key slid into the lock easily enough and he entered her house without any serious effort. The house echoed with silence as he stood there drinking in the surroundings. He wouldn't turn on the lights. He knew well enough that that would attract attention from the neighborhood. Say what you will, but small towns are known for nosy neighbors.

That might be to his advantage.

He would contemplate that later. For now, he had to find a source of light that he could use to search the premises. He walked into the kitchen and dug through drawer after drawer of utensils, bowls, old magazines, and other what-nots that she'd collected over the years. The next to the last drawer had what he needed. He found a steel flashlight, clicked it to life, and shot a steady beam of light onto the linoleum floor of Marie's kitchen.

Everything had its own place on her counters. Marie had the rep of being a neat freak about her house and cherished the fact that it was so clean it squeaked. Sean vaguely remembered a cast party she threw where she bragged about how many hours she'd spent cleaning before the party. It didn't seem to matter, though, as Tony drank too much and puked watermelon onto her bathroom floor. There had been a ruckus, but the humor of the moment won the day. Tony bragged about his hangover for weeks.

He searched every room, but everything seemed in perfect order. He knew the police had probably spent their afternoon inside the house combing for new clues. He didn't know what he would find, if anything.

But he knew he had to try and do something.

He checked the bathroom where Tony had blown chunks and the memory faded into view. He could see Tony hugging the porcelain throne and swearing upon everything that was holy in the universe that he would never, ever again do something so wicked and so foolish. That had lasted all of a month before he did it again, but the thought was there at least.

Sean leaned against the frame of the door and thought about the moments he'd spent in Marie's house in her company. Too many times differences drive folks apart and Marie had practically shoved others away with her actions and words. His times here had been too few and too far between for someone he was supposed to have known well.

Sean angled the light ahead of his feet and toward the utility room. Butterflies twisted into knots in his stomach as he approached the rear of the house and the door that led to the garage.

The scene of the crime, he thought bitterly.

The utility room had clothes strewn about in great clumps and piles. He avoided these and put his hand on the doorknob. A moment's hesitation and a quick breath and then he opened the door.

A faint mustiness filled his nostrils. He scrunched his face against the aroma and tried to shut it out. The flashlight cast giant shadows off the tools and other things Marie had hanging from her garage walls. Like the house, everything had its proper place. Rakes, hoes, and hoses lined the walls in pristine order. And most of it looked brand new or hardly used.

He followed the light's path as it ran along the length of the wall. Nothing appeared to be out of place.

What am I doing here?

He spun the light onto the concrete where her car had rested. The police had apparently moved it out already. Maybe they had it impounded until the family could do something with it. Oil spots decorated the floor like some mad Rorschach test gone slightly insane. The light played on a spot on the floor that had a different coloration to it. Sean bent down and recognized the dried blood that had coagulated on the concrete.

While unconscious, her assailant had let her lay on the floor long enough for blood to spot near the car. The impact of the instrument used had drawn blood. A queasy feeling shot through his stomach and into his legs. A moment of dizziness made him close his eyes.

She had been here. Right here.

As he knelt by the dried spot, he swung the flashlight to the cracks and crevices in the garage. She swept on a regular basis it seemed from the little to almost no collection of dust and dirt on the concrete floor. He cast the light underneath a work table on the far wall and saw the same thing. On the work bench, she had cans of screws, tubes of glue, and other paraphernalia.

Wait a minute. What's that?

He streamed the light underneath again and some kind of lumpy device cast a shadow on the back of the wall. The flashlight's beam had captured something amiss in Marie's perfectly groomed garage. He got closer and saw the handle of a tool or gardening utensil of some kind. He cast the light back onto the wall, but he didn't see anything missing from the marker outlines she had drawn around each of her implements.

What is this thing?

He bent down again and reached for it. It was a handle, all right.

Sean put it under the light and nearly fell over.

He swallowed bile and decided now would be a good time to make a phone call.

Chapter Nine

"Just what do you think you were doing, anyway?" Ric asked, obviously in a huff about things.

"I don't know. It seemed like the right thing to do."

Ric folded his arms and took an authoritative tone. "I've had to do some talking with the chief, but I think he's cool, although he has every right not to be."

"What if I hadn't found that hammer?" Sean asked, defending himself.

"Someone would have. They only started their initial investigation earlier today, Sean. They would've found it."

Sean sipped from his cup of coffee. They had met up at the all-night quick stop on the outskirts of Lyle. Ric had blown up on the phone and promised to rush down there in a hurry. He would also notify the Lyle P.D. of what Sean had found.

After an hour or so at Marie's and a score of questions from the chief, Sean had been allowed to leave the scene of the crime with a warning to call next time with any suspicions that he might have. Ric had backed him up with the chief and swore his friend wouldn't do anything else to mess up the investigation.

"You know what it means, don't you?" Sean asked.

"I know exactly what it means. Do you?"

Sean drank the last of his coffee and threw the cup in the dumpster near the quick stop. "We're all going to get questioned now."

Ric laughed at that. "Of course you are. You probably would've anyway."

"I'm scared," Sean said.

"I would be, too. Things could get very complicated in your show down there."

"And I've got to find a way to keep my mouth shut."

"You better, Sean. Keep it zipped for the time being. Let the cops here do their job. And they will."

Sean didn't want to share his doubt. He also didn't want to re-live that moment when he put the hammer he'd found into the light. The memory still caused goose bumps to pop up on his forearms and the backs of his hands.

In the glow of the flashlight, he turned the hammer over and over in his hand. And then he tipped the handle up and saw what made him almost vomit.

The letters *LCT* had been branded into the butt-end of the handle.

"She could've had it stored there, you know," Ric offered, not really believing it himself.

"No chance. Every single item in there had its own special place, man. That hammer was brought here for the express purpose of bashing her over the head."

"Don't jump to conclusions. There could be a rational explanation."

It was Sean's turn to laugh. "Uh-huh. And what does your gut tell you? I know what mine tells me. Marie didn't make it a habit of carrying off the theatre's tools for her own use. She had her own stuff in there, Ric. There were plenty of hammers lining the walls in there."

Ric countered: "It could've been carried off months ago by someone in a past show. That could explain it."

Sean shook his head vehemently. "No way, man. My gut tells me that someone down there had a grudge big enough to want to take her life over it."

"Who had one against her?" Ric asked, going into his "cop mode" as he playfully called it.

"Who didn't?"

"That good of a reputation, huh?"

"She rubbed everyone down there the wrong way. I could give you a list of all the folks down there she had ticked off."

Ric smiled mischievously and finished off his own cup of coffee. "You may have to soon enough. Not for me, but probably for the chief."

"I don't like knowing what I know, Ric. We start rehearsals tomorrow night," Sean said.

Ric patted him gently on the shoulder. "Then I guess we'll see what kind of actor you really are."

And he did have to dig deep within himself to hide what he knew the following night. By then the news had spread like an out of control blaze that Marie's death had been no accident. The usual starting time for rehearsal of seven o'clock got postponed while they all bemoaned the situation and wondered what to do. Sean listened intently to the conversation, all the time asking himself if one of them there could be a killer.

He didn't like contemplating it.

"What's happening in this town of ours?" Dora asked. She threw her script down to add emphasis. The others could only hopelessly stare and gawk in their own bewilderment.

"That changes a lot of things," Darin mumbled to himself.

"What things?" Lynn asked.

"I don't know…just everything around here. One of our own got murdered."

Our own, thought Sean. Who was he kidding? Darin had little love for Marie and made no bones about it. Now that it had been revealed that she'd been killed, they all seemed to be Marie's closest confidant and friend.

Suffering by association, Sean wondered maliciously. Some kind of twisted Baron Munchausen by proxy situation if there ever was one.

"We really should do something to honor her in this show," Tony suggested. The irony struck Sean with his sincerity and sad countenance. Every one in that room had something bitterly against Marie while living, but now she was one step away from community theatre sainthood.

"We'll think of something, Tony. Don't worry about it," Lynn offered. "Darin and I will talk about it and maybe do something in the program, or make some sort of announcement before one of the shows."

"That sounds good," Heather agreed. She took the news the hardest and a steady stream of tears had flowed since the discussion began.

"We'll talk to Mike about it, too," Darin said. "But we should really get down to it tonight and try to get a read-through out of the way and discuss some of the blocking."

"After a break, maybe, Darin," Lynn suggested, which he readily agreed to. They broke and left to find a place to sit in quiet or congregate and gossip more about Marie's death. Not once was it ever suggested that someone there had been responsible. Sean knew that if the info about the hammer was revealed, things would turn ugly at the theatre. Suspicions would darken the production and a score of accusations would fly like unwanted bats in the belfry.

Sean joined Tony out in front of the building. He sat next to him on the hood of his car. They sat in an uncomfortable silence until Tony couldn't handle it any longer.

"This is very weird, man, very strange," Tony said.

"To say the very least."

Heather and Dora joined them. Dora lit up a cigarette and blew smoke into the air. Heather continued to wipe tears from her swollen face.

"Life is one bizarre ride, guys," observed Dora. She blew more smoke out of her mouth.

"And I feel horrible about it," Heather said. "She was my friend and now I have to face the fact that someone took her life."

You aren't the only one dealing with that, Sean thought.

"It's like some wacky surrealist painting with all the colors mixed together and running into one big tornado of imagery," Dora said.

"What?" Tony asked. "What are you talking about?"

"Art stuff. Sorry. I let my art lingo get tangled up when I talk."

Heather sniffled to get their attention. "And I feel so guilty, too, guys."

"What about?" Sean asked.

"I don't know. I just...I didn't think she deserved the role she got."

"Me, either," Dora said. "One of the boys' dates, maybe, but the woman at the hotel room? I didn't see that at all."

Heather admitted: "I was mad at her because of it."

"She didn't cast it, Heather," Sean reminded her. "She had nothing to do with it."

She shook her head and wiped more tears away. "I know that. But she knew how bad I wanted it, so she worked extra hard to get it. Didn't you see her unbutton her blouse a couple of buttons the night of call backs?"

"You're kidding me?" Tony asked, completely oblivious to this piece of information. "She did that?"

"She did," Dora agreed, "and she made no bones about it. She knew if she showed a bit of cleavage that Lynn and Darin would cast her."

"Wait a minute, now. Come on, guys," Sean found himself saying.

"What are you guys talking about?" Sara asked from behind them. She had just come out to gather the troops for rehearsal.

"Nothing," everyone chimed in unison and lumbered inside for the first read-through of the show.

The reading plodded along at a steady pace. They took ten at the act break and came back refreshed to finish. Lynn and Darin finished the night by explaining characterizations and other bits of information valuable to the actors. The new people soaked it all up with vigor. The regulars muddled through distant thoughts of Marie's death. Distracted eyes darted around looking for nothing in particular in the auditorium as they dwelt on the dark subject of murder.

"And so we start blocking tomorrow night and we'll try to get act one done and then we'll get act two on Wednesday night," Darin said. "Work on memorization right now and get it done as soon as possible. The sooner we're off book, the better off we'll be for such a heavy show."

Bobbing heads moved in unison and the cast shuffled through the auditorium into the cool night. Most of the new folks said their good nights and left. Sean and the others camped out in front of the building and discussion struck up again about Marie's death.

An uneasiness crept through Sean and had been for most of the night. He had determined to keep a watchful eye out for anyone who might seem to be suspicious or on guard about Marie. But up until that point everyone there acted like he thought they would. But then again, it may have only been acting.

Looking at Sara and Darin, he decided to try and crack some of the ice. "What was going on with you two the other night?" he asked Sara.

"What are you talking about, Sean?" she shot back.

"You know. You and Marie getting into it."

Sara's mood darkened and Sean regretted asking the question. Darin put his arm around her and frowned in Sean's direction. "I told you the other day to not ask me about it, Sean."

"Sorry. I was just wondering," Sean said. It didn't help.

"Let's just say that Marie opened her mouth about some things that weren't her business," she said wearily. She leaned against Darin for support and he held her tighter.

"Why do you ask, snoopy?" Tony asked, suddenly agitated about something. Sean shrugged and tried to change the subject. "Listen, curiosity is one thing, but maybe some things are off limits. You know?"

"I was just asking."

"And I'm asking why, man. Why?" Tony said. "Don't try and play detective, Sean. It doesn't suit you."

"Who said I was?" Sean said more defensively than he wanted to.

"Guys. Don't worry about it," Sara said, trying to intervene.

"Sara was just very upset by something Marie said to her and I just wondered about it, that's all."

Darin held up his hands to avoid an argument in the group. "There are some things just not worth hashing over again. She popped off and Sara got upset about it. 'Nuff said."

But Sean knew that there was more to it. The sudden shift in Sara's mood, Tony's attack, and Darin's offhanded way of changing the subject pointed to a real problem.

Someone at the theatre is a killer. The thought made him sick.

He heard the tiny voice in the back of his mind whisper it as he stood there. He examined all the faces around him and tried to imagine one of them as a murderer. The thoughts turned bitter and he let them go for the time being. Sullen expressions of regret clouded over everyone and the gathering broke up for the evening. Sean didn't attempt to smooth anything over, but decided to call it a night and head home.

"Uh-oh, here comes trouble," Darin said, pointing off in the distance. The others turned in time to see Lynn's daughter, Angie, rush up on her scooter. She buzzed by her father and waved.

"Hey, you," he said. "What are you doing here? Aren't you supposed to be at home doing your homework?"

"Mom said to come and check on you. And so here I am."

"It's a little late to be out on your scooter, hon," he said.

She agreed. "Yeah, I know, but I need to go get some gas for it. You'd think I drove this thing everywhere or it drinks gas." She laughed.

Lynn grabbed for his wallet and passed some cash over to her. "Both." She hugged him and sped off into the night. The scooter zipped away with the echo of its motor still hanging in the air.

"And that's why I don't have kids," Darin teased.

"Here, here," Tony chimed in.

Sean opened the door to his car. Sara caught up with him and looped an arm through his.

"Hey, you. Listen, I didn't mean to get upset with you," she said.

"I'm the one who should be apologizing, not you," he countered. He swung into his front seat and put the keys in the ignition. "I don't know what I was thinking."

"Marie and I never got along very well," she admitted. "I wanted to and we went out a couple of times. She came over to MoMo's there for a while and we would sit around and drink a few. One night I drank too much and shared some things with her that I shouldn't have."

"You don't have to tell me, Sara," Sean said, reassuring her that he wouldn't pry anymore into it.

"I'm not going to, Sean. Let's just say that some things that are personal are meant to stay that way."

He rubbed his forehead with the back of his hand and slid behind the wheel. "It's just you can't seem to make any meaning of an event like this. You know?"

"I know." She patted him on the shoulder.

"And she and I didn't have a great love for each other, either, but still." He sat in silence and waited for Sara to fill it. She didn't and the quiet made them both uncomfortable. Sean started his bug and pulled the gear shift into drive.

"It kinda makes me afraid," Sara admitted suddenly as if sharing some deep secret. Sean understood that. He felt the same way. "I mean, we knew her and she got on everybody's nerves around here and we all wanted her gone and then...well, now she is. I don't know what to say about it. I mean, who would kill her, Sean? And why? Who benefits from her death?"

"I wish I knew," he said. "I really do."

"Me, too." She hugged him and he drove away wondering what he thought he had been doing. Why did he persist in knowing what Marie had said to Sara? He had to know, that's all there was to it.

Someone at the theatre is a killer.

That's why. It was simple as that. He needed to know. He had to find out. And if he played it right, he might be able to find the truth.

And that was worth more than anything else in the world.

Chapter Ten

Work kept Sean alert the next day as he ran a thousand and one errands along with all the other work he'd set up for himself. He'd been working on a new inter-office campaign involving T-shirts and bumper stickers with the company's logo on them. The company doing both had made a spelling error, forcing the items back to factory and setting his cool plan off by a couple of weeks.

In the middle of the afternoon, he took a much needed coffee break, grabbed his script for the show, and found solace in the break room. Since Marie's death, he'd had little time to contemplate or celebrate his first leading role of Willy Loman. He knew Tony had been ticked about it, but that's the way Darin saw it. He couldn't do anything about that and knew Tony would eventually get over it. As long as he felt his role had importance in the show, Tony would be utterly thrilled.

He cracked the script open and tried to commit the highlighted lines to memory. Willy started the show and Sean knew that he would have to come in with presence and strength onto the stage.

Who benefits from her death?

The thought sprang up from nowhere and he had to shut the script for a moment. The question had been asked the night before and he couldn't seem to shake it. Why would someone take another person's life? The answer had to be because that person would stand to benefit from the death. But who would benefit at the theatre?

The discovery of the hammer in Marie's garage could be explained a dozen different ways, all leading to someone else not associated with the theatre, but somehow that didn't ring true to Sean. Marie had obviously ruffled feathers. But who would be driven to do such a deed?

Who benefits from her death?

Benefits could mean a number of things. Insurance, her will, revenge, an act of anger, of passion, could all be at the core of the "benefits." Her death had brought some kind of satisfaction to someone. As sick as it sounded, that lay at the crux of the matter for the killer. That person wanted her dead. She is, so now that person's life can go back to normal, or some semblance of normalcy that the killer needed which could only be brought about by Marie's death.

Sean opened the script to the page he'd marked and got back to memorizing. Too many questions were floating around in his already convoluted mind. He knew he had to get the lines down for the first scene before tonight. Blocking would be tonight and he needed to be off book enough to write down instructions regarding where to go, where to exit and enter, and what business he needed to do onstage.

He sipped from his cup of coffee and let the lines sink into his mind, hoping they would graft onto a brain cell and stay there for the next six weeks of rehearsal time.

He shut the book and finished his coffee. The lines weren't coming. The news of Marie had unsettled him too much. A play done without Marie. When was the last time that had happened at the community theatre? He couldn't think of a time in recent memory. She had played bit and secondary roles for a long time. The last two shows had given her the chance to play the lead. Would it run smoother without her there? Was there a way to replace her on the board?

Who benefits from her death?

The thought made his stomach sour. He threw his coffee cup away and got back to work.

At home, Sean found that Ric had phoned earlier in the day and left a message on Sean's machine. He grabbed his cordless as he dug deep for a frying pan to cook up his favorite concoction of sour kraut and ham for a sandwich. Ric picked up at work and they exchanged pleasantries.

"So?" Sean asked.

"So what?"

"Why'd you call, lunkhead?"

"Hey, hey. You're insulting my mother there," Ric joked.

"I hope so," Sean teased back.

Ric cleared his throat. "Hold on just a sec." Sean heard a chair scrape the floor in the background and then the shutting of a door. The phone banged around on the other end as Ric picked it back up. "Okay. I'm back."

"That bad?"

"I just wanted to give you a heads up."

"What for?" Sean opened a can of kraut and put it in the pan. He turned the heat onto medium and let it simmer.

"I know you, bud. I know this thing is eating you up."

"Wouldn't it you?" Sean asked.

"It would. I just want you to be very careful what you try and step into," Ric warned.

"You're assuming that I'm going to try and dig."

"Come on, Sean, who are you talking to here? I know you've probably already gone over it a hundred times. I just want you to be careful. The coroner reported today that the wound to Marie's head would have eventually killed her if the carbon monoxide hadn't. And the hair fibers and blood on the hammer are hers."

Sean leaned against the counter. "I see."

"This whole thing is premeditated, man."

"How do you know that?" Sean asked.

"The crime scene and her house not being disturbed is one clue."

"So, it was planned?"

"Yes. Whoever did this is capable of mapping something like this out and then acting upon it."

"Which means?"

"They didn't do it as an act of passion, you know, a spur of the moment kind of thing," Ric said with warning in his voice.

"Meaning this person is capable of planning another if need be?"

"That's what I'm saying. I want you to be extremely careful up there."

Sean stirred the kraut and added some slices of ham into the skillet. "I'm only asking questions."

"That could get you into trouble."

"I'll keep my eyes peeled," Sean said, hoping to sound nonchalant.

"And your ears open. And don't forget to drop a line in case you do find out anything."

Sean laughed at that. "This is very unorthodox, you know."

"Dude, it's your life and I'm not about to try and talk you out of asking questions. It'd be a waste of breath."

"I'll see what happens."

"Do that," Ric ordered.

With that he hung up and was gone. Sean clicked the *Talk* button on his phone and put it back on the counter. He stirred the contents in the pan and thought about what Ric had said.

The killer hadn't done it as an accident or an act of passion. It was deliberate, calculated, and carried out by someone who had mapped it out ahead of time. No random act here.

Could this person do it again?

He would need to be ever so careful how he asked his questions.

Another night of rehearsal rolled around with an intense evening of blocking and setting the stage business in order. Darin barked out orders as if they were commandments from up on high. Lynn gophered for him as the rehearsal trudged on for over three hours. Sara and Dora whined for breaks throughout and Darin acquiesced for a couple of fifteen minute breathers.

Sean took the opportunity to walk through the shop area of the theatre. He snooped through the tools, which were scattered all over the place. All was chaos with electric cords, screwdrivers, screws, hammers (with the *LCT* brand), glue, measuring tapes, and other odds and ends strewn about as if a bomb had gone off in the place. Lynn found him and said they were resuming.

"What are you doing, Sean?" he asked, joining him.

"We have a mess back here."

"That's the way it always is. I'm sure it's the way it will always be, too."

"Who does the buying of the tools around here?" Sean asked.

Lynn grabbed a screwdriver and put it in a toolbox. "Whoever can get the credit card from Mike. I usually do it when we need something. But Darin has taken it up lately."

"I was just curious."

"Come on, let's get back to it."

Sean scribbled furiously in his script the rest of night. Darin blocked the scenes with a rag-tag precision that seemed to make some sort of sense. He made changes as he saw problems and Sean erased and re-wrote directions in the margins. Stage business had been discussed and he made notes of that as well.

"Why don't you come over after rehearsal?" Tony asked during the blocking of their scene together.

"Sounds good," Sean said without lifting his head from his script. He jotted down more notes as Darin dictated directions to him. He thought absently how Tony had given him an opportunity to do a little digging. He just hoped he could do it without ruffling his friend too much.

Afterwards, the crew joined outside and discussion turned from the play back to Marie. The usual bits of gossip were thrown around as the dialogue heated up and then cooled again. The shadow of Marie hung over them and they all knew it.

"It's almost like the play is haunted. You know?" Sara said as she clung to Darin. He kissed her on the brow and whispered something in her ear. They quickly said their goodbyes and were gone.

"She could do that with any show," Dora mused. She hopped in her car and leaned back, staring at the stars. "She'd be proud of all this, I'm sure."

"I don't think she intended to do it by dying, Dora," Sean retorted.

"Who knows with Marie?" she said bitterly.

Tony looked at his watch and tapped Sean on the shoulder. "I'm heading home, man. See ya there." He fired up his car and left.

"You guys watching a movie?" Lynn asked.

"I guess so." Sean got into his car and started it.

Lynn yawned and glanced at his watch. "Oh, man. I've got an early class in the morning. I've got a couple of things to do inside and then I'm outta here." He waved to them and entered the theatre. Sean noticed that Heather hadn't come out of the theatre and that her car was still parked in front.

Dora and Sean said their farewells and promised to see each other the next night for more rehearsal. Sean enjoyed putting on productions, but knew the drudgery of the night after night practices that seemed to drag on forever. They had just started the process, but they all seemed so fatigued already. Maybe Marie's death cast a bigger shadow then he truly understood.

Tony had cracked open a couple of sodas and had them set out. He also had a new DVD that he'd bought and was ready to watch. Sean noted that it was some sci-fi classic that had just been released in the DVD format. He loved the old movies and was ready to watch it. He drank from his ice-cold can as he watched Tony scurry over to answer the ringing phone.

"It's your dime," Tony said into the receiver. Sean could tell it was Dora by his tone and what they discussed. Apparently she had a concern about a costume item, which Tony had agreed to assist her with.

Sean leaned back on the couch and settled his head against the wall. A headache had been coming on for most of the evening, but he'd been able to work around it. Now the dull throbbing grabbed his attention. He hoped he could make it through the flick.

"No way, Dora! That can't be!" Tony said into the phone, his tone shifting suddenly.

Sean sat forward and eavesdropped. More gossip from the theatre, apparently, from the tone in Tony's voice. Tony sat at his kitchen table and listened intently for a long time. Sean noticed his bills neatly stacked in an organizer on the table.

Is it bill time already? he asked himself. He'd check his own in the morning. A yellow slip caught his attention so he walked over to the table and perused the bills. He and Tony had known each other long enough that scrounging in each other's stuff had become a matter of habit. He tilted the yellow page back and saw a doctor's name printed in the corner. Tony ripped it from his hands.

"What do you think you're doing?" he yelped.

"Looking." Sean meant it as nothing more than innocent curiosity, but Tony's reaction turned violent.

"Mind your own business." He turned his attention back to the phone. "Not you. Never mind."

Tony's agitation increased and Sean knew when to back off. He plopped back down on the sofa and drained the rest of his soda. The tone on the phone got ugly and he could tell that Tony's frustration was getting poured onto Dora.

"Lay off, man," Sean whispered to him. Tony said nothing, but pointed a finger at him. He rung off and pouted on the couch.

"What?" Sean asked. Tony said nothing, but pretended to be studying the back of the DVD box. Sean knew the routine all too well and let him go through it. Tony blew out a series of heavy sighs and set the box down with folded arms gripped tightly across his chest.

"Dude, I was just looking through your bills. No big deal," Sean offered.

"You have no idea, do you?"

"About what?"

"About anything." The words were bitter and were meant to sting. Sean let it roll off and waited.

"What did Dora want?" Sean asked, hoping to change the subject.

"Not much. She was asking about her costume and she said that Mike called Lynn after everyone left and said there wasn't as much money available for this show as he'd originally thought."

"You're kidding me? What about the musical we just did? That raked in a tremendous amount of money."

"Go ask Mike."

"He wouldn't tell me anything," Sean shot back. *But maybe the books would,* he thought to himself. If he could find them, that is.

"That guy is crooked and I get slapped down for writing a few bad things on my own website," Tony hissed. "Something ain't right in Denmark."

"What about this doctor thing, Tony? You didn't say anything about going to see a doctor."

Tony looked at the ceiling and released another one of his sighs. "There's a reason for that."

"Oh, I see."

"No, you don't, Sean."

"Is it something that you'd rather keep private?" Sean asked, knowing it was an obvious question with an obvious answer.

"Well, duh, but I'm way past that now, aren't I?"

Sean got up and threw his empty can away. He grabbed a bag of chips off the top of the fridge and dug into them. He offered some to Tony, who refused.

"What is it and who knows?" Sean asked, putting it together.

Tony grabbed the sheet of paper and folded it open across his lap. Sean sat on the couch and munched away on the chips.

"Aw, man," Tony groaned, not really wanting to discuss it, but not wanting to deny his comrade. "When Sara and I were together, we were *together*."

"I figured that. I think everyone knew."

"Well, the fun thing is that Sara just so happened to have some baggage, if you get my drift."

"Baggage?" And then the shoe dropped and Sean frowned. "I see. Did she know when you two were *together*?"

"No. She found out later and told me that I needed to go get checked out. And so I did." He handed the sheet over to Sean, who read the results. He shook his head sadly.

"Man, I'm sorry. I had no idea," Sean said.

"No one was supposed to, either, but it didn't work out that way."

"What happened?"

Tony leaned back in his chair and gazed at a spot on the ceiling. "You know, I'm not really proud of getting an STD. It's not something you wear like a crown or ribbon. And Sara isn't even someone known for *getting around*, if you know what I mean."

"I do."

"One time with some poor slob months ago and she didn't even know about it until after." He let the thought trail off as he collected his thoughts. "And now I've got baggage and that's something I'll have to deal with like forever," he said, the bitterness taking over. "And is if that weren't bad enough, Sara has to open her fat mouth and tell someone."

"Darin?"

"If only! He doesn't even know yet, which is bad enough because he's pressuring her to go all the way now and she won't and refuses to tell him why."

More drama, Sean thought sadly. *It never ends.*

"Someone else then," Sean remarked.

"Sara got chummy with one of our board members a few weeks back during the musical. They were at MoMo's and Sara imbibed, let's just say. And she shared her secret with the worst person possible."

Sean knew who before Tony told him. It had to be Marie.

"Marie," he said.

Tony shot him a glance that could freeze water. He squeezed his face with his hands and sighed again. "Yeah, Marie. And she's been, or had been, holding that over Sara ever since."

"Is that what happened the other night at the theatre?"

Tony shook his head.

"So Marie used it as something to tease Sara about?" Sean asked, knowing it had to more than just that.

"Are you kidding? She used it to get an advantage over Sara. She threatened to tell everybody down there. I could cope with something like that. Everyone down there thinks the worst of me anyway. What would one more thing be? But for Sara, it would be a different story. She's totally embarrassed and feels like a failure for having it and then passing it onto me."

"So if Sara ever got in Marie's way, she would use it against her. That's what you're saying."

"Exactly what I'm saying. She saw Sara as a threat to her down at the theatre, so she used it. And I'd had enough of it."

"Enough to..." Sean let it hang in the air without finishing it. Tony glared at him, knowing the rest of it. They sat in silence. Sean closed his eyes and tried to imagine Marie's final moments. Would a secret like this lead to murder?

"Go ahead and finish it, Sean," Tony said. A coldness had settled on him and Sean could feel it across the living room.

"Forget it."

"Oh, no, pal, finish your sentence."

"Fine. Enough to murder her?" Sean asked.

"What do you think?"

"You said to finish my sentence and I did. I wasn't thinking."

Tony laughed at that. "Oh, yes you were, pal. You were thinking too much. I didn't like Marie so you're trying to play detective and you're doing a pretty poor job of it."

Sean shrugged. He reached for his backpack and dug out a sheaf of papers. He had read them earlier in the day and highlighted some very interesting spots. Tony leaned over in curiosity and saw they were printouts of his online diary.

"What's that?" he asked.

"The evidence used against you on Sunday."

"My journal?" He reached out to jerk them from him, but Sean was too quick.

"Just wait a minute, man," Sean said. He passed through the top few pages and then came to a passage he wanted to read. "You wrote: 'and sometimes I think the best thing for the theatre would be for some folks to disappear from the scene. And I don't mean disappear in the traditional sense, meaning going onto other things. I mean like disappear as in for good.'" He folded the sheet and stuck it back in his bag. Tony sat there bewildered.

"Get out of here," he hissed.

"You'd better understand something, Tony," Sean said with growing intensity. "This is a murder investigation now. And if and when the police find this, you will be on their list of folks they're going to be very interested in."

"I can go in and change it."

"Uh, no you can't and I won't let you. You can call it blowing off steam, but she's dead now and it looks like something else. You wrote her name a couple of sentences later, man. You weren't just generalizing."

"Just get out of here."

Sean found another passage to read. "And I quote: 'Marie would be much better off if she weren't around anymore. And I don't mean just not here at the theatre. I mean some place else and somewhere permanent.'"

"Get out of here!" Tony shouted.

Sean stood up with his backpack in his hand. "You'd better listen to me, Tony. Your opinions are your business and everyone knows that. You remind us all the time. But here's the thing. You should've been smarter and shouldn't have written what you did. And no matter what Marie did, didn't merit something like this on a public site. But it's done now. And I'm just telling you as a friend that you'd better be ready because Lyle's finest are going to start questioning those who knew her and that means us."

"What are you talking about?"

"She was hit on the back of the head, Tony, before she was put in the car."

"Okay, so the paper said something about it. So what?"

"A hammer."

"Okay."

He let a dramatic pause fill the room. "One of ours."

"What's that supposed to mean?"

"One from the theatre, Tony. That's what I mean."

Tony stood up suddenly and stormed into the kitchen. Sean had calculated this as carefully as he could. He knew that if he wanted to find out anything, he would have to start dropping bombs. He also knew that before morning everyone in the theatre would have a heads up on this. It was a risk and he understood that.

He also knew that since the information had come from him, he might be putting himself in danger. He had promised Ric to hold off from spilling this piece of information, but he wanted to rock a few boats.

"Go on and get out of here if that's all you want to talk about."

"Fine." He grabbed his bag and grabbed the doorknob.

"But for the record, I didn't do it."

"I never thought you did," Sean said.

"Don't lie." Tony had known him long enough to know when Sean fibbed to him. "You wouldn't have asked all that and read from my journal if you didn't have a suspicion."

"But you do now, don't you? Your mind is turning it over. Who down there would've wanted her dead? It's a scary question, isn't it? The cops will start interrogating all of us now and so we'd better get ready for the fact that one of us down there is probably a murderer."

"It isn't me."

"Say I believe you. Look at it from their point of view. You have two strikes against you already. What you told me tonight about you and Sara and your journal. That's plenty to get the law on your trail."

"Everyone down there had something against Marie!" Tony yelled. "I'm not the only one."

"You're exactly right about that. And the implication is that someone went so far as to kill her. Someone of our own number. Someone in our own midst."

"Someone we're acting with on the stage right now," Tony said softly, almost to himself.

"That could very well be. Now you know why I'm asking."

Chapter Eleven

The investigation entered the phase of questioning all those who knew Marie. The police needed information on her movements, habits, and other tidbits of info that would lead to some kind of clue about her last remaining hours. The hammer brought an investigator to begin the process of rounding up the theatre members. He started calling and making appointments. He found Sean at his house preparing to leave for Marie's funeral.

Hello, there," the man said as Sean let him into the house.

"Come on in, officer. Do you want anything to drink?" Sean opened the fridge and handed over a soda before the officer could refuse.

"Thanks. Nice place."

"I've been working on it lately. I bought it as a fixer-upper a few years ago and have just gotten around to it."

They sat down in the living room. Sean sipped at his own drink while the officer looked through his pile of untidy notes that he kept crammed in a jacket pocket.

"I'm Officer Stiles, by the way," he said after he had his notes in order. "Adam Stiles."

They shook hands and he fumbled through his notes again.

"Not a common occurrence here in Lyle, huh?" Sean found himself asking to break the tension in the room.

"Not at all. The chief is thinking about asking for some O.S.B.I. help, but you didn't hear that from me."

"Right. That bad, is it?"

"I'm sure you know all about it," Stiles said with a smile painted across his face. "I've talked to your friend Ric from down south."

Sean laughed. "Great. Don't believe everything that he says."

"What he says is that you've got a pretty sharp mind."

Sean grunted surprise and finished off his soda. "I don't know about that. I've played armchair detective with Ric on a couple of things in the past."

"That helped him out apparently," Stiles said. "What about Marie Winters?"

Sean explained everything he knew about her and his work with her down at the community theatre. The officer seemed interested and jotted a couple of notes on a piece of paper. Sean ran through the events of the past ten days or so and described how much she was despised down at the theatre.

"And so we have a hammer that apparently is from the theatre," Stiles remarked, "unless it was made to look that way for a reason."

At first Sean laughed at the suggestion, but then thought hard about it. *Could that be?* he wondered. *Would someone go that far to throw them off the scent?*

He recalled collecting the hammer from Marie's garage and the careful etching in the butt of the hammer. No. It was the theatre's. He knew it and he told Stiles as much.

"Just a thought, anyway," Stiles said. He drank from his can of soda and set it down on a coaster on the coffee table. The coaster had a comedy face sculpted into it. "Pretty cool, that," he said.

"A gift from Marie, as a matter of fact. I directed her last season in a show and she found those for me."

"Was she generous?" Stiles asked.

"Not so much."

"Seeing anyone down at the theatre?"

Sean frowned. He hadn't thought of that because he couldn't imagine it. Was this nothing more than a lover's quarrel? Surely not. He had seen her make eyes at men down at the theatre, but nothing ever came of it.

"So no?" Stiles asked, breaking him out of his trance.

"Not that I know of. Like I said, most everyone down there couldn't stand her, so I can't imagine anyone going out with her."

"So not possible?"

"Not at all."

Stiles made another note and then began asking about Tony's online journal. He described it in such a way that Sean knew he'd already taken a look at it.

"You've seen it then?" Sean asked.

"We've been out there, yeah. There's a lot of hateful stuff out there."

"Tony can be a hateful guy sometimes."

"And you say he's a friend of yours?" Stiles studied Sean as he answered and Sean knew it.

"Look, I won't protect a killer. But I will say this, I don't think it was Tony."

"Why's that?"

"He's a talker. Plain and simple. He blusters a lot and gets it off his chest. When he wrote it, he probably didn't see anything wrong with it. He would say it was just stream of consciousness kind of stuff and let it go at that."

"But she's dead," Stiles reminded him as he made another note.

"Yeah."

"That changes things, don't you think?"

"I'm having enough trouble trying to get geared up for the funeral this afternoon, officer," Sean confessed.

Stiles churned uncomfortably in his seat. "If it was someone down at the theatre, I don't have a clue as to who it might be. I'm hoping your questioning finds some answers. It's hard enough going down to rehearsal every night thinking that someone there is a killer."

Stiles rose from his chair and thanked Sean for the cold drink. "Look, I'm sorry. I know this is terrible timing, but we're just now finding the right questions to be asking the right people."

An idea hit Sean as he led Stiles back to the front door. "Can I ask a question?"

"Sure."

"Have you questioned anyone in her neighborhood?"

"Yeah."

"Did anyone hear anything? See anything?"

Stiles shook his head. "Most were asleep and didn't hear a thing." He pulled a sheet of paper from his stack of notes. "A Mrs. Singer says she heard some kind of noise early in the morning, but wasn't sure what it was."

"Mrs. Singer?"

"Mildred Singer. Know her?"

"I think Marie introduced me to her once upon a time."

Stiles shook Sean's hand again and thanked him for his time.

"I'm sure you'll be back," Sean said.

"Most likely, yeah. And hey, if you hear anything, let me know, will ya?"

Sean said he would as he shut the door. He glanced at his watch. He had less than an hour to get down to the church to join the others for Marie's funeral. He grabbed a tie and jacket out of his closet. He fed the dogs and watched them fight playfully over the grub.

"Hey, now, Weejo," he warned as she got too rambunctious with Titan. "Cool it, now."

The dog licked his face and tried to paw at his legs. He pushed her back and shut the back door to the house. He ran a comb through his tangled hair, checked himself in the mirror, and headed out the door for the First Baptist.

He revved the bug to life and zipped through town. The church was on the other side of the school, just a few blocks from his house. He found a parking spot and killed the engine. He re-checked himself in the mirror and looked for someone that he knew.

Across the parking lot and just entering the church were Darin and Sara. Darin opened the door for her and they disappeared inside. Sara had a handkerchief clutched in her hand and wiped a tear away from her face. Sean locked up the car and hustled inside the church.

"Hey, you," Sara said, hugging him around the neck. "You see any of the others?"

He glanced in the auditorium of the building and saw Lynn sitting off by himself reading the tiny program that had been printed out for Marie's funeral. He pointed him out to Sara. Sean grabbed her by the arm and led her back outside.

"What is it?" she asked, very suspicious of him.

"I don't know how to ask, so I'll just go for the jugular," he said.

Sara folded her arms. Her face drew in and almost puckered. "What is it?"

"Have you told Darin yet?" Sean asked careful to gauge her reaction.

A steady calm spread through her and then she burst into tears. "What are you talking about?" she tried to ask through the sobs.

"It's obvious that you know," Sean said. He eased her to the side of the building and held her. "I just found out and it was by mistake."

"Tony said something, didn't he?" She dug her fists into his jacket and pressed her face into his chest.

"Does Darin know yet?"

"I told him."

"When did you tell him?" he asked. She stopped crying to stare up at him. She read his thoughts instantly.

"Don't think for a minute, Sean, that he had anything…" she said, letting the rest of it trail off.

"Tony thought he didn't know. He's wrong, isn't he? When?"

"Sean…"

"When did you tell Darin about it, Sara? It's important. Before or after she died?"

Sara paused a long time. She let go of him and stepped into the sun shining over the lip of the roof. "Before," she whispered.

"All right. C'mon, we've got to get back in there." He led her back inside.

"I'll go sit with Lynn and see if I can't round up the others," she offered. "Darin's in the bathroom. Will you tell him?"

"Sure. And I won't tell what I know either, Sara."

She touched him on the arm and entered the auditorium area of the church building. Sean sauntered through the maze of hallways and finally found the men's room neatly tucked away at the back of the building. Any sounds of loud flushing wouldn't disturb the services. The builders had seen to that. It was unlike his own church, which echoed every cough, flush, or sputter from the front of the building.

He entered and ran into Darin who was washing his hands in the basin. "Hey, man, how are you?" Darin said. They hugged each other briefly. Sean told him about the seating arrangements. Darin was about to leave when Sean decided to drop another bomb.

"I take it the police have been to see you?" he asked Darin.

Darin stared at him. "The police have talked to you?" He said it with a note of dread. Sean studied his face. "They haven't talked to me yet."

"They will. And they seem pretty determined to find out everything that's been going on."

"What's that supposed to mean?" Darin watched Sean in the mirror. Sean sensed his dread. He couldn't blame him. He felt it, too.

Sean washed his hands in the basin and wiped them off on a paper towel. "You know exactly what it means. They're going to be asking a lot of personal questions."

Darin leaned his head against the wall. "I don't know anything about that hammer. The only thing I can figure is that Marie took it home to use."

Sean let that go for the moment. "I'm not talking about that, man. I'm talking about what Marie knew."

"About what?"

"About all of us. The police are going to start nosing around."

"What do you know?" Darin looked at him suspiciously. He folded his arms casually, but the message was clear. Sean could tell he was shutting off from him.

"Darin. I know about Sara and Tony."

Darin's face turned crimson. He hit the wall with the back of his head. "That's just great!" he shouted. He hit the wall again.

"Everyone will probably know soon enough. I also know that Marie knew."

Darin gritted his teeth. "So what?"

Sean didn't say anything. He didn't have to. Darin thought about the implications and what that could mean for him. He moved around Sean and splashed some water on his face.

"Sara opened her mouth when she shouldn't have," Darin said after he wiped his face dry.

"That may be true. But the question here is what you'd do about it."

Darin threw the paper towel away. He gripped the sides of the basin as tears sprang to life in his eyes. "Sean, I never would've done something like kill her."

"The police are going to ask a lot of questions, Darin. A lot."

"I know that. What are you doing grilling me, anyway? They're going to be talking to you, too. Why get on me?"

"It's obvious. Think about it. We're not talking about petty jealousy here, man. We're talking about someone's life messed up and Marie knowing about it."

"Sara's life isn't messed up!" Darin retorted.

Sean pushed harder. He could feel he was getting somewhere. "Okay. Not all the way, but it's something that she has to think about now. Something that you both have to think about. And Marie knew. And she used it to her advantage. She used it the other night to catch Sara off guard. You knew it. Tony knew it. How long would it be before the whole thing blew up? Can you answer me that? Believe me, people have been killed for knowing less."

Darin blurted out something completely unintelligible and threw a punch at Sean, who half expected it and fell backwards against the opposite wall. Darin struck air and whirled around. He fell against the wall and sank down to the floor with his head buried in his hands.

"It isn't going to take much for them to find out everything. And they will start pushing the buttons," Sean said quietly.

"What do you want me to do?"

They both ignored Darin's outburst. Sean had grown accustomed to them.

"Tell them what you know. Tell me."

Darin chuckled and snot ran out of his nose. "I don't know anything, man."

"Don't lie, Darin. I've known you too long."

More tears ran down Darin's face. He held his knees close to his chest and rested his chin on them. "Sara went to see her that night," he finally said reluctantly.

"You have got to be kidding me."

"No. She went over there to talk to her about everything."

Sean opened the door and glanced at his watch. "Come on. Wash your face and let's find our seats. It's about to start."

"Sean. I'm sorry."

Sean squeezed Darin's arm and looked at his face in the mirror. "This is a big mess. And it's going to take some doing before the truth can come out."

"That's what I'm afraid of. And Sara, too, for that matter," Darin said softly.

"It doesn't matter now. And it won't to the police, either."

Darin shook his head and stuck it into the basin. He turned on the water and scrubbed the tears on his face. "I'll be out in a minute," he said.

"Okay, man. We're sitting with Lynn."

The funeral ran through the usual program of obit, songs, and sermon. The preacher, who obviously didn't know Marie very well, talked about how life could be taken away at any moment and that we all needed to prepare. Sean whole-heartedly agreed, but knew that it fell on deaf ears on his row. The theatre gang had gathered and blithered away with tears and tissues galore. He knew to expect this, but simply observed the small production that the others were giving. Lynn wiped an occasional tear from his face. Darin and Sara held onto one another for comfort while Tony sat looking on. Tony had a cream-colored handkerchief that he used to cover his eyes from time to time. Heather, Dora and Mike sat at the end and they both shed a steady stream of tears.

Sean didn't know whether to marvel at the display or count it as a blessing that they actually had feelings for her and missed her presence.

If only, he thought to himself bitterly. He knew that deep down they each had regret over not getting along with her better, but he also knew that someone in their bunch—and maybe sitting right in this very row—sat relieved that she was dead and gone.

The service wrapped up and they reconvened at the graveside. Similar words were spoken and prayers were offered up. Sean and the others told the family how much they felt their loss. He watched as they all filed through. The family sat in a detached trance as the coffin rested in front of them. He walked to his car and had his key in the ignition when Dora came over to him.

"I think we're all going over to MoMo's for dinner before rehearsal if you want to join us."

He nodded his head. "Yeah, that sounds great. Come on. You can ride with me."

She hopped in beside him and cranked the radio up to the alternative station. He eased it down some as he drove through the narrow passage through the lines of cars. They waved to the others and promised that they would meet them there.

"This stinks," Dora said out of the blue.

"What stinks?" he asked. He turned the radio down to where it could barely be heard. He couldn't stand Dora's kind of music.

"This," she said as she waved back at the cemetery. "All of this. This shouldn't be happening."

"But it did."

Dora dug diligently for a stick of gum from her purse. "Want some?" she offered. Sean took a piece and stuck it into his mouth and marveled at how strong the peppermint flavor was.

"Marie apparently upset someone very much," Sean said. He turned onto Main Street and pointed the car toward MoMo's.

"And the cops think it was one of us," Dora said angrily. She stared intently out of the window and chewed sporadically on her gum. "How can they even think that?"

"They've questioned you?"

"They caught me this morning," she said. "They're definitely convinced that the answers are in our little group."

"Are they?"

She jerked her head at him for just a fraction and then relaxed some. Her eyes fluttered shut as she leaned against the headrest of her seat. "I don't know, Sean. What do you think?"

"A lot of things, I'm afraid."

"Darin said as much."

"When?"

"Right after the funeral. He warned us to be careful what we said around you. He said you had a friend on the force."

"Not in Lyle, though, Dora. I'm just curious. Aren't you?" Darin's warning couldn't be a good thing.

Should he continue digging? If things progressed, he could get close to a killer and what then?

"Then wherever. What does it matter? A killer and a snitch in our group is too much to take."

He laughed maliciously at that and quietly reminded her of all the times secrets had slipped out of her own mouth.

"That's different," she offered matter-of-factly.

"How so?"

"It just is." She blew a bubble and then sucked it back into her mouth for another cycle.

"Be that as it may, Dora. We've all got a lot to answer for in this thing."

"How's that?" she asked, suddenly curious. She tensed up again, ready for his questions.

"You didn't like Marie all that much."

"Like that's a news flash, Sean. Who did?"

"I didn't mind her that much."

"That's one then," she whispered.

He shook his head to himself as he turned the blinker on before he spun into MoMo's parking lot. "What did you have against her?"

"I've answered these questions already today, officer," she said with a twisted smirk of her mouth. "Why do I have to answer them for you?"

"I want you to, Dora," he said mildly. He tried to approach her as delicately as possible. She melted again. "I know Marie could be vicious sometimes, but she isn't the only one."

Dora chomped on her gum. "She bragged, Sean. Bragged all the time about what she knew about folks. What she found out about Sara."

"You know about that?"

"About what? She never told me. I don't dare ask Sara. But she loved to let me know that she knew things." She blew another bubble in a fury. Sean parked the car, cracked the windows, and killed the engine.

"Implying what?" he asked carefully. He knew from her tone that Marie had threatened Dora.

"What are you talking about?" she threw back. A tear appeared in the corner of her eye.

"Come on, Dora. I know how competitive it is for the women to get parts."

"That's because you guys pick shows that are primarily men. Just like the one we're doing now." She pulled a loose strand of hair out of her face angrily and bit harder into her wad of gum. "And she bragged about being the prettiest one of the bunch. And Heather, her so-called best friend, just sitting there and taking it like some idiot. It was horrible the things she did to Heather before a tryout."

"Did she do anything before this last one?"

She bit off a bitter laugh. "What do you think, Sean? She had Heather near tears back stage before we came on to read for the show."

"What did she say?" Sean asked, careful not to push too hard.

"The usual stuff. How she was prettier and how Heather needed to lose weight. How she'd gotten a little too hippy lately."

"Yeah, I noticed that, too," Sean said before he had time to censor himself.

Dora glared at him. "And that's the reason why we have the reputation of being so heartless."

"What? I said I just noticed. Look at me. I'm no Adonis."

"That's true enough," she spat at him.

"I'm not trying to rile you, Dora."

"Too late."

"Just tell me what else happened. Please."

She boiled over in her seat, chomping down even harder on her stick of gum. Nervously she tugged at wisps of hair that framed her face. Sean had always admired her good looks, but had never told her so. He knew Dora to be a hard girl, but with good intentions. She drank too much and liked a little weed now and again, which he didn't approve of, but he understood her to be a genuinely good person underneath all that.

"Sean. It was hard for me to watch. Marie kept teasing and taunting her like some bully would."

"She could be that way."

"She wanted the part of the woman in the hotel room, that's all there was to it. She was going to do anything to get it, too. And then she opened her big mouth about Heather's ex."

"Jeff? What about him?"

"That he was a lunatic who needed to be in an asylum somewhere."

Sean shook his head at that. Jeff had threatened to kill everyone down at the theatre over a year ago if Heather didn't get away from them and start staying at home where he felt she belonged. Heather had gone through a horrible break up and had tried desperately to build her life again. Jeff's shadow hung over her and if Marie had used it against her, it had been a low blow.

"Did you say anything?"

"I did then. She had no right to say anything about him. Especially since we were all scared half to death," she admitted.

"And especially since Mike held out on us as long as he thought he could without scaring us."

"And doing it anyway."

He thought of those dark days. Everyone had kept watching the front doors waiting to see if Heather's mad husband would come in and start mowing them all down with a gun.

"What did Marie do?" Sean asked. Those thoughts from a year ago haunted him still. He had held a grudge against Mike for a long time after that. They all had. He had felt as if Mike held their lives in his hands and hadn't warned them about the fact that he did. Sean hated being in the dark on anything and that incident had put him off Mike for a while.

"What she did best. She turned on me then. Said hateful things about how I looked."

Sean scoffed. "What about your looks? You look fine. You always have." He shut his mouth and chided himself for not censoring his thoughts before they came flying out of his big yapper. He thought of how they had playfully splashed each other with paint the other day at the theatre.

She smiled at him. "Thanks, Sean. I appreciate that."

"I mean it, Dora."

A heavy silence ensued and filled the car. They both understood what it meant, but both backed away from it. Now was not the time or the place.

"Anyway," Dora said finally, "she mentioned that I had put some of my weight back on and that it would take more than just morning aerobics to lose it. She also mentioned that I was too much of a mooch and should learn to take care of myself."

"And she said all of this before you guys went on the stage to read?"

"Oh, yeah. She also undid a couple of buttons on her blouse to let some cleavage show. She said Darin and Lynn would appreciate it, especially Lynn."

"Why Lynn?" he asked quietly to himself.

"Why Darin? Who knows?" she answered back. "And then she rags us one last time before she heads for the stage."

"Was she hateful about it?"

Dora waved a hand. "You know Marie." She stopped and thought about that. "*Knew* Marie. She said it with a smile and honey dripping off her tongue, but you knew the guile she had underneath."

"How did it affect the tryouts?" Sean asked as he imagined the scene playing out.

"Heather had to go up front to the restroom and have a good cry. The thing about Jeff really got to her."

"And you?"

"It only ticked me off. I went out there to strut my stuff."

Sean smiled at the memory. "You did do that."

She bit into her next bubble thoughtfully. Secretly she knew Sean to be one of the last true gentlemen—modest, clever, and handsome. She hadn't played on it before because she thought him out of her league. But with his generous smile and outpouring of understanding and sympathy, he endeared himself even more to her. Maybe she did have a shot after all.

"What happened after that? Anything?" Sean asked, breaking the moment.

"Marie felt really good about the tryouts, so she asked Heather out for lunch the next day."

"What did Heather do?"

"Before or after she asked?"

"Both."

"I've never heard Heather cuss much, but she did that night. As Marie read on the stage, Heather stood in the wings calling her everything she could think of. And with Heather, I was surprised she knew so many things to call her."

They both laughed at that. Heather had been known to curse a blue streak.

"And after?"

"Friends as usual. But you could see the hurt in Heather's eyes. It was still there," Dora said. She looked out the window to break eye contact with him.

"Enough to do her harm?" Sean asked quite suddenly.

Dora mulled it over and shook her head. "Heather isn't known for violence, Sean."

"Good point. But then again, none of us were until this happened. And now they're looking at us for their suspect."

"It's spooky, you know?" she confided, trusting him.

"Yeah. I appreciate you being honest with me about it, Dora," Sean said.

"Any time, Sean. You know that." She reached into her purse for a pack of cigarettes.

He grabbed them away from her. "I hope you don't take this the wrong way, but I think you'd be a lot more attractive if you quit these things."

A tear streamed down her face. "You're probably right."

"I know I'm right. Who needs these, anyway?"

Another tear glistened in Dora's eye. Sean wiped it away with an invitation for him to buy her dinner. She readily agreed as she eased herself out of his car. *Funny how things change*, she thought. *A death and a conversation later and I'm wondering what it would be like to be with him.*

Sean shut the car door for her and put his arm through hers leading her to the restaurant. She stopped him and hugged him on a whim. He hugged back. They stood there, squeezing the life out of one another as the others arrived with catcalls and whistles galore.

Chapter Twelve

Rehearsals that night were tension-free overall except for the occasional barb from Tony over a blocking cue or where the doors would be set. He enjoyed trading insults with Darin, and although things were not back to normal, they at least tried to lighten things up for the rest of the group. The ones in the cast who didn't know Marie all that well offered condolences which were readily accepted.

Sean began to hit his stride with the blocking as he and Sara worked through the scenes that they had with each other, which were quite a few. They had worked together before and it was as easy and comfortable as a pair of slippers. Darin sat amazed at how well they got on together with an almost jealous look plastered across his face. He knew that Sean only tried to help earlier at the funeral and he knew perfectly well what the situation looked like to the police.

They took their first break and scattered to the far corners of the theatre to talk, work on lines, or get a smoke. Dora sat on the hood of Sean's bug and lit up. He frowned at her.

"What?" she asked, obviously defensive.

"You really don't have to do that, you know," he said. He sat beside. She leaned her head on his shoulder.

"Why not?" She blew a ring away from his face and stared up at him.

"You just don't have to."

"I get bored too easy. That's all."

"We all do, I guess. It's just we don't all need a habit."

She chuckled and blew another ring. "I do, I suppose."

He stuck his face close to hers and whispered: "You don't. Not at all."

"You bugged me earlier about it. Why the sudden concern?"

He smiled and bit off a remark as Tony joined them.

"Howard really sets things in motion," he said, half-expecting some kind of refutation from Sean. He didn't get one. "Willy has nowhere to go and then Howard sets it all off. He's a very important role in the show."

"Very important," Sean mumbled.

Lynn and Heather came out of the theatre and whisked away to his car. They got in and started talking to each other. It appeared as if a long-time married couple were off parking somewhere.

"Those two need a room," Tony muttered. "It's disgusting."

"They're just talking, Tony," Dora said.

"And you know what that leads to," he answered back. She blushed and blew another smoke ring. She crushed the cigarette out half-finished, which she typically never did. She hated waste, but for some reason it didn't taste the same. Not now, anyway.

"Are they seeing each other?" Sean asked, remembering how Lynn had hung onto Marie just a few days earlier.

"Not officially," Dora said. "But she wants it real bad. Since her hubby flipped out and she got the divorce, she's been very lonely."

"And Lynn?" Sean asked.

"He's the perpetual lonely man. Or, didn't you know? His divorce was a pretty rough one from what I understand."

Tony coughed and added: "It was. He confided in me about it." The tone he had meant he had information that the others weren't privy to. Dora glanced at Heather and Lynn in his car and smiled to herself.

"How long ago was that?" Sean inquired. "About five years ago?"

"Yeah," Tony answered before Dora could open her mouth. "But they stay pretty close for Angie's sake. She's young and needs her parents."

"Yeah, but her re-marriage didn't do him much good," Dora said.

"Yeah, he took that hard, too," Tony said.

Sean stared just long enough before it got too rude. They had an easiness around each other that he admired in couples. He'd had that once, and only once, in his life and he missed it desperately. He glanced at Dora and grinned at her.

"What?" she asked, quietly enough for Tony not to hear.

"Nothing." He looked at the couple again. Lynn had his arm around Heather as she buried her head into his shoulder. It had no sexual connotation to it. The embrace held a sweetness and sincerity that reminded Sean of the great romances portrayed in the movies and on TV. Lynn kissed Heather on the cheek and they came out of the car.

Tony applauded mockingly at them. "Bravo. Another show, please."

Heather opened her mouth to say something hateful, but Lynn stopped. "It's okay," Sean heard him say to her. "He's only playing."

Off in the distance a buzzing sound could be heard. All ears turned attention to it and Lynn smiled. Angie drove up into the parking lot and stopped in front of her father.

"Hey, dad," she said as she took her helmet off. "How's rehearsal?"

"Fine. How's homework?"

"Ah, dad, come on."

"Come on nothing. You're supposed to be over at your mom's doing homework."

"I got bored."

"Hi, Angie," Heather said, stepping close to Lynn to make her presence known.

"Hi, Heather," Angie mumbled. Her body became rigid. Sean sensed her discomfort with the situation. *Little wonder*, he thought to himself.

"Heather and I are going to get some ice cream after rehearsal. Want to come?" Lynn asked.

"I better not. Mom wanted me back pretty quick."

"Okay."

Heather walked away from them to give them some private time to talk. She rolled her eyes at Dora and Sean and said, "She doesn't like me that much."

"I wouldn't say that," Dora said, trying to encourage her.

"I would," Tony said.

"Shut up, T.T.," Heather mumbled.

"I don't like to be called that, you know," he said without much force. He knew when to leave well enough alone—for the time being, anyway. Everyone there felt Heather's desperation and concern.

"Just take it one day at a time," Sean offered.

"You sound like a Hallmark card," Tony mocked.

"It's good advice, especially for someone like you, Tone," Dora said. He rolled his eyes and left to go back into the theatre.

Lynn's voice raised just a fraction, sending their attention back to the man and his daughter. Angie pulled her helmet on angrily and started her scooter.

"We'll see you this weekend," he promised.

"We? You mean you and Heather?"

"Yes. We'll go out and when you come over for my weekend."

Angie snorted and said something the others couldn't hear. Lynn bowed his head in defeat. He couldn't think of what to say to his daughter to change her mind.

"At least she's not like the other one," Angie said and sped off into the night.

Sean wondered at that. Who was she talking about? What other one? As far as they all knew, he hadn't been seeing anyone before Heather. The others either didn't hear the comment or chose to ignore it because no one asked him about it. Lynn joined them. Heather gave him a playful hug, but he wasn't in the mood.

"I'm going back in," Dora said. She squeezed Sean's arm and winked at him. *What was going on with that?* Sean reflected to himself. He'd worry about it later.

"Wait up," Heather said as she slid off the hood and through the door behind Dora.

"Don't ever have kids, Sean," Lynn joked.

"She's not so bad. You guys are doing a great job with her."

"Yeah. I guess."

"And since when are you and Heather…?" Sean let the thought trail off. Lynn didn't answer at first. He studied the palms of his hands for a moment and looked at Sean.

"I don't know what's going on with that just yet, Sean. She's been flirting for quite a while now, but I guess I'm just now noticing it. I've never been a Casanova by any stretch of the imagination."

"Oh, now, I hear the college girls just love you," Sean teased. They laughed, but he could sense that Lynn carried pain underneath it all. "I didn't mean to offend you, man."

Lynn slapped him on the shoulder. "You didn't. Really." He looked at his hands again and held up his left one. He referred to the third finger with a scowl marked on his face. "I used to wear a ring on that finger. You know?"

"I know. Divorce must be hard."

"You have no idea. When we busted up, I thought that was it for me. And now Heather comes along and talks to me. I mean, she talks to me, Sean. She doesn't talk at me. And she listens. I can't get over it."

"Sounds like you're hooked."

"I don't know. I better take it easy and not count anything before it's hatched."

"Surely you've been dating around some, though," Sean asked, digging for something there.

"Not really. Nothing serious. Dinner here, a dinner there. Not a big deal."

"Oh."

Lynn glared at him. "Oh, what?"

"I just overheard Angie mention someone else that you may have been seeing before Heather."

Lynn's lip twisted up and Sean anticipated a thorough chewing, but one didn't come. Slowly, Lynn shut his eyes to the world and began to laugh quietly to himself.

"What's so funny?" Sean asked.

"Nothing. Nothing at all, Sean. I only wish I had been seeing someone. Angie is at that age where she thinks every female friend I have is my next fling."

Sean took the plunge. "Who did she mean then?"

Lynn opened his eyes back to the world. He folded his arms across his chest with that scowl forming on his face again. "No one, Sean. I think she probably means someone up at the college. That's all."

He got up and entered the theatre without another word.

Why's he lying?

Sean knew it had been a lie, but why? What was the big deal unless he had been taking out someone he wasn't supposed to? A co-ed maybe or another faculty member. That had to be why he kept his mouth shut about it.

Darin stuck his head out the door, breaking his train of thought, and announced it was time to get back on the stage.

The rest of the rehearsal went very well. It flowed smoothly and each minute got used in a positive way. Very few rehearsals down there had been that way and Sean counted it as a blessing.

Just as things wrapped up, a figure appeared at the back of the theatre and took a seat in the last row. Lynn and Darin exchanged glances, but proceeded to notes with the cast. Sean peered into the darkness and made out the shape of Detective Stiles. The questioning obviously wouldn't take place during normal business hours. He assumed that the detective had come to see him, but as the group broke up, Stiles approached Darin and introduced himself. Everyone looked nervously around waiting to be the next one interrogated.

Stiles felt it from them and put up his hands as some kind of peace offering. "I just thought I'd catch Mr. Peters and ask a few questions. It's no big deal."

"We don't have to stay?" Heather asked. Her knuckles had turned bone white as she gripped the strap of her purse.

"Oh, no. Not at all. We'll be in contact if we need you. Thanks." He shook hands with Sean and then he and Darin took a walk toward the lip of the stage.

"I was afraid of this," a new voice said from the darkness.

Dora nearly jumped off the floor it scared her so bad. "Who is that out there, anyway?"

"It's me," Mike said. "I thought I'd come down and see how everything's going on with the show."

He joined them and they got into a discussion about the rehearsals, Marie's death, and other items that had been on everyone's minds as of late. Even though members of the group held grudges and were backbiters galore, they fell into an easy patter of talk about the theatre and its business.

"When are we going to have our next meeting, Mike?" Sean asked.

"Very good question. And I'd like to be included in this one," Tony said bitterly. He and Mike had come to some sort of agreement. What it was, Sean didn't know, but they at least stayed in each other's presence without looking for the nearest exit.

"I don't know yet," Mike said.

"We need to discuss the finances," Heather said. A score of voices agreed with her, causing Mike to suddenly look for the time on his watch.

"I don't understand, Mike, why we have to cut it short with this show," Sean said. He watched closely for his reaction.

"We've just had a lot of bills. You guys don't know all the bills we have around here."

"That's why we'd like to see the financial report at the next meeting," Dora said. They all began to see Mike's caginess about the topic.

"We will, we will," he assured them. "But hey, we had huge heating bills we got just a couple of months ago and then we had all that duct work done."

"Which was donated to the theatre, Mike," Tony reminded him.

"That's right," Heather chimed in. *Wow,* Sean thought, *something Tony and Heather can agree on.*

"I thought the musical would've brought in loads of money," Dora said. She dug for her packet of gum and offered it all around.

"It did. But the rights were really high for it," Mike said. He refused the gum and said he had to get going. They followed him out.

"So are the records in the office then?" Sean asked. He knew the answer he gave to Marie a few days ago, but he wanted to check his reaction.

Mike chuckled almost too forcefully. "Oh, no. I've been going over them at home." He grabbed his keys from his pocket and locked the bolt on the office door. The others didn't think anything of it as he did it all the time, but Sean took it in as a sign of guilt.

Why is he lying?

And why is that becoming a habit around here as of late?

Mike said his goodbyes and left the theatre in a hurry. Heather and Lynn left to get ice cream, invited the others out of courtesy, but Sean knew they wanted to be alone. Two lonely people who had found each other. That suited them both just fine.

"What are you thinking about?" Dora asked him as he opened the door to his car.

"Oh. Heather and Lynn."

"I think it's great."

He didn't answer, but thought of his exchange with Lynn at the break. Had there been someone else? And why did he feel the need to find out?

"Hello in there," Dora said, waving a hand in front of his face. "Earth to Sean."

"Sorry. Lost in thought."

"I noticed."

The door opened with Darin leading Stiles out of the theatre. Stiles thanked him about something and left.

Sean waved as he left. Sara joined Darin as he locked up. He was agitated about something.

"What's up?" Dora asked. "Did you get grilled?"

Darin pulled Sara to his car. "I'd rather not talk about it. See you guys." They got into the car and left.

Dora dug for her watch in her purse. "I've got to get going, too. A big day at work tomorrow." She looked at Sean for some kind of invitation to go somewhere, but none came. "Bye."

"Wait," he said, suddenly snapping out of his thoughts.

"What?"

"Sorry. My mind was off in outer space there for a minute." He grabbed her by the arm and walked her to her car. Dora couldn't remember the last time a guy had done that for her. He took her keys from her and unlocked the door. He caught Tony making faces at him from the corner of his eye. He waved him away as he opened the door. Tony gave him the okay sign, got into his own car, and left.

"Thanks," Dora said quietly, almost to herself. She couldn't get used to guys with manners. She spent most of her time at work fending for herself as she fought off those who clawed at her and made derogatory comments about her breasts or butt. But here standing in front of her was someone she had known for quite a while now, but had never really noticed before. Why hadn't she? *Maybe*, she thought, *because she expected him to treat like every other male did.*

"Listen, let's do dinner tomorrow night," he said. He didn't plan to ask right then. It just flew out of his mouth.

"I'd like that. MoMo's?"

"Uh, no. Too many eyes and wagging tongues. How 'bout the Italian place on Main?"

"Sounds great. I'll meet you there." She quickly did a tally of how much was in her bank account. Could she afford to go to dinner? He saw the trepidation on her face and smiled at her.

"Dora. This is on me."

"I wasn't..." she said, letting the thought trail off.

"You were. This is a date, okay?" Before she could say anything, he kissed her.

Chapter Thirteen

In the middle of the night Sean tossed and turned from side to side in his bed. Titan and Weejo both could sense his unease so they plopped down on the floor at the foot of the bed and nodded off. Sean rolled over from time to time to check his alarm clock. It seemed as if the universe stood still and refused to move forward. He sat up and rubbed his temples, massaging his head.

"This isn't going to work," he muttered, then got up, and used the bathroom.

He tried television, but that only agitated him more. The last thing he needed was the tube right now. He made a sandwich and poured a glass of milk. Usually the dogs would be begging for a crumb, but they remained in the bedroom asleep.

Too many lies tonight.

He could be a good judge of character and people's behavior. Even if people lied to him, he had a knack for detecting it. Why so many lies? He ate half the sandwich and drained the milk in a couple of gulps.

Mike had been the worst of the lot. Sean knew he had lied about the finances. He could see it printed on his lying face. And then the locking of the office door as some kind of symbolic token of refusal and a demonstration of his presidential authority.

We've got to do something about that.

He wrapped the sandwich remains, put them in the fridge, and stalked back to bed. He made another bathroom trip and sat on the edge of his bed.

Wait, this isn't going to work, he thought. *I've got to go see.*

He dressed himself in sweats, his cross-trainers, and a jacket. Titan barked playfully, waking Weejo. They both licked at his heels, begging for attention.

"All right, come on. Let's go."

They exited the house and hopped in the bug. The clock on the radio told him it was just after two in the morning. He spun out of his driveway and down the street.

His suspicions flew everywhere. Every word that came out of people's mouths he hung on and digested with some kind of psychological dissection. Why did he say that? What did she mean by that? Did she know Marie that well? The questions went on and on making him paranoid about the entire group. He knew that deep-down most were trustworthy, but one had broken trust and faith by taking Marie's life.

He hit Constance Street without anyone at the light and whipped the bug into the theatre parking lot. Someone had turned on the outside light to keep burglars away. He hoped the surrounding neighborhood slept heavy, or at least wouldn't suspect a crime in progress.

He unlocked the door with his official issued key with the dogs right behind him. They playfully bit at one another as they entered the lobby. He ordered them to sit and behave while he checked the office.

For some unknown reason, Mike had purchased a bolt lock for the theatre office, justifying it by saying they kept a lot of private material and it shouldn't be seen by the general public. Lynn and Darin had pushed hard for board members to have a key, which Mike fought, but lost. He wanted to have the only access and Sean began to wonder why.

His key slid in easily enough and he heard the heavy click of metal on metal as the bolt clanked back into its slot in the lock. Sean opened the door, clicked on the light, and didn't waste time by mulling over what he was doing.

Don't think about it, just do it.

If he contemplated his actions too long, he would walk away. He knew he would. Even though he sat on the board, and had for some time, he felt like an errant thief in search of booty or hidden treasure.

He plopped down behind the desk and quickly pulled on the center drawer, which had been conveniently locked. The desk had a main lock on the center drawer that locked every other drawer in it. He needed the key, but he knew it wouldn't be here. Surely Mike wouldn't have hidden the key in the office. Or, had he?

Sean tore the place apart looking for the desk key. He searched every book shelf and through every play, book, and manuscript on the shelves. He found nothing. He tipped the chair over, half-expecting to see the key taped to the bottom of it, but it wasn't there.

This is ridiculous.

He was now more determined than ever to get the desk open before he left there. He jerked on the center drawer again, rattling all the contents inside. The dogs rambled through the door, disturbed by the noise.

"It's all right. Go on back in the lobby," he said. They left with tails wagging.

Studying the lock, he knew he couldn't break the drawer open without it being detected. He had to get in and out without Mike knowing. He grabbed for a letter opener in a plastic pencil holder on the edge of the desk. The letter opener wouldn't fit into the lock. Despairing, he threw the opener back into the holder knocking the whole thing onto the floor. Pencils, pens, rubber bands, paper clips, and other office supplies crashed to the floor.

Sean bemoaned his clumsiness as he picked it all up off the floor. Buried in a wad of rubber bands he saw a key.

He'd left it after all.

He fit the key in the lock and slid the drawers out. A mountain of neatly filed papers and folders were stacked in each drawer. He checked each of them. Files for each play had been meticulously kept. At the back of one of the drawers he found a folder that had been labeled "Reviews." His curiosity got the best of him and he pulled it out and spread it on the top of the desk.

He gaped in wonder at the stack of newspaper cuttings that Mike had kept for the reviews. Why had he done that? He found another folder in the drawer that had been next to the *Reviews* file. It hadn't been labeled, but Sean had a hunch.

"Eureka, baby," he whispered. "The mother lode."

Sean pulled out printed sheets with dates on each of them. He checked and compared them to the articles snipped from the Lyle paper. They matched. He'd inadvertently found proof of Mike's reviewing the shows for the paper. He spread the printed sheets from the folder and found a hand written note on a slip of paper with different ideas for the pen name. He had scratched a couple of others before circling, "Clara Ann Hillway."

"Unbelievable," he whispered to himself. But what should he do now? He had broken into the office and the desk. What kind of moral ground could he stand on if he presented this to the board? Wait a minute, he chided himself quickly. I'm not breaking into the office. Mike shouldn't keep a locked desk. This is universal community theatre property. It is an organization for the *community*, not just one man.

But still, he couldn't take the folders without looking like a thief himself. If he wanted Mike to play ethically, he had to, as well. He put the folders back with a shudder of disgust at the man's gall and got back to searching for the financial records.

He found the ledger in the opposite drawer. Carefully he followed the entries with a keen eye and a sharp memory for purchases and invoices. He found a score to the local Sherwin Williams for paint and brushes. They did go through a lot of paint for each of the shows. There were entries to a fabric company. That was for costumes, he knew. He ran a finger along the list of utilities they paid and whistled at the high cost of the heating a couple of months back. Mike didn't lie about that apparently. They had paid a pretty penny for the heat that month.

Flipping through the pages, he read through entry after entry of purchases the theatre group had made for shows. And then one of them caught his attention. Why in the world would they have a three hundred dollar phone bill? He checked the date on it. Almost two years ago. *Wow,* he thought, *who did we call?* He dug into the drawer and found a file marked "Phone Bills." Mike had catalogued them in order by month. Luckily they went back two years.

He found the month and his jaw dropped.

What in the world!

A list that ran over a page recorded the calls made that month. He counted quickly and came up with twenty that had been made to one number. He shook his head, not believing what he'd found.

Someone in the theatre that month had been calling a 900 number. He wrote it down on a stick-it note and shoved it into his pocket.

Mike had been over-confident in leaving the files in the office. But then again, how many on the board actually asked to see the books? None, except for Marie, and she was dead.

He swallowed that thought down. Surely she couldn't have been killed because of that?

Retrieving the ledger, he fumbled through the pages looking for the credit card receipt list. He found the sheet near the back of the book without one single entry listed. How could that be? Everything else from the theatre account had been recorded into the ledger. He frantically searched through the drawers looking for a credit card receipt file. He didn't find one. Those receipts had obviously been removed from the premises. Why?

A ready answer wouldn't come to him, so he returned everything to its proper spot in the desk. First a high phone bill because someone called a 900 number. And second, no records for the theatre credit card. The implications didn't bode well for Mike, but Sean decided to be patient with it. Maybe Mike had a legitimate reason for having the information elsewhere.

Sean knew it couldn't be true, but he held out hope for the best.

As he slid the key into the center drawer lock, another thought hit him. The credit card information had to have been filed somewhere. Maybe not the records, but at least the application for it.

He couldn't find it, either.

Wait just a minute here.

Sean went back through the invoice files finding one to Sherwin Williams. He knew for a fact that they had bought paint for the musical from there with the credit card. Printed neatly at the top of the invoice was the credit card number. He wrote it down on another sticky note, along with the type of card that it was, and put the invoice back exactly where he'd found it. He didn't dare risk Mike suspecting that someone had rummaged through the desk. He would build his case and decide what to do with it.

He stuck the key back under the wad of rubber bands and put the chair back where he'd found it. He puckered his lips to whistle for the dogs when the lights went out.

"Aw, crud," he whispered. "Not again." Recently, the theatre had had trouble with keeping the lights on all the time. A faulty fuse had been to blame, had been replaced, but hadn't fixed the problem. They had mentioned calling an electrician to look over their box, but as far as he knew, they hadn't done it yet.

Fumbling in the darkness, he stepped out of the office. Warm, wet lickings met him and he told the dogs to go on and get to the door. He locked the bolt on the door. As he tripped through the blackness, he heard steps coming up from the direction of the auditorium.

How could that be?

The steady rhythm of his heart raced as he heard each quiet step echo through the recesses of his mind. Did he imagine them? Was his mind playing tricks on him? Steeling his courage, he slid down the length of wall to the auditorium doors, which had been staked open. His eyes adjusted to the dark, but that wasn't saying much. He couldn't see anything. Weejo trotted over to him and stuck her head through the auditorium doors. She growled and the footsteps stopped. Titan joined his partner and let out a bark.

Nothing happened. No one moved. The dogs continued to peer into the darkness. Sean wished that he had their eyes at that moment. He nearly opened his mouth to ask if anyone was out there, but thought better of it.

He squinted his eyes hard into the pitch black auditorium, but he couldn't make out a shape of any kind. He heard some kind of scraping on the floor inside the theatre and nearly panicked. He didn't recognize the noise, but he knew he couldn't stay in there a minute longer.

"Time to go," Sean whispered. He ran to the door with the dogs following right behind. From the auditorium he could hear running steps up the center aisle approaching the front doors fast.

The dogs jumped through the open window of the car before Sean could get his hand on the door handle. Without looking at the door, he started the car, revved the engine to keep it alive, and shot out of the parking lot like his life depended on it.

Chapter Fourteen

By four, he finally fell asleep. His fear had melted away slowly. The dogs kept close to him, sensing his fright, which made him feel better. His eyelids fell heavy and he slipped off into dreamland.

Morning came too soon, but Sean dragged himself into the shower and started off the day. While he lathered shampoo into his scalp, he pondered the figure in the theatre. Did he really hear someone in there? The dogs saw something of that he was sure.

Why didn't I call the police then?

He didn't have the answer to that one, but he decided to stay quiet about it for now. Why, he really didn't know. It just seemed the right thing to do for the time being. His newfound bravado gave him something else to fear. He knew he shouldn't play hero. Heroes only lived in stories. And this wasn't another play they were performing.

The dogs sat begging for a bowl of food in the kitchen so he obliged. He fed them outside and watched in amazement as they gobbled away. The phone ringing from the kitchen broke his concentration on them.

"Morning," he said.

"Hey, you," Dora purred back. "How'd you sleep last night?"

He needed to keep quiet about everything. He knew that. Even from prospective dates. "Fine. How 'bout you?"

"I did."

"What's up?"

"Listen, I know this is silly of me, but I just wanted to call you this morning." She let it hang in the air and a moment of silence passed between them on the phone.

"I'm glad you did."

"And I'm glad you asked me out," she said awkwardly. He could tell from her tone that it took a lot of courage for her to do this. "It came as quite a surprise."

"I'm just sorry I didn't do it earlier."

"Me, too."

"Look, I need to get going around here..." Sean said.

"Oh, right, sorry. Me, too."

"I'm not trying to cut you off or anything. I've just got a packed day ahead of me."

"I hear you."

"And hey," he said with all sincerity.

"Yeah?"

"I'm glad you called. You've made my day."

"And you've made mine. 'Bye."

He hung up and cursed himself for being so melodramatic with the whole "you made my day" junk. It didn't matter, though. He meant it.

Before Marie had been killed, he hadn't seriously considered taking anyone out—especially down at the theatre. But since her death, he had taken a hard look at life, and his specifically. Why had he been alone for so long? He didn't know the answer to that, but he had just had a friend die in a violent way and it got him to re-evaluating his life.

And the other day in the car with Dora had opened his eyes to something that he hadn't known before—he had a thing for her and it was reciprocated. And even with all of the horrors of Marie's death and the things he'd discovered at the theatre in the office, she had indeed made his day.

On the way to work he got the sudden whim to run back by the theatre. A hard knot of nerves erupted in his stomach, but he had to see. He whipped across town in his bug, zipping in and out of the morning drive. He spun onto Constance Street and into the theatre parking lot and left the car running. He jerked the key to the door of the ring and entered the place.

In the morning the theatre somehow felt cold, indifferent to him. It was a rare occasion for him to be there during the day. At night the building breathed a life all its own like another character in a play. He found himself listening for noises and chided himself for his fear and foolishness—a deadly combination, he thought. He rushed through the side door around the men's room and was in the scene shop for the theatre. Avoiding flats, chairs, tables, props, and other pieces of theatre scenery, Sean dug through to the back wall where the main fuse box was.

Checking for any kind of tampering on the outside, and finding none, he cautiously opened the lid like it had been wired to a bomb. The faulty fuse that was the usual culprit hadn't popped. His eyes widened in silent horror.

The main power switch had been pulled.

Sean spent the morning at work preening and posing in front of every mirror that he passed at work. At first he didn't know that he was doing it, but then by mid-morning he caught himself slicking back his cow-lick. He never did that. It was a losing battle and he knew it, but there he stood in front of the mirror in the men's room trying to make it stay down on his head.

What am I doing?

He had pushed what he'd found at the theatre that morning out of his mind—or, he'd tried to, anyway. He turned his thoughts back to Dora.

It wasn't as if he didn't go out on dates. He did. It had just been a while. He had settled into a routine of working, eating, going to rehearsals, and playing with his dogs. His life had been full. But now he felt giddy.

It's only Dora, come on.

No, it wasn't only just Dora. She had a beauty all her own that he had admired for some time, but didn't have the courage to pursue. She also had wit and character, which attracted him to her even more. But since she had shown her vulnerability with the situation with Marie, he had a need to be with her. And he'd never felt that.

Throughout the morning he found his thoughts returning to her and distracting him from his work. The boss had seen him earlier and asked him to prepare a PR campaign with local merchants over an art exhibit they were sponsoring in Lyle. He blocked himself in his office and pecked away at the keyboard, but couldn't stay focused. He leaned back in his chair, grabbed one of his toy basketballs, and shot it into the goal mounted on the wall in front of his desk. It sank through the net and into the basket he'd placed under it. He grabbed two more balls and repeated the routine.

He had to get to work. He chided himself for his laziness, leaned back toward his computer, and finished writing a letter to the mayor of the town about the event. He edited it, hit the spell-check, and printed off two copies. One to mail and one for his boss to go over. The name of one of the artists caught his attention so he returned back to his computer and typed in his name. His website popped up and he took a few minutes to look through the man's wide array of work that he would be bringing to Lyle.

And then a thought hit him.

He clicked back to the homepage of the search engine he used. He zipped the mouse over to "Images" and clicked on it. He typed in Marie's name.

Nothing. She hadn't kept a site and there weren't any pics of her out on the web except for on the community theatre's website that Mike maintained. He scanned through a few pictures of her and then clicked back to the search engine.

He typed in another name and hit "Search." A score of images flew across the screen. He ran through page after page without seeing any faces he recognized.

On the fourth page he saw a pic that caused him to sigh out loud. He leaned his head on one hand and studied the photograph.

Lynn had been lying.

On a company website where Marie had worked were a series of pictures from a recent inter-office party. He remembered Marie mentioning that someone down there updated their site with things like that.

Standing there holding a drink with Marie's arms wrapped around him and her lips pressed against his cheek with a faraway romantic look was Lynn. They both looked a bit intoxicated and Marie had the red eye, giving her a possessed, demonic look. Why had Lynn lied? It didn't take a genius to figure out that the two had something between them in the photograph. The pose had an intimacy beyond a simple kiss exchanged at a New Year's party, or something similar. No, this had the appearance of something deeper.

Who would have known about this?

He grabbed the phone and tried to recall Heather's number. As quickly as he'd snatched it from the cradle, he set it back down. He wouldn't call and ask her about it. The photo was enough to make him understand that something had gone on between Marie and Lynn. What, he didn't know, but he would add it to his list of things to pursue.

Ric's voice rang out in his conscience telling him to dial the police and tell them what he'd found. His morality pushed for him to do just that, but a strong part of him held back. In his search he'd come across an array of facts that reflected poorly on the community theatre group. His church friends had wondered why he hung out with such a crowd, but he couldn't find the words to justify it. He just did and that was enough.

He studied the picture again, hoping that whatever he thought he saw had only been a fleeting thing. Maybe that's why Lynn had been tight-lipped about it. He flagged it in his *Favorites* folder in case he needed to refer to it later.

There were other things that he needed to check out. He checked his calendar for the day and its emptiness caused him to celebrate. He could allocate some work time to doing a little "researching." He dialed MoMo's and asked for Sara.

"Hello, you," she said. "What's up with you?"

"How about some lunch?" he asked.

"All right, sure. Any special reason?"

He thought of one: "The play."

She moaned and said she'd have his chicken-fried steak ready for him. He hung up and reflected on the real reason he needed to see her. He trusted Sara. They had grown close through their work at the theatre. He wanted to find out what Stiles needed from Darin last night. He knew his curiosity would get the best of him, but he had to find out.

"Yes, I need to check my account," he said in a rush into the receiver. He had dialed the credit card company. He asked for a purchase list and amounts, but the woman on the other end at customer service required a password from him.

"It's a company credit card, ma'am," he explained.

"All the more reason to have a password. You see that, don't you?"

Of course he did, but it didn't make it any less frustrating. He hung up and thought of how he could get the password from Mike.

That won't happen.

Leaning back in his chair, he pulled his cell phone from his pocket and fiddled with the keys. He slipped the 900 number from his pocket and made sure no one was passing by his office. He couldn't see anyone through the frosted glass beside the door so he dialed it and waited.

A bead of sweat popped on his brow. He anticipated the worst and he somehow felt all the more dirty for it. The phone rang twice before a recorded voice answered and gave him a selection of choices by pressing one, two, three, or four. His frustration with the situation manifested itself as he covered his face with his free hand.

Someone had used the community theatre line to call a phone sex service.

With a renewed sense of serving justice and his rabid curiosity, Sean took off a half hour early for his lunch hour, promising himself to return that afternoon to focus on nothing but his job. He wove through the city streets until he was on Marie's. He parked a block down from her house and tried to recall Mildred Singer's address. He knocked on a door and an elderly man pointed him to the next house over.

Carefully stepping through a maze of kids' toys, bikes, and dolls strewn in the front yard, Sean came to the front door and rang the doorbell. A host of tiny voices sang adulation at someone come calling. A cute doll of a girl with sandy hair answered the door.

"Hello, there," she said.

"Hi, there. Is Ms. Singer in?" Sean asked politely.

An older woman swung the door wide with a toothless grin. "Hello. What can I do for you?"

Sean introduced himself and told the woman why he was there.

"Well, come on in," she offered. "You want a cup of coffee?" He refused saying he was about to meet a friend for lunch. "Well, come on in, anyway." She opened the door for him and he paraded through a score of little bodies.

"Hi!" they all chattered at him. He raised a hand and waved.

"Some of my grandkids. Their parents think I'm running a daycare," Mildred Singer said. "Back in my time, parents raised their own kids."

Sean couldn't think of a response so he just smiled. "Ms. Singer…"

"Oh, call me Mildred."

"Yes, ma'am. Mildred, I understand that you heard some arguing over at Marie's the night she was found."

"That's right. I heard Marie yelling something wonderful at someone out there. It was just after dark. I went to the door to make sure no one was getting killed over there." A tear sprang to life and ran down her wrinkled face. "And she got killed, anyway."

"Could you make out who it was?" Sean asked.

"I got one good look, but that was it. I told the police already." A grandchild came and begged for some juice. She acquiesced and poured the little one a cup of it. She handed it off and the kid took off back to the living room with the others.

"If you could tell me, ma'am."

"Well, whoever it was stood behind Marie's pear tree, so I couldn't make out much of anything. All I know is that it was a woman about medium height."

That was her one good look?

"Nothing else?"

"Not much more. Whoever it was yelled a bit, too. She was upset just like Marie."

"Did you hear anything that they said?"

She giggled and put a hand to her mouth. "Oh, I don't know if I should say." She actually blushed and put a hand to her chest.

"Did you tell the police?"

She shook her head that she didn't. "I was embarrassed half to death and I didn't see the woman's face that well. I didn't think it meant anything."

"Would you be willing to tell me?"

"I don't know."

"It's important, ma'am," he said. She studied him thoroughly before she said anything to him. She saw something she trusted.

"I couldn't believe it when I heard it," she said as she grabbed a child playing at her feet.

"What did you hear?"

"I heard Marie tell whoever she was talking to that she was awfully glad she wasn't the one going around town giving folks herpes!" She said it and then stuck her hand to her mouth as if she'd said something horrible and nasty.

"I see." Now he had something else to talk to Sara about at lunch. "Is that all you saw or heard?"

"Well, just like I told the police, after midnight I heard something that sounded like a chainsaw that came from the other side of Marie's house. I was awake with my arthritis and got up to check it out."

"A chainsaw?" Sean asked. "Are you sure about that?"

"Or, something like that. Some kind of motor. But I couldn't tell just by hearing it. Sorry."

He thanked her for her help and left. The kids followed him out the door and waved goodbye to him. They craved attention more than just from their grandmother, he thought. They had her run ragged. He could tell from the condition of her house and yard. She had raised children once and now she was doing it again. He hoped her kids appreciated what she did for them.

He secretly dreaded confronting Sara with what he'd found out, but she'd kept this from the police. He knew that she hadn't been questioned about seeing Marie that night. She hadn't said anything, like he knew she would, and Ric had said nothing.

He made a mental note to call Ric and touch base.

Speaking of touching base...

He speed-dialed Darin and listened to the ring.

"Yello," Darin said. "What are you doing?"

"I'm out and about when a thought hit me."

"Shoot."

He could hear the tension from Darin, but he decided to ignore it. He knew that Darin would need time to get over their confrontation in the bathroom at Marie's funeral.

"If I need to buy paint or something with the theatre credit card," Sean began with all innocence, "do I need to give them some sort of confirmation number or password since it's not my credit card."

"Haven't you used it before?" Darin asked.

"You're kidding, right? You know Mike. You, he, and Lynn seem to be the ones who use it the most."

"Are you buying paint for the show? Did Lynn set you up to get some stuff for the play?"

Sean couldn't bring himself to lie. "No, but I was thinking when I had to direct." That would work. He was on the schedule to direct soon after *Death*.

"No, man. You just go and buy whatever and sign it. Mike takes care of it from there."

"And no code or number or anything?" Sean asked again just to make sure.

"Nope. That's all you do. Just like a regular credit card."

"Then what am I thinking of? I'm totally confused," Sean said. Now that was a lie and he instantly felt guilty about it.

"I don't know. There's a password that's used when you activate the credit card. That's the only one I can think of."

"Oh, yeah. Like your mother's maiden name or something like that."

Darin laughed at his obtuseness. "Yeah, Mike used his wife's maiden name when he set up ours. Lukens, I think."

Thank you, Darin.

He patiently answered a few of Darin's questions about how he thought rehearsals were going, how he thought Darin did as a director, and a list of other questions before he was able to hang up.

He pulled into MoMo's and killed the engine. Approaching Sara about her encounter would be difficult. He knew how she would react, but he had to know what they'd talked about.

He silently prayed for strength and entered the restaurant.

Chapter Fifteen

After the customary small talk of how the work day was going and other bits of gossip and news, Sara and Sean settled into the quiet of two old friends munching through a light salad with fresh-baked bread. Everything tasted great and Sean told her so. He could remember when MoMo's had been run by MoMo himself and how the quality of food had declined as the owner did. But the namesake had been on the building and in the town for three generations and when Sara bought the restaurant, she refused to change the name. It was a wise business decision and everyone in town told her so.

"How is everything?" she asked, anticipating Sean's glowing complements, to which she was not disappointed. He went on about how the salad was fresh and the bread was worth dying for. "You know exactly what to say to a struggling restaurant owner," she said.

I only wish I knew how to ask about Marie.

The main dishes came out and Sean smothered his chicken-fried steak in a thick layer of white gravy and black pepper. The cook at the restaurant had perfected the recipe and it remained the hottest item on the menu. He savored the first bite and washed it down with a deep draught of iced-tea.

"So, what's up?" Sara asked. She could read his off-handed remarks about nothing in particular and his habit of not looking at her as a sign that he had something to say.

"My curiosity, I guess," he began weakly. He took another bite.

"Go ahead. I assume it's about Marie."

"Why would you assume that?"

She bit into her club sandwich. She said through the chewing: "We've all noticed that you've become an overnight sleuth."

He blushed at that and couldn't think of what to say. "Yeah, I guess."

"The police are working us all over, you know. You don't have to do it, too."

He sighed, studying the condensation on his glass. Tiny droplets oozed down the glass and onto the tablecloth. "I guess I feel I can do something."

"What?"

"Ask questions," he answered. His voice had dropped in volume almost to a whisper.

She studied his face intently, the way friends do when trying to get each other's thoughts when the words just aren't there. "You have your suspicions, don't you?"

"I'm working on it."

She broke eye contact and studied her own glass. "You think one of us did it."

He answered with silence.

"Don't you?" she asked. "You think it was someone at the theatre."

"I'm just asking questions, Sara. I don't have a clue. I'm in the same boat as the police are."

She laughed bitterly at him. "Not true. Not true at all, Sean. You're one of us. You're down there and are privy to everything we say and do." She paused to catch her breath. "And our secrets."

"I'm not trying to betray anyone's trust, Sara, especially yours. You've been a good friend for way too long."

She refused to answer, instead stuffing more food in her mouth.

"Why didn't you tell the police that you saw Marie the night she died?" he asked finally. His eyes never left her face. He could read her and they were both aware of it. She didn't try to hide her consternation or frustration.

"That's none of your business," she said after she got her food down.

"It may not be mine, but the police need to know. There was a witness."

Her eyes welled up from the grief. She pulled back away from the table.

"They will find out one way or the other," he said quietly.

She scoffed at him. "Because you'll open your mouth, you mean. I'm trying to keep things quiet about my...*situation*. I don't want half the town knowing."

"Listen, Sara, you don't go to a woman's house and have an argument with her in the front yard and her ending up dead later without coming forward and saying something. You were seen yelling at each other about what she knew."

Sara flung her napkin onto the table. Sean knew to let her have her moment of anger. He shut his mouth and set his attention back on his food. Sara pushed away from the table and left.

Oh, just great.

Sean sat embarrassed at her dramatic exit and examined the other patrons in the restaurant to see if they had witnessed it. No shocked eyes or accusing stares met his gaze so he assumed they had been quiet enough in their confrontation. He pushed the food around on his plate trying to muster up the nerve to finish it. He couldn't. His appetite had evaporated like the dialogue with Sara.

In a few minutes she returned with puffy, red eyes. She wiped at her face with a white handkerchief. Sean waited in muted silence while she calmed herself down.

"You have no idea how hard it is," she said suddenly, breaking the dead air between them. "I had always prided myself on being the good girl in the neighborhood. In high school I didn't do anything. Didn't drink, didn't smoke, and certainly didn't sleep around. And then I got into college and started drinking some and hanging around the wrong crowd." She stopped to smooth out her face with the handkerchief. "And all the while I'm still teaching my Sunday school class. And then I met this guy...one thing led to another and I wasn't innocent anymore."

"Sara, you don't have to give me a history lesson, hon. I know all about it."

She slammed the table catching the attention of the elderly couple eating next to them at another table. "No, you don't. Stop pretending and quit trying to make it easier somehow. It isn't."

"I was only asking..."

"I know exactly what you were asking, Sean. The same question I've been asking myself."

He reached over for her hand, but she jerked it away.

"Just don't. Okay?" she said. Her eyes rimmed with fresh tears again. "I get a degree, I get involved at my job, I get a loan and I buy this place. And all the while I'm doing the best that I can to be that good little girl that I was. And I'm failing at it. I'm failing at it every day."

"Sara, please," Sean pleaded. "You don't have to do this. Not now."

"Oh, no. You wanted it, so you're going to get it. All right? So last year I meet this guy from out of town. He's nice, he's clean-cut, and he's a coffee drinker. We stay up half the night in the restaurant talking. We make a date and we started seeing each other."

"I met him. I remember."

Sara took a deep breath, all the while looking down at her plate. "And then it happened. I got caught up in everything. I got wrapped up in what he said and what he did and before you know it, I'm sleeping with him."

Sean could sense the elderly couples stare deepen from the next table.

"And then he disappears from my life as quickly as he came into it. She stopped to study her fingernails on her right hand. She got agitated with something she saw and tore at it with her thumbnail.

"Sara, I can't tell you how sorry I am."

She cackled, almost witch-like. She acted like it was the funniest thing she'd been told all day. "It's irony, you know? Pure irony. I try and try to keep an image of being a good person, and then it never fails. I don't. So then Tony comes into my life and sweeps me off my feet with his passion and fire and his words. And I'm in the sack again."

"You're only making it worse for yourself."

"Let me! You wanted this. I'm getting to Marie. Marie, who let me know how much she cared about me the night she saw me on the verge of a nervous breakdown. I was here at the restaurant and Tony and I had been busted up for about a couple of weeks or so. And I start…well, having some signs…so I go see the doctor. I was completely devastated when he told me."

"And then you had to tell Tony," Sean said almost to himself.

"He blew up, but we promised to keep it between us and then I opened my big fat mouth to Marie. She was here at the restaurant right after I had made the call."

"And you told her," Sean muttered.

"I told her."

"Why go over to her house and have it out with her?"

Sara cracked a painful smile. She folded her hands giving the appearance of someone about to pray. "She sent me an e-mail apologizing for ragging me about it at tryouts, but she got what she wanted and we both knew it. And attached to this e-mail is a link to a chat room for people with similar problems." She laughed her witch's laugh again. "I couldn't believe it. So I decided to go over and let her have it. And I did."

Sean mulled it over, pushed a lump of mashed potatoes on his plate, and searched desperately for the right response. He drained his glass of tea and crunched on a piece of ice.

"What do you want me to do?" Sara asked. "It was only an argument. Nothing more. I said some hateful things to her, but so did she."

"Did you say anything that could be conceived as a threat?"

"What did the neighbor hear?"

"Enough to think you two were going to brawl right there," he said. "I don't know how these things work exactly, Sara, but you need to tell the police about it."

"They'll make me a suspect."

"Who says you aren't already one? Who says we all aren't?"

"What do you want me to do?" she repeated.

"Go see Detective Stiles and make a full statement. It will help them get a picture of her final moments maybe. I don't know."

"You've seen too many episodes of *Poirot*," she teased.

"You may be right," he said with a smile.

Friends again.

"Can I ask question?" he said.

"You have been."

"What did Stiles want with Darin last night?"

A flicker of agitation passed over her face and then evaporated. "He didn't really want to talk about it."

"What?"

"Oh, he opened his mouth."

"Darin?"

She shook her head. "He said something to a co-worker about Marie being gone. You know, macho stuff. Stiles interviewed a few people who knew Darin and this guy was one of them."

"So he verified Darin's comments, then," Sean posited.

"Yeah."

He folded his arms and rested his face in his hands. His stomach had stopped churning and his appetite returned, but the food had grown too cold to eat. He chided himself for not asking her about Marie until they had finished.

"Why is it that none of us seemed to really care about Marie?" he asked out loud, but meant for the question to remain unspoken.

"Good question. I guess she just seemed to intentionally rag on folks to get her kicks. She just couldn't stop herself."

"Unlike who else down there?"

"Another good point. I don't know why, Sean. Does it matter?"

"Enough for someone to kill her, Sara. And that's the cold, ugly truth about it."

"I don't like to think about it." She hugged herself as though a stiff northern breeze had blown through the restaurant.

"Let's go for a walk tomorrow before rehearsal," he suggested.

She looked back at her hands. "Let's don't. Not tomorrow. Give me a few days." She got up and took his plate. "And lunch is on me."

"No, Sara, that's all right," he said, but she was already out of ear shot.

She needs space. Give it to her.

He questioned the intelligence of digging into his friends' lives like he had the past few days. The things he'd been finding out about those he associated with most were enlightening him in ways he didn't want to be. Marie had her nose into everyone's business down at the theatre. But which one killed her? And why?

She knew so much about them all it seemed. She knew about Sara and Tony's dilemma. She suspected trouble with the finances, which stepped into Mike's territory. Apparently she'd been seeing Lynn at one time, but they'd both been tight-lipped about it. He needed to verify that little nugget before he did anything with it. What else was there? She could intimidate and use Heather when the fancy struck her. And she would push on Dora when she felt like it.

Dora.

He checked his watch. He had to get back to work, finish the day, and get ready for dinner with Dora.

In the Volkswagen he wondered what Marie had on or against him. But for some strange reason he hadn't been in her path to get scathed or wounded. But almost everyone else in the "gang" down at the theatre had had a run-in with her. Mike, Lynn, Tony, Darin, Dora, Sara, and Heather had all been at odds against Marie at one time or another.

And what about everything else he'd been finding out?

The phone bill and the missing credit card receipts?

He gunned the bug for the office to make a phone call.

"Lukens," he said to the customer service operator on the phone. He had shut his door again to the rest of the world and had immediately dialed the credit card company that had the theatre's account.

"Yes, sir," the woman said politely from the other end.

Another world away.

He spilled out nonsense about a filing system that had gotten lost and begged her to walk him through the past few months of purchases. He hated the lie, but knew the truth would take too long and too much explaining.

"Why, sir, we have a new system where you can check your account online. Let me get you set up to do that," the woman chirped from the other world, so far away from his own.

"Let's do that. And hey, thanks."

In front of him on the screen were the purchases and account balance for the theatre's credit card. He couldn't believe it. *No wonder the receipts have disappeared,* he thought. If and when the others found out, there would be blood. He scrolled down from one month to the next and tried to discern the justifiable purchases with those that fell under the frivolous category.

Someone had been going out to eat at some of the restaurants in Lyle and the surrounding area and charging it on the theatre's credit card.

Unbelievable. The gall of the person.

The sums weren't all that big, but over a few months they had accumulated into quite a figure. In fact, the total amount owed was just over a thousand dollars. Now wonder Mike said there wasn't enough money for

Death of a Salesman. He needed to pay for this bill so no one would know about it.

He assumed Mike to be the culprit, but he wanted to keep an open mind. Who knew very well, though, that if Mike had been the one who found these charges he would have called an immediate emergency meeting and banned the perpetrator for life.

It's got to be Mike.

He hated the accusing thoughts, but all the fingers pointed in one direction. Mike would have a lot to answer for when this finally came out. The other members of the board would have a field day with this. He scanned back to the previous year and found out how the elusive and controversial phone bill had been paid. Mike had charged it on the card to keep it out of going through the bank in the checking account. Mike had been having fun with everyone else's money.

Not even that.

It was the community theatre's money. And who did the theatre belong to? The community, that's who. *Oh, Mike, are you up a creek*, he thought morosely as he sat examining the list of purchases.

He saved the document to his hard drive and then printed a copy to his printer. He looked through the stack of sheets, stuck them in a folder, and buried it deep within his file cabinet.

Did Marie know about this? Surely not. She would have cried bloody murder to everyone else at the theatre. Marie obviously couldn't keep her mouth shut when it came to her co-performers down at the theatre. And she would burn Mike in a minute.

He remembered their confrontation a few nights ago in the office. She had pushed for the financial records and Mike had scurried away as fast as he could. She suspected, all right, but she didn't know for certain. Sean knew Mike well enough to know that he would do anything he could to keep his spending of the theatre funds a secret. Mike could be vicious and cruel when he had to be. Didn't the incident with Tony prove that? He hadn't waited to hear the other side before he let the ax fall.

But would he have killed Marie over this?

The possible answer chilled him. He couldn't concentrate on anything work related, but he knew that he needed to. There were too many deadlines creeping up on him. He closed the file on his desktop and tried to look busy, but all the while his thoughts wandered back to that horrible scene in Marie's garage.

And each time he played it in his mind, he saw one of their faces as the killer—Mike, Lynn, Heather, Sara, Tony, Dora, and then himself.

He shut his eyes and prayed.

Chapter Sixteen

"I thought that, too. It was horrible."

"Very much so. As far as sequels go, it was the pits."

"And all I kept thinking was that I paid money to see this thing," Sean replied.

She looked at him and they held each other's gaze for what felt like a small eternity. He hadn't planned on talking about movies, but there they were, doing it just the same. He could see tiny flecks of yellow and gold bursting around her the pupils of her eyes and wondered why he hadn't noticed them before.

"Do you want some dessert?" Sean asked. He broke their connection and studied a menu card framed on the wall beside them. "They have something called 'The Devil's Chocolate Sundae.' What do you think?"

Her face brightened. "I've had it. It'll kill you, Sean."

"Let's get it then."

"Oh, we don't have to," Dora said. She really wanted one, though, and hoped he would order them one. She liked the way his hair had a shagginess to it right at the part on the side. She couldn't believe she hadn't taken note of it before now.

"Let's spoil ourselves." He waved the waitress over and ordered their dessert.

"And some coffee, please?" Dora asked politely. She had been impressed when Sean had ordered the meal for them both. He took initiative that she didn't know he had.

"Me, too. Coffee," he said to the waitress right as she turned to go back to the kitchen. He hadn't realized that Dora could be so polite and kind. She had a persona of being a bit rude when it suited her, but now she had no reason to put on that façade and Sean was grateful for it.

"I won't be able to make it through rehearsal, I've eaten so much," Dora moaned. "I can never perform on a full stomach."

"I hear you. I have to nibble on a salad or something when it's a performance. But what's one rehearsal?"

"Right." She had the urgent need to light a cigarette, but fought it back. He didn't like the smoking and she didn't want to turn him off. She bit the inside of her mouth and promised herself one after they got to the theatre. He had asked for the smoking section for her sake, but she knew it would mean more if she didn't.

"This is weird," Sean mumbled, embarrassed at the revelation. "Strange."

"What is?"

"This." He hastily took a drink to wash any other awkward words that he may have wanted to let fly out of his mouth.

She found his shyness enthralling and cute. Sean was the kind of guy who stood on that line between hard masculinity and being considered a geek. She didn't like that term, but she knew what she meant by it. He could in one moment change from a timid child-like person to a man determined, full of intention. She liked the contrast. It was something that had made his performance as Willy Loman so interesting. She hadn't told him yet, but she would.

There wasn't anything simple about Sean, she thought. *There's just something about him.*

Sean mulled over the turn of events the past couple of weeks and couldn't quite grapple with all of it. Why had he known Dora for so long without any thoughts of asking her out? Did Marie's death make him look in the mirror and ask himself where he thought he was heading. Did death do that to everyone? Could all of this just be fallout from that? His emotions had been running high, which could influence him. Was that it?

Not at all.

He'd just finally found the guts to do something about it. Dora always held allurement for him, but he never had the gumption to do anything. Stranger things had happened so he wouldn't question it.

"The others are getting antsy," Dora said out of the blue.

"About what? The show isn't for another five weeks or so."

"Not that. Everything with Marie."

He sighed. More talk about Marie. They couldn't escape it and he didn't help any by stirring up things.

"Are you off somewhere?" she asked, breaking his trance.

"I guess we all are," he said. His enthusiasm for the conversation waned and Dora sensed it. "It's everywhere we turn around, isn't it?"

"Sorry. I didn't mean…"

"No, that's fine. She's been on my mind a lot lately." He didn't want to tell her that he'd spent most of his day dedicated to searching for clues, facts, something to go on for the police. His fear of her reproving him kept him silent.

"We've noticed," she said with a playful smirk.

We've noticed?

"Who's *we*?"

"Come on, Sean, everyone down at the theatre is wondering why you keep asking so many questions."

He opened his mouth to tell her, but the fear came back.

"I guess I'm just in shock by it all. I don't know."
He couldn't bring himself to lie to her—he wouldn't,
anyway, but the words of truth refused to form in his
mouth. "There's so much that I didn't know about."

"And that's probably a good thing."

The dessert came and attention got diverted to the
mound of brownie, ice cream, and whipped topping.
The dove into it with shovel-sized spoons. Dora giggled
at the enormity of it while Sean remained quiet and
removed from the entire scene.

*I pressed someone's button. The theatre last night
proved that...*

"Hello in there," Dora said, apparently repeating it
again. "When you zone out, you're really gone."

"Sorry," he said, completely embarrassed for zoning
out yet again. "Really, sorry. You have my full,
undivided attention."

She reached over and took his hand in hers. Both of
them sat timidly, but connected by her one gesture of
affection. Her hands were smooth and soft. The warmth
washed through his fingers and into his palm.

"Listen, Sean, I didn't mean to say anything…"

"No, that's fine."

"No. Please. Let me say this. I know you care about
what goes on down there and that includes Marie, even
though I know she was hard to care about."

"Too true."

"That's what I've always admired about you," she
admitted.

"What's that?"

"The fact that you care about those who are alone,
isolated…distant from everyone else. The outsiders."

"I didn't know I did that."

She looked away awkwardly. A small tear shed and
dripped down her cheek.

"What? What is it?" he asked.

"You did that for me."

"What are you talking about?"

"You probably don't remember the first time I came down to try out for anything, do you?"

He laughed at the memory. Of course he remembered and he told her so. "*Rumors* by Simon."

"That's right. You remember." Her hands wrapped around his tighter.

"You were great," he said.

"You were the only one who said anything to me at the tryouts. I thought I had brought in the plague the way everyone acted."

He remembered that, too. "That's the way they are."

"But not you. Not you, Sean. And I know Mike cast me because you put in a good word for me."

"I don't know about that."

"I do." She rubbed the hair on the back of his hand. Her feathery touch sent a chill up his back. She grabbed her spoon and held it up like a weapon.

"I'll race you to the bottom of the bowl!"

At the first break, Sean left by himself to go to his car and retrieve his cell phone. While rehearsals had been going on he felt guilty for not calling Ric and getting him up to speed on things.

"Hey," he said.

"You pooped out, or what?"

"No."

"You sound like you are," Sean said.

"Tough day. What's up?"

So Sean told him everything he had discovered in his casual (he thought, anyway) digging and snooping.

"You are going to get yourself into a lot of trouble," Ric reprimanded him.

"I may have been imagining someone in the theatre, Ric. I'll watch myself."

"You do that."

A long pause followed, both knowing the serious of the situation but neither relenting on what had to be done.

"Why are you doing this again?" Ric asked. "Remind me."

"I don't really know now. It started off as some quest to see things right with Marie, but now I've stumbled onto so much in our little group that I can't seem to stop." And that was true. He had been amazed at all the secrets and confused dealings that all of them had with each other.

"Listen, I'm going to call the chief on this and he'll probably get his man over to talk to you."

"Stiles, you mean?"

"I think that's his name, yeah. You have got to be careful, Sean. Really. You don't know what's going in this person's mind."

"Why don't they just charge someone?" Sean asked, beginning to get concerned with his well-being. Ric had a habit of making him look over his shoulder.

"Not real life, Sean. They need something to work with."

Exasperated, Sean said: "What about everything that I've told you?"

"I told you I'd make a phone call. They'll have to decide what to do from there. You just be careful. And, that's an order."

Darin rushed out of the front door and tapped on his watch. "Break's over, gang."

"Gotta go. *Mein Fuhrer* is signaling me to come in."

"Who? Darin?"

"Ah, you remember *Il Duce*, huh?"

"I do. Sounds like it's business as usual down there." *If only.*

"C'mon, Sean," Darin ordered, waiting at the door.

"See ya," Sean said and hung up the phone.

"We don't have all night, Sean," Darin hissed at him.

Hissing at me? Since when?

All night Darin had taken extra time during rehearsal to throw barbs at him, criticize a line, make him re-do an entrance, and anything else he could think of to agitate Sean. It took fifteen minutes for Sean to get his first entrance down right for Darin's liking. Sean knew that Sara had filled him in on their ill-fated lunch. Darin could be protective to the point of alienating everyone around him, or anyone remotely associated with him.

Back on the stage the deluge of criticisms started all over again. Sean took it as patiently as he could, reminding himself that it had very little to do with him and everything to do with Marie.

The black cloud cast by her murder still hung heavy and dark over all of them. Even the brightest light on the stage couldn't wash her shadowy image from their minds. Everywhere any of them looked, they saw her there. The makeup room, the dressing rooms, the stage, and even the lobby held some hazy etching of her face, the echoes of her words. Sean thought that the shroud that had been cast over them could be visible if you only looked.

"Again, Sean, and this time do something," Darin commanded. Lynn leaned over to him and whispered something. "I don't care, Lynn," Darin almost shouted. "Do it again."

"No problem," Sean mumbled. The others recognized the struggle between them and could only sympathize.

"Man, I'm sorry," Tony said, putting a playful arm over his shoulder. "He's hacked off at somebody tonight."

"Yeah, and that someone is me," Sean said. He made direct eye contact with Sara, but she looked away.

She knows what's going on.

"Come over for a movie, man. I bought one off the cheap rack this afternoon," Tony offered.

"No thanks. Let me get through tonight first." Tony could be selfish, hateful, and even cruel, but he did know how to ease his friend's troubles. Maybe that's why Sean still felt a connection to him and had remained his friend.

He sucked in a deep breath and re-entered the scene they were working on. Willy Loman had to confront Howard (for the umpteenth time) and lose his job, sending him through a fit of anger and loss. Sean did the scene with Tony with ease. He could use all the frustration from Marie's death plus Darin's rantings as fuel for the scene. Tony sensed his outrage and played off of it well. They had a chemistry that even those waiting in the wings wondered at. Dora, Heather, and even Sara stood transfixed to the events unfolding on the stage.

It was a good scene and everyone there knew it.

"What in the world are you doing?" Darin demanded from the auditorium. Lynn put a restraining hand on his shoulder, but he shrugged it away.

Tony and Sean remained silent on the stage.

"Hello, I'm talking to you," Darin said. He posed at the lip of the stage like the dictatorial commander of a platoon at war.

"I assume you're talking to me," Sean said quietly.

"Yes. I'm not looking at Tony, am I?"

"What's the problem?"

"What isn't? Where's your head tonight, Sean?" Darin stood waiting for an answer, but Sean refused to give him one. He would let him get this night out of the way. He knew what was really going on underneath the bluster and rage.

"Hello!" Darin yelled. "I'm talking to you, Sean."

"No, actually you were yelling at me," Sean said. "There's a big difference, by the way, just so you know."

Everyone sucked in a deep breath. They had seen these types of confrontations before and they knew that what Sean had done was return fire. The battle would now commence.

"Excuse me," Darin raged. "I am the director trying to shape a show here."

"We've just begun rehearsals here, Darin," Tony said.

"I'm not talking to you, T.T."

"I don't like to be called that, Darin."

"Well," Darin continued, ignoring Tony, "do you want to share why your head isn't in it tonight, or shall I?"

You wouldn't dare.

Sean saw Sara's head pop out from the wings trying to decide to intervene or not. He hoped she wouldn't. He wanted to see just how far Darin would be willing to go.

"I could re-cast it, you know. Don't think that I can't," Darin threatened. Another collective breath filled the stage.

Now I know how far.

Sean carefully put his script down on the desk in front of Tony. Dora and Heather stepped onto the stage before he could say the words, but they were too late.

"Then do so," Sean said and slowly walked off the stage, into the auditorium, and out the front door.

Just as he cranked the engine of his car, Lynn bolted out and stopped him.

"Don't," he said.

Sean merely shook his head. "You know what's going on in there, Lynn. I'm not sticking around for that. Sorry. This is supposed to be community theatre, not some version of a concentration camp." He knew the comparison was over-exaggerated, a perfect example of melodrama flourish, but he didn't care. He needed to get away and nothing was going to stop him.

"Let's talk about it," Lynn offered.

"You guys can. Have fun." He put the car into gear and drove out of the parking lot. Just as he pulled onto Constance, he saw Dora framed in his rearview standing outside the front door with a baffled look of consternation across her lovely face.

"Go outside, you mongrels," he growled at Weejo and Titan. When he got home, they attacked him and expected some play in return. Instead, they received grumblings and an order to get outside for a while. They bounded through the back door into the dark and disappeared.

Sean quickly changed into sweats and a T-shirt. He leaned back in his favorite chair and tried to breath. The anger that coursed through him made his hands tingle. He didn't like that feeling so he tried to breathe and relax his body. Shutting his eyes to the world, he imagined sunny skies and inviting beaches. He remembered a biofeedback trick a college professor had taught his psychology class and he used it regularly to try and calm down.

Warm sand and cool water from the ocean.

No matter how he tried, the scene on the stage kept replaying in his head. He saw a movie screen unfurl from a vaulted ceiling with carvings of angels and demons on every side. The screen descended and the movie rolled. He made all the necessary edits and fast-forwarded to the confrontation on the stage and him placing the script down and walking away.

Quit thinking about it.

The community theatre had more than its share of drama. No one would argue that. The mysterious details surrounding Marie's demise proved that. But they had always had drama of some kind or another. The thing with Mike and the reviews and his sensitivity to the finances, Dora's past mooching, Darin's moods, Sara's infidelities, Tony's rants, and on and on and on it went. He made a mental list on an imagined piece of paper in his mind.

He tried breathing again and seeing the beaches. The spray sprang up in the air like it had been shot from a cannon. He could almost feel the sunshine glaring down on him as he created it in his mind.

His aggravation with the evening's events had ruined the dinner with Dora. He couldn't even bring himself to think about her. He fried in his own juices of feeling sorry for himself and anger at Darin. He couldn't get away from it. He replayed the fight again and again. His hands balled up until they turned white from the strain.

"Okay, this is stupid," he said, flinging himself up from his chair. He stripped down to his skivvies and walked into the bathroom. He blasted hot water into the tub and pulled the metal stem to divert the water to the showerhead.

He stepped into the cascade of blistering water, letting the heat wash over his body. The steam from the water burned his nostrils, but eased the tension away. He spun the dial down a bit because the skin of his belly had turned a bright pink. He tried a steady rhythm of breathing again, trying to clear his head.

I hate conflict. I hate it with a passion.

And that was true. Any kind of argument anywhere and his gut twisted into aching knots of anxiety. He wanted everyone to get along, but knew the impossibility of that. Didn't the preacher at church talk about it from time to time? *You can't make everyone happy or everyone like you*, he was known to say from the pulpit. And Sean knew just how true that was.

He shut the water off and stood there watching the droplets spin and fall off of his body into the tub. He grabbed the towel off the wall hanger and dried himself off. Staring at himself in the mirror, he quietly wondered if he should walk away from the theatre all together. He shook the thought away and chided himself for being so melodramatic. If he didn't watch himself, he'd turn into another Tony. And the theatre could only handle one Tony at a time.

Putting on a fresh T-shirt, sweats, and socks he studied himself closely in his bedroom mirror. His eyes had a haggard look to them. A harder edge lurked there, which he was unaccustomed to seeing. The reflection had a twisted appearance to it like something burned to get out of his skin.

I've got to quit doing this.

He found an open can of soda in the fridge and sucked it down in one swallow. He eased back in his chair and shut the lamp off next to him. The nerves had settled down some and he could feel a yawn coming on. He grabbed a foot blanket and covered himself and counted entrances and exits until he passed out.

A noise exploded in his ears waking him up with a start. He had jerked in his chair like he'd been hooked up to an electrical outlet. The shock disappeared and he pulled the blanket tighter around his shoulders. Sleep came back to him as the noise repeated itself. Knocking came from the front door—someone not willing to take "no one home" as an answer.

He wearily trudged to the small foyer in his house and peeked through the frosted glass window inset in the door. He could make out the shape of someone with longish hair and agitated features.

Dora.

Reluctantly he swung the door open to let her in. The only reason he hesitated was because he knew he had looked like a jerk at the theatre and he didn't want to look her in the eye just yet.

"Hello to you, too," she said.

He led her into the living room. "I was asleep."

"Oh. I'm sorry. I thought you were just ignoring me." She set her purse on the floor and took a seat on the couch. He sat in his chair and attempted to shake the sleep from his brain.

"I feel like I owe you an apology," he said.

"That's funny; I was about to say the same thing," she said and laughed.

"Why?"

"For Darin's behavior tonight."

"You aren't responsible for Darin."

"I know, but I just felt so sorry for what he was doing to you. That's all."

"I appreciate it." He expected coldness between them, but there wasn't. She had come to see him in good faith and with an apology on her lips. "Hey, sorry, my manners. Do you want something to drink, or anything?"

"No thanks. I'm still full from dinner."

"Yeah, and that mountain of brownie and ice cream."

"No kidding," she said with a chuckle. A sudden spark of seriousness flooded her face. "Look, Sean, he's not going to get someone else. He's just mad at you about something with Sara. We all talked about it after you left."

Sean leaned back in his chair and stared at the ceiling. "I've been opening my mouth a lot lately, it seems."

"He'll probably call you some time."

"Not tonight, I hope."

"No. Not tonight. They all went down to MoMo's to have a cup of coffee and some pie."

"Why didn't you go with them?" he asked, clueless as to the reason.

She smiled with white teeth showing. "I would think that's pretty obvious," she said.

"I didn't mean to bust up rehearsal. I'm the one who needs to apologize to everyone. It was childish of me to leave." It embarrassed him to admit these things to her, but he knew that she truly understood.

"Well, I just came over to check on you. I was worried about you. We don't have to talk about it unless you want to."

Okay, call me the slow one.

He got up from his chair and sat beside her on the couch. Putting his arms around her, he pulled her close to his body. They held each other like that for a long time before either one of them moved. And then it was Dora who gently pushed back and touched her lips softly to his. He responded in kind and they settled into the routine of getting to know each other without any words needing to be spoken.

Her kisses came freely and easily as he pulled her back close to his chest. The warmth of her mouth spread into his delicately, passionately. Sean couldn't remember the last time he had kissed someone with so much anticipation and longing. Her arms wrapped around his neck and her fingers dug deeply into his hair. He could feel her fingernails caress the nape of his neck. She broke away and took a deep breath.

"Wow," she said.

"Wow, yourself." He kissed her on the cheek and lightly touched her cheek with his own. He could feel the flush in her face and the heat from it. The lull in conversation made him uncomfortable. He opened his mouth to speak: "I don't know what to say...I know it seems pretty silly to say it, but you came around at a good time."

She didn't laugh at him. She lifted his face up to hers and grinned. "And the same goes for you."

He laughed at himself. "I better not say anything else or I'll start sounding like a soap opera."

She batted her eyes melodramatically and held an arm over her eyes. "Oh, Sean, hold me before I break!"

He followed the act as he pulled her head back and lightly kissed her on the neck. "Oh, Dora, the days have been so long without you!"

They shared a laugh and giggled until tears streamed down their faces. They had both been so lonely for so long and to finally hold someone again made them giddy, and even a little ridiculous.

They settled back on the couch. She leaned into him and rested her head on his shoulder. He massaged her scalp with one hand while he caressed an arm with the other. She kicked off her shoes and let her breathing fall into a rhythm with his.

"This is nice," she whispered.

"Very."

"I'm glad I came over here."

"Me, too." He rubbed the tips of her eyebrows softly, caressing her forehead gently, lovingly.

She burrowed her face into his shoulder, staring up at his jaw line and wondering why it intrigued her so much. She ran her finger along the edge of it.

"This whole rehearsal process...is it me, or do I miss Marie being around?" she asked out of the blue.

Sean found that funny and told her.

"I know, I know," she said. "But there was just something about her being around. Something about her crassness and being rude all the time that I just came to expect."

"She got you a few times, as I recall," Sean commented. He didn't need conversation now. He enjoyed just sitting next to her and hearing her breath. Everything came back to Marie.

"She did, yeah," Dora said, tensing up in his arms.

"What is it?"

"Just remembering."

"Yeah. As I recall she nagged you about being a mooch."

Dora pulled back to look in his face. "Yeah, and?"

"That's all I'm saying. I just remember that."

"And so did Tony. And you did a couple of times as I remember," she said, the agitation rising within her.

"Hey, now, wait just a sec, I didn't bring it up," Sean said. He knew that the "mooch" thing really did crawl all over her so he tried to change the subject. It didn't work.

"I was out of a job, Sean."

"I know that."

"I was laid off out at the radio station."

"I know that, too."

She jerked back completely away from him. "Then maybe you'd know what it's like to have nothing in the fridge to eat." Remembering it made her angry, but admitting it to Sean kindled it even further. She couldn't believe she was opening up like this to him. But she couldn't stop the anger rising deep within her, either.

"Listen, Dora, I'm not trying to start anything. You brought it up and I was just trying to tease you. That's all." Sean could see that anything he said only made it worse.

"So what are you suggesting, detective?" she asked with a scowl on her face. "Are you saying that I killed her because I mooched off of her and she wouldn't leave me alone about it?"

"I didn't know you mooched off her."

Dora jumped off the couch, tugged her shoes on, and headed for the door with Sean trailing fast behind. She grabbed the door open and he shut it.

"Dora, we don't have to do this. I didn't say anything." *And it was true,* he thought sadly, *he hadn't.*

"I don't care. Marie held that over my head until the day she died."

"Held what?"

She grabbed the door again, but he wouldn't budge. She jerked hard but he held fast. "I would like to go, please."

Sean refused to move.

"I said I would like to go," she said, this time with a snarl on her mouth.

"What did she hold over you?" he asked.

"I am not doing this with you, Sean. Forget it. Forget everything."

He tried to pull her back to him, but she had gone completely cold. The smell of faraway roses drifted from her hair, but he couldn't do anything about it.

"Dora, I'm asking you…"

"And I'm saying to let me out of this house, Sean. Right now."

He stepped away from the door dumbfounded as to what had just happened. The words of apology tripped along his tongue but couldn't find their way out of his mouth. He watched her step out and jog to her car like she had a dog chasing her out of the yard.

The dogs.

He hadn't heard them in a while, which wasn't like them, and he wondered what they were up to. Dora slammed into her car as he slowly closed the door and locked it. So much for the new woman in my life, he thought. He peered through the smoky glass and saw the last of her tail lights glow red at the stop sign at the four-way next to his house and then out of sight as she left his neighborhood.

How had this night turned into such a disaster? First Darin, and now Dora running away from him. If he continued on his present course, he'd burn every bridge down at the theatre. Those folks could hold grudges. He had another wave of loneliness fill his heart.

He grabbed a couple of doggy treats from the pantry and exited the house through the back door to find Titan and Weejo. He called for them, but they didn't come. That was hardly unusual. He squinted into the darkness of the oversized back yard, but couldn't see them.

"Titan, Weejo," he called. "Treats, babies. Come on."

Still no movement flickered in the dark. What's going on here? Did they get out again?

"Come on, Titan. Weejo."

Off from the far corner of the yard he heard whining sounds. Were they playing with each other, or had they tangled with the neighbor's German Shepard again? The harder he listened, the more he figured out they weren't playing. He trotted over to them and saw Titan lying on the ground trying to rise up from the ground, but not able to. Weejo stood over him whining and beginning to yelp as Sean approached.

"What's up, boy?" Sean asked, not allowing his anxiety to take over. "Come on, boy, get up now."

The dog couldn't. Sean couldn't see much, but he could feel. He ran his hands along the length of the dog's body. When he reached his head, he sucked in air and gasped audibly.

"Oh, no, Titan. All right, boy, all right." He knew what he had to do. He ran toward the back door full throttle, having completely forgotten the scene with Dora. Weejo ran after him, but he ordered her to stay with Titan. She whined again but did as she was told.

Sean found his keys and shoes, ran to the bug, and had it around in the alleyway in less than a minute. In the dim lighting of the car, he could make out the stain of blood on his palm and fingers.

"All right, Titan. Come on now, boy. I've got you." He continued talking tenderly to the dog and eased him into his arms. Weejo barked and whined the entire time. He told her to hush, but she refused. He reached for a leg blanket on the front floorboard and draped it over the front seat of the car. He carefully placed Titan on the seat and got a better look at his skull. Blood streamed freely from a gash on Titan's head.

Without being told to, Weejo hopped over the driver's side window and jumped into the back seat of the car. Sean drove slowly out of the alley so as to not jar Titan too much. He had the vet's number called on his cell phone before he reached the main street in front of his house.

"Sean, don't you think it's a bit late?" the vet said, obviously aided in his identity by caller ID.

Sean quickly explained the emergency and the doctor readily agreed to meet him at the clinic. The doctor knew Sean and his dogs on a first name basis. Sean took great care in seeing to their health needs. The vet got onto him from time to time for not letting them just be dogs, but Sean knew that he was only teasing.

Sean kicked the car faster as he jogged onto the main drag through town. The vet had his clinic on the outskirts of town where he could have a big corral for the larger animals that people brought to him. Sean ignored the speed limit signs and hoped the police were busy with something else.

He got out to the clinic in less than five minutes—it usually took him over ten—the vet had already arrived and had the lights on in the main office of the compound.

"Dr. Terry, he's in the front seat," Sean said. He sounded frantic and he knew it immediately. He took a deep breath and tried to count to ten. It failed.

"It's all right now, Sean. Let me have a look," the doctor said. He clicked on a flashlight and ran it along the dog's body. "Okay. I see it now," he whispered, now understanding Sean's urgency on the phone. "I can see why you called me."

"What do you think?" Sean asked, fully knowing the doctor couldn't tell him.

"Let's get him inside, Sean, and I'll take a look at him. What happened?"

"I have no idea." In all the confusion and the shock of finding him, Sean hadn't even thought of what happened to him. A lump of nerves sat cold in his stomach.

What had happened?

"Let's get him inside," the doctor said. "And we'll see how bad it is."

He sat reminiscing about the first time he'd set eyes on his dogs. When he got them, he'd been going through a bout of isolation and detachment from the world. He went to work, went home, made it to church, but that was about it. The rut he'd fallen into was deep so he decided he needed to try and fix it.

The previous dog he'd owned had been one an old college flame had bought for him one Christmas. It had papers, but that didn't matter much to him. He liked dogs, always had. When the dog died, he vowed to let it alone for a while. It had been the isolation and loneliness talking. The death of the animal brought on memories of the girl who bought it for him, which brought on other things, and so and so on.

He had the names for them as soon as he saw them. Something in their carriage, their being had determined that for him. As soon as he brought them home, he could feel the change take over in him. So they were dogs? So what? He had renewed energy and purpose and that beat watching late movies until all hours of the morning.

Pretty soon he took them with him in the car and out to the city park. They filled a void where he had created one. And that had been enough.

He slowed down as he drove up to his driveway. He killed the engine and with Weejo in tow he grabbed a flashlight from his kitchen drawer and walked out into the back yard.

The vet had told him to either go home or drive around. Either way he didn't want Sean hanging around bugging him. The vet knew him well enough to know that he would. Sean reluctantly agreed and determined to find what had happened to Titan.

"What is it, Weejo?" he asked as the dog sniffed around where Titan had fallen. He flashed his light to the spot and saw the darkness of the blood on the grass. Weejo whimpered at something near the back gate. Sean stepped cautiously to Weejo and knelt down on the ground. An imprint of a shoe had been pressed into the soft earth where he had been watering earlier in the week.

"It's not mine, Weejo," he said, reassuring his pet. "One must assume it's the person who hit Titan," he whispered to himself. He touched the footprint with his fingertips. Whoever made it had a medium to large foot. They weren't his, that he knew. He tried to make out a pattern or letters in the earth, but couldn't. The ground hadn't been that soft.

He checked the alley for tire tracks, but knew they'd been covered (if there were any to speak of) by his own when he drove around to pick up Titan. The helplessness he felt overwhelmed him. He couldn't think without picturing his dog's wounded skull pressed down on the vet's examination table. Weejo licked his hand, to which he responded to by rubbing her neck and back.

"Thanks, baby girl," he whispered.

The cool night blew its light breezes across his face and arms, sending a chill through him. He shut the light off and locked the house up for the night. Whoever did this had known exactly the effect it would have on him. He knew that all too well. His instincts or impulses, or whatever, told him that much.

This has everything to do with Marie.

The thought of it angered him to the point where he needed something to hit or break. He hadn't had a good tantrum in months and one came on him now. He beat his fist against the bar top and rued the decision to do so. What was he to do? Sean despised feeling this way. It burned him up and made him feel weak, inferior in some way. From the living room Weejo whined at seeing him like this. He took a breath, tried to feel the rhythm of his heartbeat in his fingers, and sat down in his chair again.

How could this night get any worse?

And as if on cue, the phone rang. It had to be the vet.

"Hello, how is he?" he asked before the other party could say anything.

"Uh, excuse me? Sorry. This is Detective Stiles."

"Oh, sorry."

"What's wrong, Mr. Maston?"

Now was not the time to tell the detective. "Nothing. Sorry. What was it you needed?"

"We've gathered some of Ms. Winters' items from her work place. Date books, calendars, notes, and that kind of thing. And there's an item or two I'd like for you to look over for me."

Sean could hear his voice from far away, but nothing seemed to compute.

"Mr. Maston?"

"Yes. Not a problem. When?"

"How 'bout now?"

"No. Now's not the best time. In the morning maybe?"

He heard some scribbling in the background. "That'd be fine. Her family is going to go through her stuff at the house tomorrow. They're going to look out for anything that might seem out of place or suspicious."

"Okay, fine." How would they know what was "out of place or suspicious?"

"Tomorrow morning then."

He hung up the phone and stared at the receiver.

What about tomorrow morning?

Right, right. Go see Stiles at the police station. He petted Weejo until she curled up at his feet. He registered her steady breathing, but that was it. He couldn't erase the bloody images of Titan out of his mind. He reminded himself that it was only a dog, for goodness sake, but he couldn't stop himself. He had tied a lot of years, care, and love into that animal. And that part of him wouldn't let him stop himself.

This had everything to do with Marie.

Someone's trying to send me a warning. He knew very well it couldn't be a prank from the neighbor kids or the rowdy bunch that lived down the block. They didn't do things like that. Who would? Someone sick and twisted enough to let him know they didn't like his inquiries. Someone knew what would affect him the most. He heard the message loud and clear, but knew it would only fuel him on to find the guilty party.

Desperation begat ugliness, of that, he knew. Ask the uncomfortable questions and people reacted in hurt, anger, and even fury. His wounded dog pointed to the latter. Someone out there didn't like Sean digging around in Marie's murder. And this someone struck in a place where it would send the loudest message.

What else did it mean? That this someone sent a warning only. It could have been much more. It could have been another killing, and not of his dog, either.

Death can only bring heartache and despair.

He closed his heavy eyes and fell to sleep.

Chapter Seventeen

The morning came too soon, but it shot its bright buttery sunshine through the curtains anyway. Sean stretched and yawned, which woke Weejo from her light sleep at his feet. He hadn't made it to his bed. The entire night he'd slept in a contortionist position in his chair leaving him an enormous crick in the neck and a sore back. He checked the wall clock and decided it was too early to call the vet. A shower, breakfast, and then he'd make the phone call he dreaded.

"Out, Weejo," he said, opening the door and releasing the cooped up dog to the outdoors. He shut the door, but then had second thoughts. He walked back outside to the fence near the alley and took a closer look at the ground where Titan had fallen. He examined the foot print again, but still couldn't make out any discernable characteristics that would point him to anyone in particular. The gate told him nothing more. No signs were left there or anywhere else.

One thing, though. Whoever did it knew the layout of his address, how to get to his back yard, and where his dogs stayed during the night. Maybe he wanted to force those facts to be true, but he knew deep down in his darkest of hunches that it had to be true.

The killer knows you're getting close to the truth.

The thought stopped him cold, not even the sunshine could warm him. The impression of where Titan had fallen could be made out in the grass and another wave of chills spread over his body.

The killer knows...

What had he done or asked that had gotten the killer worried? The other night at the theatre had been one thing, which could be explained in some morbid way. But the dog? No. That was something altogether different, unless the person in the darkened theatre had planned his demise that early morning.

The killer knows...

Something he'd found out, maybe, had sparked the murderer's actions? What had he found out? *Too many things,* he thought dramatically. Coffee, he needed a cup desperately.

He brewed up, still weighing conversations and confrontations he'd had in the past couple of days. Everyone that he had a discussion with about Marie had turned on him in some form or fashion. Marie's legacy had been cancerous. Her fingers spread throughout the entire clique and wouldn't let go, even from the grave. She knew things about people and used it against them. She threatened, cajoled, and bullied her way into roles. She'd done a good turn now and again, but held it over the person's head like the sword of Damocles. She refused to forget, or forgive, anything.

The killer...

Something she had done or said or knew (or all three) burned the fuse to her life. But what? Everyone had something that they protected and held close. Marie exploited those things in cruel and vicious ways. He'd been a witness to that.

He barely tasted the coffee as it slid over his tongue and down his throat. The bitterness of the situation had overwhelmed him—yet again.

Grabbing the phone, he punched the numbers rapidly to the vet's office.

"Yes, Sean?" the voice rattled from the other end.

"Well?"

"It's a pretty good skull fracture, Sean. Titan got clobbered with something hard."

"I figured that much," Sean snapped. He took a breath. He didn't need to get angry with the doctor.

"I know you hate to hear these things."

"I'm sorry. I'm just mad."

"You should be. Whoever did this meant to hurt your dog pretty bad. An inch back on the skull and Titan wouldn't be lying down in my clinic."

"I'll check on him later, doc. Thanks. Is there anything I can do?"

"Just be patient. I know it stinks, but there you go. My best bedside manner at it again."

"Thanks, doc. Really. Thank you."

He hung up contemplating the news. Not good, but definitely not bad. He could tell from the report that there was hope, and that was enough for now. Hating to do it, but feeling the need, he called into work and explained his situation to his immediate supervisor, who just happened to be another animal lover. Taking the day off wouldn't be a problem, to which he thanked him profusely.

"Now, for some good old-fashioned routine," he muttered to himself.

He hopped in the shower, shaved, and dressed in casual clothes preparing himself for a busy day. The face he saw in the mirror had an edge to it now, a haggard appearance. His constitution could only handle so much. He shrugged it off and made some toast with strawberry jelly. It was the only breakfast he could stomach.

As a cautionary gesture, he put Weejo in the house. He knew that it was probably a silly thing to do, but how could he know for sure? There was a doggy door in the utility room that led into the garage where he had water, food, and a big box for potty trips. The dogs had become accustomed to it in the winter months as Sean spoiled them by letting them stay inside. *I spoil them all the time,* he thought. He rubbed Weejo's ears, received a wet sloppy kiss from her, and locked the front door behind him.

The sun blazed in the sky, boding of good things to come, or at least he hoped it did. Bright days brought better things for him and he needed it today.

The bug fired to life and he eased out of the driveway, trying to decide what do to first for his busy day. Checking his watch for the time, he figured it to be too early to see Stiles. His mind wandered to the movie playing in his head about last night's ugly events. He knew it sounded like an odd combination—*Dora and then Titan*—but it meant something to him.

He pulled onto the main through street of Lyle and watched the frantic workers returning to their shops and businesses for another day of work. The town had its share of stores and offices, which gave it character. The odd junk shop next to the diner, which sat next to a doctor's office had always appealed to him as being pleasantly unique. He waved at folks he knew, and even some he didn't, as he cruised along the main drag.

In a few minutes, he found himself driving along an all too familiar street. He slowed down and wondered what had brought him here.

The killer knows you're getting close to the truth.

He saw Marie's house up in the distance and decided to drive on by for the time being. He would wait to talk to the family. As he drove by, a woman walked out of the door with a box weighted down in her arms. Without thinking about it, he pulled over to the curb and killed the engine.

"Here, let me help you with that," he offered to the stranger.

"That'd be great," she said, handing the box over to him.

"Where do you want it?"

"The curb for now. Thanks a lot."

He set the box down and shook her hand. "I'm Sean Maston."

"I saw you at the funeral. Co-worker?"

"Huh? Oh, no. Marie and I were at the community theatre together."

She laughed and then snapped her fingers in recognition. "I saw you in the musical you guys just finished up there."

"Yeah."

"What brings you to this neck of the woods?" A certain cautionary tone took over and Sean knew he would have to be as delicate as he could. "I'm Sheryl, by the way."

"Marie," he said simply.

"Were you close?"

"Not really. To be honest, she didn't get along with a lot of people that well. If you don't mind me saying."

"Who, me? No. I knew Marie. I know how she was. She did the same thing to her family." She paused to think it over. She didn't know if it was right to speak ill of the dead. "I'm her aunt, by the way."

"I see the resemblance," Sean said, hoping it to be a compliment.

"Yeah, she's my sister's oldest daughter. *Was*." She wiped a tear from her eye.

Sean felt like an intruder on private, hidden grief. "I better go…I…"

"Nonsense. I've just put a pot of coffee on. You want some?"

"That'd be fine." He followed her to the front door and opened it for her.

She smiled at him. "I'm glad to see chivalry isn't dead."

"My mother would rise up out of the grave and whip me if I didn't." She laughed at that and led him into the kitchen. Boxes of clothes, books, and other possessions flooded throughout the living room.

"You know, maybe you could help me sort through some of this stuff. I just don't know what to do with all of it. Marie's mother didn't want to do this. I can't say as I blame her. You know?" She looked at him for an answer, which he didn't have ready to give. He couldn't tear his eyes away from the mounds of stuff piled all over the room. The life had gone out of them somehow now that Marie was gone. Is that the way of material possessions?

"She had a lot, didn't she?" he remarked.

"She did. Just like the rest of us, huh?"

"Here today and then into the fire," he mumbled. She heard him, but didn't comment.

"Here," she said, giving him a hot cup of coffee. The smell of it made him feel welcome, comfortable. "It'll put hair on your chest."

He sipped it, actually tasting the coffee this time. "Thanks. It's great."

"Columbian Supremo. There's no other way to go." She drank her own. They waited in silence wanting the other to say something to keep the conversation moving, flowing.

Sean blurted out suddenly: "I've been asking questions about Marie's death."

Sheryl pondered it a moment before answering. "That man Stiles had mentioned that someone at the theatre had been nosing around some. He thought it was a dangerous idea. As do I. Let the professionals do what they're paid to do."

Sean thought of Titan and couldn't agree more.

"But who am I to judge, right?" she said. "I'm surprised they haven't made an arrest yet."

"Why's that?"

"I don't know. I just assumed with Marie's personality that it would be easy to find out who was responsible for her death."

Sean smiled bitterly and she saw it. Her own bitter grin spread on her face. "That's just it. She got on a lot of people's nerves," he said.

"Boy, did she ever," she conceded. "But someone killed her. That person, to me anyway, should stick out like a sore thumb."

Sean mulled that over and wondered why the killer didn't. At least, not to him. Why was that? Could it be that he knew folks down at the theatre too long and had become prejudiced? That had to be it. He hadn't approached this in the most objective way and it had gotten him into trouble. The murderer had been able to mask himself in the very fact that Sean knew the person. Nothing out of the ordinary had been detected. If there had been anything out of sync, would he have noticed it anyway? Chewing on it, he knew that a big part of him just couldn't fathom anyone he knew and cared for killing someone. That fact had lurked in the back of his conscience mind the past few days, especially when confronting his friends.

"Where did you go off to?" Sheryl asked, snapping him out of his trance.

"Pondering the universe," he said with a vague stare off into space. "I have a habit of doing that."

"You think you know the person responsible."

"That's very perceptive of you."

"You have an easy face to read."

She had such an easy, straight forward way about her. Sean knew if she stayed in Lyle, he could become fast friends with her. She didn't have one bone of pretension in her body. He liked that in people. He knew his own trouble with it, but admired others who were just what they seemed.

"There are a lot of things that point to it."

She set her cup down on the counter, looked at the pile of boxes, and sighed heavily. "I really need to get started on this stuff."

"Are you taking it to good will?" he asked, following her into the living room.

"Most of it. The rest the family will want to go through and separate."

Sean picked up a box and headed for the door. "The corner?"

"Oh, wait." She looked in the box. "No, that one goes in my car. Here, I'll get the trunk for you."

They deposited the box into her vehicle and returned for the next one. This continued for a while, which Sean didn't mind. He enjoyed her company and helping someone who needed it. Sheryl had readily accepted him on faith and trust, which he didn't encounter often.

She grabbed a box of bathroom items, thought better of it, and set it down in the middle of the living room floor. "Can I ask you something?"

"Sure," Sean said, coming back from another trip to her car.

"Look in this box and tell me if anything seems out of place," she said. She sounded like she had been hiding a great conspiracy of some kind. She pulled the box over in front him. He knelt down beside it and shifted through the stuff.

All kinds of bathroom and toiletries were stacked neatly into the cardboard box. He assumed that the aunt had gone to great effort to keep things separately in such a meticulous way. Everything in the box had order and design to it. The floss, three tubes of toothpaste (including a whitener), and teeth drops suggested Marie worked very hard on her award-winning smile. The irony struck Sean hard as he rummaged through the rest of what was in the box.

"Well?" Sheryl asked. She found his intense expression intriguing and mysterious as he examined every item in the box. Funny how a stranger she had just met over a half hour ago could feel so close to her so fast.

Sean's face fell a mile. Buried underneath some feminine products and other items he found a box that looked new in comparison to everything else in the collection. He held the box up and looked inside. Two had been used.

"I thought you might react that way," Sheryl said. "That's how I reacted to it, too."

"I didn't know she was active."

"Very."

"She never breathed a word about it up at the theatre," Sean said, still dumb-founded by what he held in his hand.

"It's known to happen and still keep quiet about it."

"But Marie," he countered quickly. "You'd think she would've broadcast it to the world."

"If she was actually pregnant."

Sean turned the pregnancy test box over in his hands. "It's a shocker."

"She was worried enough to buy that for some reason."

"And tested twice."

"Unless she dropped the first one down the toilet," she said, laughing at the thought. "But yeah, I thought of that, too."

"The box doesn't have that aged look, as silly as that sounds."

"It doesn't."

Sean sat down to digest the endless possibilities. What in the world did this mean? Did this point to anything concrete? "No, it doesn't," he said out loud.

"What doesn't?"

"Oh, nothing. Thinking out loud."

Sheryl sighed and grabbed a seat across from Sean on the couch. "I haven't had the heart to ask her mother. It'd kill her to think that Marie had…" she let the thought trail off.

"I know."

Okay, so Marie had been fooling around, or so he assumed. She certainly wouldn't have the pregnancy kits over at her house for a friend. Who could trust her? No, it was for Marie. He knew that. Who had she been seeing that seriously? He almost choked on the laughter. He couldn't be that naïve about things. She could very well have had a one-night stand that had gone too far. This meant that she suspected it. You didn't keep this around for kicks and giggles.

"A penny for them," Sheryl said.

Sean told her his suspicions. She listened intently with a blank expression, suggesting she'd had enough time to think this all through for herself.

"Marie could get around back home," she said. "She had a scare or two back when she was in high school, freaked her dad out half to death. Her mother never knew."

"But you did?"

"Yeah. Funny how those things work out, isn't it?" She held out her hand for the box and studied it for herself.

"Surely the autopsy would've shown something," Sean said quietly, thinking of the implications if it were true.

"What's that?"

"The autopsy."

Sheryl's face twisted and the wrinkles around her eyes crinkled up and spread. The thought made her ill.

"If it is, then the police know and are playing that angle. But I haven't heard about it," Sean pondered.

"Maybe we're just reacting to the actions of someone who's dead and not quite grasping who and what she actually was in life."

Sean heaved a deep breath that went all the way to his toes. "And you know, I'm about tired of that, too," he said. "Thinking you know someone pretty well and then you begin to find out that you really didn't have a clue. It's sad."

"That was Marie for you." She leaned forward and pulled out a scrapbook that had a dark, aged look to it. "From a baby to a girl to a teenager, and then—wow—a young woman. And you think you know all about her. Then you find it's all been some kind of façade to hide something that she didn't want the rest of us to see."

"Which we saw plenty of, I guess."

"I suppose, but just like you said, you didn't really know all about her."

"Yeah, you're right. It's like we saw one half, which you didn't see and vice versa."

She didn't answer for a long time. Something in the scrapbook caught her attention. She thumbed through pages that represented years and accomplishments, markers and time passing. She held it up and then placed it dramatically back into the box.

"One life all in one book, compact and neat with pictures to guide the way," she mused. "I'm not sure I know what it's all for."

"Now you're getting philosophical," Sean told her.

"Yep, that's me all over," she said.

"Have you told the police?"

"Are you kidding? I've been trying to get my mind around it all morning long. I still don't know what to think. What was going on? Why would anyone kill her?"

"All the same questions that I've been asking."

"And the police," she reminded him.

"And the police."

He checked his watch and realized he really needed to go. She sensed it and stood up.

"You need to go somewhere?" she asked, hoping he didn't, not just yet, anyway. She enjoyed talking to him.

"Yeah, as a matter of fact, to see the detective." He made it sound like he had been rejected from something important.

"Tell them, will you?"

"I thought it might be a good idea." He stood up and shook her hand.

She held onto it longer than what was considered polite. "I can't even find the strength to pick up the phone."

"I understand."

"And her mother. What do I tell her?"

Sean didn't have an answer. None came to him. What could she tell her? That Marie had been pregnant when she died? They didn't even know that for sure. Everything still rested in the hands of speculation, but the assumptions were made nevertheless. This woman's eyes spoke the volumes of pain and anger that come with losing a loved one in such a violent way. The only question that keeps repeating is why, and that is never an easy one.

He hopped back into the bug and wondered what further revelations would be made that day. He waved goodbye and watched the cautious hand of understanding and friendship waving back at him.

Even with that, some mornings weren't worth waking up to.

Stiles had another cup of coffee poured for him when he arrived, but he refused. He couldn't handle any more caffeine intake. He only hoped that Stiles wouldn't take offense by not accepting his hospitality. You had to be careful in Lyle, and pretty much everywhere else in Oklahoma, when it came to being hospitable. It would be extended graciously and willingly and it had to be received in the same fashion.

Stiles waved him over to a chair by a window and started with small talk. Sean engaged him as best as he could, but the cloud of hanging about at a police station wouldn't leave him. He knew the conversation would shift to business and that prospect just didn't settle well with him.

"There's a couple of things on this deal with Marie that I want to go over with you," Stiles said. He drained the last of his coffee and put it in a drawer in his desk. Grabbing a pen and a notepad, he settled back into his chair with legs crossed in front of him. For some reason Sean didn't like the look and tried to ignore it.

"A couple of things?" he found himself asking. He still couldn't fully digest what he'd seen at her house with her Aunt Sheryl.

"She was pregnant, wasn't she?" he asked, not quite blurting it out, but enough so that Stiles shot forward in his chair.

"Where did you hear that?" Stiles demanded. He stood up from his chair to search the room for someone that Sean couldn't see.

"Sit down, detective." He rubbed his temples and massaged the pain that throbbed there. "No one here told me."

"Then who?" Stiles planted his fists on his hips in such a dramatic way that Sean thought he would make a perfect photo for a play poster or flier. He found it funny, but hid his laughter from the disgruntled Stiles.

Sean held up his hands as a way of finding a truce. He told Stiles what had happened at Marie's house. As he got deeper into the story, Stiles' tension released and he sat back down again. Sean described the entire morning, adding every detail, whether he deemed it necessary or not. Stiles soaked it in and made a note or two on his pad.

"Yeah, we gave Marie's aunt permission late yesterday afternoon to start packing up her things," Stiles mumbled. "Somebody's going to get a severe butt chewing. You don't overlook something like that. A pregnancy test box is a clue."

"How often do you have a case like this in Lyle?" Sean asked carefully.

"Not often. It doesn't matter. It's murder and that means by the book all the way. We don't go through a person's belongings for kicks and giggles. And you say two of the tests had been used?"

"No, just that two were out of the box. I just assumed they'd been used."

Stiles twisted the pen in his hands, ignoring the fact that it bent under the pressure. "Come on back here with me, Sean," he said.

They walked to a conference room at the end of a short hallway. Stiles shut the door and pointed to a chair for Sean to sit in. He did so, noticing the two stacks of material in the center of the table.

"Some of Marie's things," Stiles offered. "We'll get to that in a minute."

"What things?"

"First thing. Her autopsy said she was pregnant."

"How far along?"

"The report stated about six weeks."

"I thought the box looked pretty new. It didn't have that beat up look like everything else in the bathroom cabinet," Sean said. He weighed that out for a minute.

Six weeks. That would put the time of conception at the beginning of rehearsals for the musical Marie starred in. Suspicions floated in his mind, a thousand possible scenarios to explain her murder. Could these two be connected? A possible birth and a death? He found the possibilities too endless to contemplate.

"Did she know do you think?" Stiles asked as he took a chair across from Sean.

"She obviously suspected. We have to assume the tests were positive."

"Assuming the box was new as you noted," Stiles said. "It took two tries?"

Sean thought about that. "Who knows? Maybe she dropped the first one in the tub or something. Or, she got a positive test, couldn't believe it, and then tested again. That sounds more like it." And it did. He could envision Marie being completely baffled at finding out she was pregnant and then re-checking just to make certain.

"Who's the father then?" Stiles asked. "Anyone you know?"

"I don't have a clue. I didn't think Marie was seeing anybody. She didn't act like she was."

"Why hide it?"

Again, Sean weighed it out. It didn't make a whole lot of sense. Why would she hide it? Did she have to hide it? Had she messed around with someone married or taken or was she just plain secretive?

He fell into the trap of posing too many questions without any answers to fill in the blanks.

Conservative Lyle society would suggest keeping things like this (whatever this could be) quiet and behind closed doors. But Marie had a very hard time of keeping her mouth shut. Why would she suddenly hide something like this? And what about the show? In another six weeks she would be showing some. The pregnancy wouldn't be a secret then, but a matter of simple observation.

It wouldn't have been like Marie to choose silence. It had to be the man she got involved with who had her keep quiet about it. Marie would sing it from the rooftops, unless something serious from the other end prohibited her from spilling about it.

"It's a mess," Stiles muttered. "We keep finding out things about his woman. You know? Just one thing after another."

Sean agreed. "I keep thinking that maybe I don't know any of those people down at the theatre like I thought I did."

"We've run through them all again as far as questioning goes and nothing sticks out."

"The when and the how have been established. But it's the why that's got everyone fooled."

"It's usually the 'why' that leads us to the killer's door." Stiles slid a thin notebook over in front of him, touching the cover lightly with his fingertips. "Everything about this murder says it was done out of hate. The violence at the scene, the methodical way in which it was done, and not a lot behind to go on."

"But the hammer," Sean retorted. "That was the first clue to anything on this."

"I think it's a plant. I think it was put there to lead us to the community theatre. There's plenty of you down there who knew her, so what better place to spin our wheels."

Sean laughed and pulled the hair back on his hair until he thought it would rip out by the roots. "But that's just it. There are a whole lot of us down there who had every reason to want to kill her."

"That's true. I'm only speculating, anyway. And that leads me to this." He slid the notebook over in front of

Sean with his hand still resting on the cover. "Now, you say you and Marie were friends?"

"Acquaintances mainly. She let me stay at her house once when I had to vacate mine for a little while. Why?"

Stiles tapped the cover of the notebook. "Because I don't think you're going to like what's inside."

"What is it?" He put his hand on it, but Stiles wouldn't let it go just yet.

"Most of this stuff on the table is from her things at work. We thought this notebook had some interesting things in it, but I'm unclear on some of it. I'm hoping you can help me with it." He let it go for Sean to peruse through.

The first page of the notebook had Lyle Community Theatre scribbled at the top. Underneath were a list of dates, names, and details that Marie, for some odd reason, found interesting. She had started the notebook almost two years ago. Sean thumbed through it before examining the entries. She had almost filled the thing up. He turned back to the first page and read. Within a couple of minutes, he shut it and rubbed his temples again.

"You know something? I think I could use that cup of coffee," Sean said.

"I thought you might."

There are some people in this world who are very meticulous in recording the things that are done to them. Some can remember a grudge that dates back twenty years and can tell you exactly what the other person did to deserve their hatred. There are others who are unforgiving if they feel wronged by another person and simply shut them out of their lives. And then there are some who literally kept a list of wrongs, interesting run-ins, or important details about other folks that they deemed important to jot down and remember.

Marie fell into the last category.

Page after page of entries were left behind for someone else to find and gape at. And that someone was Sean. He read every single line looking for the hint, the clue. He read grievances against Mike, Darin, Tony, Heather, Sara, Dora, Lynn, and even himself. One that he found intriguing had been a night at rehearsal where he didn't say hello. If the police needed motive, here they found it on every page of her notebook. She kept track of who got cast and speculated as to why. There were lines attributed to those she felt owed her something, including Dora. He found the entry about her loaning money to Dora. The amount listed at over fifteen hundred dollars.

He knew she bugged Dora about being a mooch, but this was beyond that. No wonder Dora had blown up at him last night. Her guilt at owing a dead woman stung. He would track her down and apologize. He had to.

At the end of his second cup of coffee, he finally came to the end of the notebook. He couldn't process all of it. There had been so much. Everything from Sara's dalliance with Tony to Mike's fumbled finances, which she found out from a friend at the bank, to Heather's trouble with her husband had been recorded. Marie even jotted notes to the side. Little comments littered the margins, and most of them none too nice. He had come out fairly unscathed, except for the fact that she had actually done this, but the others were cut to pieces.

"I wish you hadn't shown this to me," Sean said. He pushed it back to Stiles who sat through the reading session waiting for Sean's reaction. "This is ugly."

"Are you surprised?"

"Yes and no. Yes, that Marie was the kind of person who would do something like this, but no because I'm completely hurt and baffled that she actually would."

"It kinda caught me off guard, too. Anything there that screams out at you?"

"The pregnancy isn't there," Sean mused.

"Was it, do you think?"

Sean glanced back at the notebook. In the spiral were pieces of paper left from sheets that had been ripped out of them. "I see what you mean, but we're just guessing."

"That's all we're doing. But let's assume that it was," Stiles mused.

"She didn't want it found."

"Or someone who knew she kept this and found the entry."

Sean shook his head. "Too film noir for me. I don't buy it. She probably needed paper for something at work. The pregnancy isn't there because she didn't want it in there."

"It was too important then?"

"It had to be something she wasn't recording for future use. Look at the margins. She makes snide comments about what everyone was up to. And a lot of it sounds very familiar," Sean observed.

"She bugged everyone about these things?"

"Some of them, sure. Others I didn't know about, or don't care to know about. I apparently wronged her by not saying hello."

Stiles laughed and thumbed through the pages. "Yeah, and you didn't offer to buy her supper one night after a show when she forgot her cash."

"She could get miffed about anything."

Stiles pulled a desk calendar off the table and slid it over to Sean. "The date is marked. That's important."

Sean found the sheet and looked at the "to do" list for Marie's day two weeks ago. She had jotted down a doctor's appointment. He shook his head slowly. This confirmed the theory, maybe.

"Her gyn-o?" he asked.

"Her what?"

Sean laughed. "That's what the girls at the theatre call their gynecologist. It's a running joke down there. They don't like going."

"Oh. And yeah, it is."

"Have you called yet?" Sean asked.

Stiles blushed. Sean knew the look. "I have a female officer going over there this morning."

"I understand. I don't think I could go, either." They both felt uncomfortable at the thought and changed the subject.

"This whole deal is sad," Stiles said. "From every angle. No one gets out of this thing unscathed."

"Unbelievable what we do to each other, isn't it?" Sean asked, not expecting an answer.

"Yes, it is. Some of us are even willing to kill. Those are the ones who scare me."

"I appreciate you trusting me with this," Sean said. He leaned back in his chair and studied the dots on the ceiling. He couldn't shake Marie's handwriting from his mind.

"I knew you could help out with it."

"I didn't."

"You did. It points us right back to the theatre."

"I thought you said that we were just a red herring?"

Stiles grinned and stood up from his chair. He walked over to the window and pulled the shades up to let in the light. "I'm just throwing things around to see where they land. That discarded hammer seems so convenient somehow."

"This is a first time killer then. He hits Marie and she falls, bleeding on him and on the floor. He's close enough that he has to grab her as she falls back. He drops the hammer or kicks it out under the work table. He stuffs her into the front seat and has to hold her in place while he starts the car. He shuts the door, runs out, remembers the hammer, but panics and runs."

"Sounds good, but is that what happened?" Stiles countered.

Sean pulled his hair again. "I've seen too many late, late movies is what's happened."

"I appreciate you coming down here. Are you off work today?"

"I am." The reminder of being off made him think of Titan. His grim expression spoke volumes.

"What is it?"

Sean didn't want to tell him about last night, but he could hear Ric's voice in his head telling him to. He knew that he had to report it. The events of the past week were all tied back to Marie's death. He spilled the details to Stiles, who stood soaking them up.

"Why didn't you call last night?" he asked when Sean finished.

"I had other things on my mind."

"And this morning?"

"Same thing," Sean mumbled.

"Has anything else been going on?"

Sean grinned innocently, but knew it wouldn't throw the detective off.

"What?" Stiles asked.

So Sean told him about the night at the theatre and the figure looming in the dark. He mentioned the lights going out and checking the box the following day.

"You needed to report that, Sean," Stiles said, chiding him. "It's important to the police that you do."

"I just did," he said, trying to make a joke.

"Someone at the theatre?"

"I just don't know. Not yet, anyway. No one's been acting strange down there. Well, not any more than usual."

"A burglar?"

"Again, I just don't know. My gut tells me no."

"Mine, too."

"You have that look that tells me I should back off some," Sean said.

"Is it that obvious?"

"It is."

Sean's cell phone rang an odd melodic tune. He flipped it open and answered with dread. He heard the vet's voice on the other end speak from some world very far away.

"But I thought..." Sean said, letting the thought trail off.

He listened intently to every word, but didn't hear a thing. Fragments of info about swelling of the brain and other explanations didn't compute. Stiles backed away from the window and eased over to door just in case he needed to give Sean some privacy.

He hung up the phone and returned it back to his pocket.

The killer knew I was close...

The random event explanation would make it go away so much quicker, he thought. But this is another act of premeditated mayhem and murder. He had learned so much in the past few days, but which thread had he pulled that had unraveled the killer? To kill his dog had been a desperate act of a dangerous person. Stay out of this had been the message.

"Was that your vet?" Stiles asked.

"Yeah, my dog didn't make it."

"Sorry to hear that."

"Yeah. Me, too." It sounded empty and he knew it, but he couldn't muster much else. The news had come out of nowhere, so unexpected.

"And now let's file that report about it," Stiles offered.

"Sure."

"We'll find him."

Not if I get him first.

Chapter Eighteen

Sean drove around aimlessly, not knowing where to go or what to do. He kept telling himself that he had just lost a dog—not a friend or a family member. It didn't do any good, though. He had invested too much time, energy, and love into Titan to not be devastated. He had the urge to flip his phone open and call someone and tell them in order to get some sympathy or a shoulder to cry on. He thought of Sara, but they were still not speaking to each other. And, of course, Dora would be out of the question. The thought of phoning Tony faded before he could even give it serious consideration.

The breeze rushed through his hair as he hit the highway outside of town. He craved the open road. He knew his bug wouldn't go as fast as he wanted, but it would do. After a half hour he returned to town and turned into the drive-in off of Main. He ordered tots and burgers, hoping the grease would clog every artery he had. The woman who brought him his food sensed his mood and quickly got away from him. He ate in silence, just praying for something else to go wrong.

He filled the next two hours wandering around town running errands or doing mindless things like shopping at the music store and getting a couple of paper backs from the Book Trader. Nothing helped.

As he drove through town, he found himself on Constance Street. He had gone to the theatre so many times it had become second nature to him. Parked in the lot were Mike and Darin's cars. He pulled in and slid into a spot behind Mike's small Toyota.

"Hey, what's up?" Darin asked. "What are you doing down here?"

"What about you?" he shot back, not meaning to sound ugly, but doing it nevertheless.

"What's up with you?"

"My dog just died."

"Which one, man?"

"Titan."

Darin put his arm around him. "I'm sorry, man. What happened?"

"I don't want to talk about it right now. What are you up to?"

"First thing's first, okay?" Darin said. "I'm sorry about last night."

"Not as sorry as I am," Sean answered back, but he didn't know if he meant leaving rehearsal or Titan getting hit.

"There's no other Willy Loman. I was upset about everything that's been going on."

"So am I. We all are," Sean muttered.

"Come on."

"Fine. I need a break from just driving around."

Darin led him through the lobby to the stage. "I'm working on the set. I have to hang a couple of lights above center stage. There are a couple of specials I want to set to shine on you at certain parts of the show."

Mike came out of the office and said hello. Sean mumbled something under his breath, not feeling the need to speak to Mike. Darin and Sean walked through the auditorium studying the lights shining on the stage. Mike followed in earnest.

"I've spoken to Lynn about the budget for this show," Mike said. "I'm sure he's mentioned it to you."

"He has," Sean answered for Darin. "That seems pretty strange with all the money we took in on the musical, Mike."

Mike chuckled in a patronizing way and slapped Sean on the back. "We have bills, you know, Sean."

Sean didn't need this and Darin sensed it.

"Hey, Sean, go up in the booth and get ready to hit a couple of cues. If you've got the time," Darin suggested, but it was little use. Sean came prepared for combat.

"I know, Mike. Boy, do we have bills," Sean said. He knew he sounded vicious, but he couldn't stop himself. He needed to blow and Mike would do just fine.

"The heating was very high a couple of months back," Mike said.

"Yeah. And that phone bill of ours. Wow," Sean shot back.

Mike stepped back to get a better look at Sean's face. He tried reading it, but Sean stood there stone-faced. "The phone isn't that much."

"It has been in the past. Why I think we had one some time back that was three hundred dollars."

"Say what?" Darin said, not believing a word of it. "How is that even possible?"

"What are you talking about?" Mike asked, suddenly very nervous and looking for a way out of there. "You're out of your mind."

Sean pointed at his chest. "You know exactly what I'm talking about. You have the audacity to ban Tony for his diary, but what you did, or allowed, is a lot worse. And the board is going to hear about it."

"I have no idea…"

"Yes, you do, Mike. You do. And the longer you lie about it, the worse it's going to be. I'll see to that."

"We had a phone bill that was three hundred bucks?" Darin asked.

"Talk to Mike here," Sean said. "He's the bright boy."

"I have no idea..." Mike repeated. "Really, Sean..."

"Yes, you do. And there's also some funny purchases on the credit card. A few restaurants and specialty shops out of town, as I recall."

"How dare you!" Mike yelled.

"Deny it, Mike. I can guarantee that the board is going to hear about it and we'll see if you'll even be allowed in the building!"

"Hey, now," Darin said, trying to intervene.

"Deny it," Sean said. "Go on. And, oh by the by, I also have proof that you're our phantom critic. And isn't that funny since your shows get the best reviews. I wonder how that happened?"

Mike yelled something unintelligible and threw a punch at Sean. Darin tried to step in between them, but got thrown out of the way. He landed in one of the seats and had the breath knocked out of him. Mike uppercut Sean under the chin, but fell down in the aisle when he did. Sean had a perfect opportunity to kick him in the gut and get some of his back, but he refused. He would never hit another person back, no matter the offense.

"Your days are numbered here, Mike," he said quietly. "The double standards that you set in place around here are over. You have things to answer for and you might as well get ready."

Tears streamed down Mike's face as he tried to say something in response, but no words came out of his mouth.

Sean lifted Darin out of the seat and dusted his back off.

"I'm getting out of here," he told Darin as he got him on his feet. "As far away from you hypocrites as humanly possible."

"That might be a good idea," Darin sputtered.

He walked back to the lobby and turned around to see Mike storming out of the back exit.

The pain returned to his temples with a fury. He waved goodbye to Darin and left the premises.

The pretty day of sunshine and cool breezes didn't help his temper any. The thought of forgiveness crept up and he tried to accept it. He knew that Mike had been a convenient target for his wrath. He displaced all of his fear and frustration on someone undeserving of it. Although he had Mike on the credit card and reviews, he didn't have the right to taunt and threaten him. It had been a foolish gesture of bravado, which would only hurt his reputation. He had always tried to be the peacemaker in the group and for one solitary moment he'd turned his back on it and lashed out.

The drive out to the vet's place seemed an eternity. He parked beside a truck and trailer full of cattle ready to be ear tagged, given shots, and others castrated. The doctor looked busy and there really wasn't much he could do. But he had to come out and see Titan one final time.

He entered the office area and the secretary apparently had been expecting him. She looped an arm through his and led him back to a room in the rear of the building.

"I'm sorry, Sean," she said and left him alone. "That Titan was a good one."

Fearing he couldn't do this, he stood outside the door and waited for the nerves to pass. They didn't and he wouldn't expect them to leave any time soon. He gripped the doorknob until his knuckles turned white.

It's just a dog.

He heard some tiny voice say it from the back of his mind, but he just couldn't accept it. Titan had been much more. If he'd been run over or gotten sick, that would have been one thing, but to have been struck down intentionally, that hurt. And the sick feeling came from the fact that he felt responsible for it all. He had stepped into an open murder investigation out of a sense of doing the right thing, or whatever he used in his heart to justify his actions. It didn't matter. Not now, anyway. It couldn't be taken back and on the other side of the door lay his deceased dog.

He turned the knob carefully, slowly and entered the room.

Chapter Nineteen

"Would you meet me in the park?" the voice pleaded from the other end of his cell phone. "Please?"

"I can. Sure."

"The usual spot?"

"That's fine. When?"

"Twenty minutes?"

"That's good. I'll be there." Sean rang off and turned off on a side street to take him toward the park. Sara sounded desperate on the other end and he couldn't refuse a friend. Their last meeting had been a disaster, so he hoped for the best. What did she have to talk about that she couldn't just tell him over the phone?

The killer knows you're getting close.

The thought sent a chill through him. Meet her at the usual spot? Could that some foreboding warning of horrible things to come? He shook the thought from his mind. No. He wouldn't suspect her of wanting to harm him in a public place in broad daylight.

Could she be capable of killing Titan?

More importantly, could Sara have killed Marie?

In his searching and digging he hadn't seriously considered her except as a source of information and dirt about everyone else in the theatre directly connected to Marie. But why exclude her? Just because she was his friend didn't mean anything.

Did it?

He parked the bug and killed it. He stepped out into the brightening sunshine and let the warmth of it spread over his face. The pain in his skull had dissipated some, directly linked to him calming down and a couple of aspirin. He saw her car approach and caught himself tensing.

"Hey," he said, raising a hand in greeting.

She approached cautiously with arms folded across her chest. Leaning against the hood of his car, she reached out for his hand. He took it and they stood there for quite some time before either one said anything.

"I heard about Titan," she said, shattering the heavy silence between them.

"How?"

She squeezed his hand. "Detective Stiles just got through questioning me down at the restaurant. It was the last thing that he asked me about. I think he was trying to catch me off guard."

"Did he?"

She squeezed his hand again. "Yes, he did. I wish you would've called me, Sean."

"I didn't think we were on speaking terms."

She smiled wearily but slung an arm over his shoulder. "That doesn't mean that you still aren't one of the best friends that I've ever had. Come on, Sean, this is me you're talking to. Okay?"

He smiled sheepishly, not able to handle the compliment. "You're just saying that, Sara. You were upset with me the other day. I mean, livid. And I don't blame you."

"Now I'm not. And I'm sorry about Titan. I know how much he meant to you." She wrapped her arms around his neck in a great bear hug. He had needed some kind of affection from someone since hearing the news. He was glad it was Sara.

"Did Stiles tell you how Titan was killed?" Sean asked.

"He did." She pulled back from him, but held his hand in a death grip. "Come on, let's go for one of our walks."

"Sounds great."

They took off down a narrow path that wound through the woodier part of the park. The seclusion appealed to them when they came down for their walks. It gave them privacy to talk and to share ideas.

"I suppose I should apologize for the other day," he said, being careful not to tread too closely to her feelings like he had the other day. "In fact, I am. I'm sorry."

"I want to say that you had every right, but I'd be lying," she said. "I know what you're trying to do. It's just making everyone nervous, that's all."

A group of squirrels were rummaging at the base of an oak tree. Sara stopped and watched them scurry and scratch in the dirt. She squatted down to get a closer look. One of the squirrels pounced on some scrap the other wanted and they both zipped up the side of a tree.

"The problem with Titan," Sean said, airing his thoughts out loud, "is that I must've stumbled onto something that has our murderer scared. That's the only explanation. That's the only thing that makes sense. If I wasn't close to the truth, why bother trying to scare me off?"

"Then let Stiles handle it."

"I have been, Sara. I've only been asking a few questions."

"And what about the other night with someone in the theatre with you in there by yourself? What about that?"

He sighed, grabbed her by the arm, and led her off down the path again. The squirrels shot in all directions with cheeks bulging from their foraging.

"Stiles has a big mouth."

"He's worried about you. He's afraid you're going to wind up dead, too."

The thought hadn't been considered in his wild imagination as of yet. Sara mentioning it brought a cold reality to him and he didn't like. He had been warned with Titan, but if he continued, what then? The prospects made him shudder.

Sara tapped him gently on the shoulder. "And I'm worried about you, too."

"I hear ya. I do. I just thought I had stumbled onto something. I mean, there's been so much in all of this. So many secrets and so much animosity that I just didn't see before. Why does there have to be so much *drama* in drama?"

They shared a laugh and continued down the path.

"We are around each other so much it's a wonder we can keep anything secret."

"My thoughts exactly."

"Myself included," she said sadly.

"Look, I'm really sorry. I am. I had no idea about your situation. But Marie knowing was a terrible mistake."

"Tell me about it."

"She made it a practice to get the dirt on everyone down at the theatre," he said.

"But none of us knew too much about her private life."

"She was good at keeping that a secret."

"Very much so."

They walked into a grove of pine trees that towered into the sky above, blotting out the sun. The shade chilled them both as they trudged through the opening in the forest. *What a perfect place to get rid of someone*, Sean thought morbidly. He shot a glance over his shoulder, not out of anticipation, but out of stone cold fear.

He grabbed Sara by the elbow making her stop. He shushed her with a finger to his lips and listened.

"You weren't followed here, were you?" he whispered.

She strained to hear something in the woods, but didn't. "You're getting antsy."

"With good reason."

"Come on, you, quit imagining things."

She pulled him back onto the path and they continued on through the park. He hadn't really heard anything. He didn't think so, anyway.

"This whole thing is one big nightmare," he said. "The night in the theatre with someone standing in the shadows was just the beginning. I'm finding myself looking over my shoulder everywhere I go."

"You had to get involved, Sean."

"Yes, I did, Sara."

"You can't swoop in and save everyone, you know?"

He nodded in agreement. "I'm beginning to see that."

"If only." She slapped the top his hand with hers. "You and your sense of justice. You try so hard to be that knight on the steed."

"Is that such a bad thing?"

"I've got news for you, sweetie, not everyone wants saving," she surmised.

They veered off the pathway into the light and the edge of the small lake that had been constructed to be the centerpiece of the Lyle Park. She grabbed a handful of rocks and tossed them into the water, watching them skip along the surface of the water. He grabbed a stick and flung it as far as he could and watched it splash and float aimlessly.

"Did Marie ever talk about who she was seeing?" Sean asked. "Ever mention it at all?"

"I kinda figured you'd eventually ask that."

"Why do you say that?"

"Because I've been wondering the same thing."

"What?"

"If it was someone she'd been dating. Somebody she spurned."

Stiles hadn't told her.

If he had, she would've mentioned it. He decided to keep the pregnancy a secret for the time being.

"Did she spurn a lot of guys?" Sean asked.

"She claimed she got around." She grabbed another handful and started the routine of humming them along the water's surface. The ripples blipped in and out of existence as the rocks hit. "But I usually thought those were just stories. You know Marie." She caught herself and frowned. "*Knew* Marie."

"She never said anything around me."

"No, just around the girls."

"You and Heather then?"

"Yeah. She talked like a man when she bragged about who all she was seeing," she said. "It was dirty, and that's saying something."

He laughed at her remark. "What's that supposed to mean?"

His laughter didn't faze her. "She got around and liked everyone to know it. I saw her with a lot of different guys down at MoMo's. Guys from work, mostly."

"She was a one-night stand kind of person then?"

"I don't really know. I don't think so. She liked the dinner dates and going out, but she also liked the other, too. She liked the idea of falling in love. But once she did, she was ready to get out. That was her way with men."

"Anyone at the theatre?" he asked.

She turned away to scrounge for more rocks. He could detect her reticence and waited. She threw a rock in a high arc and watched it fall near a flock of ducks in the water. They laughed at the squawking and flapping, but Sean wouldn't let it go. Sara knew it, too.

"Well?"

"You're asking the wrong person. Ask Heather."

"I'm asking you."

"I thought you'd know."

He stared at her. "I have no inkling. What are you talking about?"

"The last cast party thing got pretty crazy." She threw another rock, this time far away from the ducks. "Almost juvenile."

"Not the musical, right?"

"Right. The Simon play a few months ago."

"I missed that one. I had to get up early the next day for a convention I had to go to, as I recall."

Another rock spun from her fingers and plopped into the water. "There were all sorts of pacts and promises made to keep our mouths shut," she disclosed as if she wasn't supposed to.

"Since when does that work with this outfit?"

"Since it was your buddy Tony."

"Say what?"

"You heard me."

"How is that even remotely possible?" he asked.

She grinned and cocked an eyebrow. "They were shooting tequila like they were still in college. That's how. Made idiots out of both of them."

She watched as he sat down at the edge of the water and threw in the rest of his rocks. She eased down beside him, watching the shimmer on the water. The news hit hard, just like everything else about this situation. She knew to let him soak it in and wait.

"He never said anything," he said after a time. "Not one thing."

"They both claim nothing happened."

"What does that mean?"

Sara closed her eyes trying to envision the whole thing again in her mind. "They had been drinking too much. That was the excuse."

"It always is."

"Yeah. Darin and I tried to get them to slow down, but they were in a race with each other to see who could drink the most. She raced him shot for shot. He was on the verge of getting sick when she challenged him in other ways."

"What other ways?" he asked. He rolled his eyes. He knew exactly what she meant.

"So they went into a back room and were in there for about an hour or so."

"He never said anything to me," Sean whispered. *More and more secrets*, he thought viciously. He couldn't escape them.

"They came out later. Both of them looking very upset about something. We tried teasing them, but neither one would have it. They swore nothing happened and we all dropped it and promised not to bring it up again."

"Which I find hard to believe."

"You weren't there. You would've thought someone had died in that room. I don't know what happened with them, but whatever it was, wasn't any good at all, Sean."

"I'm afraid to ask him about it."

"Are you really?" she asked.

"I probably shouldn't say anything to him about it."

She sighed. "But you will, won't you?"

He faced her forcing a grin. "I'm sure I will."

"You're convinced that one of us did it, aren't you?"

"The more I find out, the more I am, yeah. Everyone there had a run-in with Marie. Some were no big deal. Others were catastrophic. She held things over people's heads. She manipulated and used. She threatened and cajoled. I don't think any of us really knew her at all."

"Or, maybe that was just Marie. Have you ever thought of that? Some people thrive on other's misery. They can't live without it," she observed.

Sara checked her watch. She had to get back and grabbed Sean to his feet. He followed her along the foot path on the edge of the lake. She found the main path back through the park's wooded area and took off back toward where their vehicles were parked.

Sara unlocked her door and swung it open. "I want you to know that I'm really sorry for what happened the other day."

"I am, too."

"Marie hurt me really bad. I'm not going to sit here and deny it. But Sean, I would never have killed her. Never. I hope you believe me about that."

"I do. I really do, Sara. But what about Darin? He protects you and cares a lot about you."

She rolled her eyes. "If only that were true, Sean. If only. He's like every other guy I've ever gone out with. Don't kid yourself. When it comes right down to it, he wants what every other guy has wanted from me."

"But…"

"We seem so happy? Well, yeah, I guess on some level we are. But if I ever find that guy out there who wants me for just me, I'll stake my claim and never let him go."

"Would he be capable of something like this?" he asked.

"You talked to him. What do you think?"

He shook his head. "I just don't know. I wish I did. We're all so hard to read."

"We're a bunch of actors. Some of us are pretty good at hiding things."

He thought of Tony again. "Yeah."

She glanced at her watch. "I've got to get back. We're expecting a birthday party for Charlene Haslow's boy."

"Oh, yeah? They go to my church."

"That's right. Well, them and half their family are going to be there for this party. We're going to be busy," she said.

He pulled the door wide for her as she slid into her seat. "Let me ask you something, Sara."

"Go ahead. What?"

"Could you see anyone of us capable of doing this?"

She thought about it carefully before she answered. "I do. Yeah."

"One more thing."

"What is it?"

"Do you think it's one of us? Capable is one thing, but do you really believe that the killer is down there with us at the theatre."

"Yes, I do, Sean. And it scares me half to death."

Chapter Twenty

When he pulled up into his driveway and saw who was on the porch, he nearly swerved off the street and hit the tree in his front yard. He got it back under control and parked the Volkswagen waiting for his courage to return to him. It didn't so he got out of the car anyway. He walked slowly to the front porch with the keys dangling from his index finger. Each step he took made a jingling sound.

"Hi," he said.

Dora sat very still on the porch step. She didn't say anything for a long time. She had her arms wrapped around her chest. Sean couldn't think of what else to say past hello. He stood there dumbfounded with his next move.

"I took off work to come over here," she volunteered.

"I see that."

"I heard about Titan. I'm so sorry."

"Thanks. Who called you? Sara?"

"Yeah. She thought I'd want to know."

"Why's that?"

She looked up at him like that was the dumbest question she'd ever heard in her life. She opened her mouth to tell him so, but thought better of it.

He sat next to her, still waiting for her to address last night. She didn't. He wondered at her ability to just sit without saying a word about much of anything at all.

"Look," he said, knowing he had to broach the subject, "I know about what Marie did for you. Don't ask me how. Not yet, anyway. I just know. I know how much, too."

She opened her mouth again to let the words blast him, but again, she thought better of it.

"I'm not judging, or condemning," he said. "I know and that's all there is to it. If I thought you were capable of killing her, I wouldn't be sitting here beside you." He wanted that last bit to be true. He hoped he'd at least made it sound sincere. In his heart of hearts, he just couldn't imagine Dora grabbing a hammer and smashing Marie in the skull.

And he knew she couldn't have hit Titan. She had been in the house with him when it probably occurred.

"I just thought we were at the beginning of something," she said. She had been so quiet that Sean had to lean over to hear her. "At the very start of..."

"We were. Are."

She ignored him. "I don't like being reminded that I had to mooch off of people, Sean. It hurts my feelings. I'm embarrassed by it. And I was really embarrassed to have you know about it."

"Don't be."

"I was. Still am. I can't help it."

"Don't worry about it."

"I want to say I'm sorry."

"Don't do that, either. I'm the one who should apologize. And I do. I'm sorry. I didn't want you to think that I was accusing you. I wasn't."

"You won't let me be embarrassed. You won't let me apologize. What will you let me do about this?"

"Not a thing."

"Not good enough," she teased.

"Oh, okay."

She leaned her head on his shoulder. "At least let me cook for you before rehearsal. I can at least do that."

"That you can do."

"How does lasagna sound?"

"Wonderful."

She grabbed her keys from her purse. "I'll go to the store and I'll be right back."

He grabbed her before she left the porch. "I think I have all the stuff inside."

She frowned at him and he knew he brought the issue back up without meaning to. "I'm going to store, Sean, and I'm going to buy everything we need. Got it?"

"I got it," he said with a wisp of grin. She stepped off the porch and he pulled her back again.

"What?" she asked.

"Just this." He kissed her softly on the mouth. She pushed back, putting her head on his cheek. He goosed her and made her jump.

"Hey, no fair."

"It never is."

He grabbed her close to him. He caressed her face and kissed her again.

"I'll be right back," she whispered.

"Good."

While the lasagna baked in the oven, they chatted about anything but the affair at the theatre. Dora talked about work incessantly and all of the new responsibilities that she'd been given as of late. Sean took it all in, enjoying the chance to discuss nothing of great importance. Sometimes you just had to do that, especially when so many dark chasms surrounded you on every side.

Dora flirted and flitted around the place like she practically owned it. The kiss on the porch had done something to both of them. It hadn't been just any kiss. It had the passion that meant something deeper and more meaningful had sprung to life in both of them. It meant more to them than just some casual dating experience. He admired the way she moved about and her determination to cook a good meal. The only female that he'd been used to in the house was Weejo and that didn't much count.

And what if Marie hadn't been killed? Would he still have found his way into her heart? That day outside of MoMo's on the day of funeral might never have happened. He didn't care about fate enough to contemplate it, so he turned his attention back to her. Her movements in and around the kitchen were lithe and light. Everything she did at that moment appealed to him in some way.

The meal she set before them steamed and filled the dining room with wafts of tomato sauce and hints of spices. They dove into it without the need for conversation. The silence between them spoke more than any words could. He savored every bite and thanked God for the very act of forgiveness.

But someone out there couldn't...

He tried to shake it out of his head, but failed. He couldn't help himself but come back to Marie. His work had been put on hold because of it. He had risked losing friendships over it. And now every waking moment of his day continued to turn back to Marie.

The killer walked up behind her and struck her on the back of the head.

The images rolled onto the movie screen in his brain. He saw Marie sashay into the garage with her killer right behind her holding the hammer tightly. The blow struck hard and deep enough for blood to spot onto the concrete floor of the garage as the killer set Marie down to open the door.

"Wait just a minute," he muttered, setting his fork down on his plate. "Wait just a solitary minute."

"What is it?" Dora asked, fearing another confrontation. "What's wrong with the lasagna?"

He snapped back to reality. He kissed her quickly on the cheek. "Not a thing. It's perfect. Excuse me a minute, will you? I need to make a phone call."

Dora watched him leave the dining room and disappear into the back part of the house. Was there something really wrong with the lasagna? She took another bite, tasting it carefully, and knew she'd done her best work with it. What had snatched his attention away?

In his bedroom, Sean speed-dialed Ric. Impatiently, he waited for an answer on the other end. None came. He clicked the line dead and dialed up his cell phone. If Ric had left the office, he would surely have his cell phone with him.

"Your dime," Ric shouted from the other end. "How are you?"

"Question."

"Uh-oh. I know that tone. Stiles called and told me he let you in on everything. And I heard about Titan. I'm sorry."

"Me, too. I just wish…" He let the thought trail off and disappear.

"What?"

"I don't know. Nothing, I guess."

"It's all right to grieve over your dog, man." Ric sensed Sean's reluctance to admit how hard he'd been hit, but he understood. Ric had a St. Bernard that had become a part of his family. He understood too well what Titan had meant.

"I have a question for you."

"Shoot."

"Did Stiles tell you why Marie and her killer went into her garage the night she was killed?"

"Why? What do you mean why? To kill her."

"No, that's just it. Think about it. I think everyone down there has been concentrating on the how so much that the why has been forgotten about."

Ric sighed for dramatic affect. "Look, man, it's called hatred. You and I have already been over it."

"No, you're not listening to me. Why did they go into the garage in the first place? What was the reason for going into the garage?"

A silence filled the other end. "That's right. No signs of struggle in the house."

"And no blood, either. That was in the garage. Why did she and her killer walk into the garage in the first place?"

"Good question," Ric said.

"That's why I'm asking it."

"Have you called Stiles?"

"I wanted to call you first. I figured you'd know something I didn't. Stiles sat on the pregnancy thing. Why wouldn't he on something else?"

"Right." Sean heard Ric mutter something under his breath and squealing tires echoed in the background. "Gotta call you back." And click, he was gone.

"I think I have an idea," a feminine voice said from the doorway.

Sean jumped a half mile. "You scared me half to death." He put the phone down and put a hand on her shoulder. "And it was supposed to be a private phone call."

"Sorry. I was curious. I'm curious and nosey about everything. Is that going to bother you?"

She made it sound so permanent. It sounded nice. "What's your idea?"

She led him back to the dining room and they both sat back down. He funneled in more of the lasagna while she swished a spoonful of sugar into her tea glass.

"If Marie and this person, the person who killed her, were walking back into her garage there would be a couple of possibilities," she began.

"Okay. What are they?"

"She and this person were going out. You know, for a drive or for a donut, or something like that."

"Right. Dippin' Donuts, the all-nighter. I'm with you."

She stopped stirring her tea and tested it. "Or, she had something in the car or garage that belonged to the other person and they came to get it."

"That late at night?" Sean asked. He couldn't believe that someone had come over in the dark of the night for something borrowed.

"Marie was a night person. Stayed up late a lot of the time. There are those kind of people out there, you know." She smiled deviously at him and drank her tea. The syrupy sweetness of it tasted wonderful.

He thought about flicking his breadstick at her, but changed his mind. No sense playing when she was on a roll. "Just because I'm an old fogey."

"You are, but that's what's so cute about you," she purred.

"Okay, I've had the same inkling myself. But what was in Marie's car?"

"We just closed the musical, right?" she asked, leading him to make his own conclusion.

"Right. Struck it right down to the boards."

"Including the costumes."

He rubbed his temples and let that sink in. What had Marie worn during the show? He hadn't been on the costuming crew so he hadn't paid that much attention. And it had been Taffy—Marie—who'd made it even less interesting to everyone else in the cast.

"Do you need a hint?" Dora asked, enjoying being on the other end of knowing things for a change.

"Just a sec," he said. He snapped his fingers and left the table again.

"Now what?" she said as she followed after him.

"Another phone call." He dialed the number and waited for the ring. "Detective Stiles, please." He stood silent with Dora standing next to him with her hand over his shoulder, rubbing the nape of his neck.

Stiles got on the phone and the questions flowed. Yes, there were some articles of clothing in the trunk. No, he hadn't really considered why Marie and her killer would waltz into the garage so late at night. A drive, maybe?

"I don't think so," Sean said. Dora could only hear murmurings on the other end and couldn't wait to know what Sean had found out.

"This is all tying into together, Adam," Sean said. It was the first time he'd called the detective by his first name. "Marie's badgering and berating, her mysterious and recent pregnancy, and now this. The links are there."

Dora moved in to try and hear, but he turned away from her and held up a hand. He mouthed, "just a sec" and listened to the other end.

"I know that," he muttered into the receiver. *Stiles has a lot to say*, Dora thought. From outside the house a motorcycle drove by. Sean perked up and ran to the front door. Dora gaped after him, but followed. She saw him gawking at a small dirt bike at the stop sign by his house. *A neighborhood kid*, she thought, *out for an afternoon ride*. She hoped the parents knew.

"There's also something else," Sean said. He paused, listened to the other, and shook his head as if Stiles were in the room. "Let me call you right back."

He rang off and walked back into the kitchen.

"Hello in there," Dora said. "Anyone home?" He had gone back to rubbing his temples again. She grabbed him by the wrists. "I'm talking to you, Sean. What's up in that head of yours?"

He picked up the phone and put it in her hand. "I want you to make a couple of calls."

"What for?"

"Why else? We're going to catch a killer."

Chapter Twenty-One

"Question," Sean said to a baffled Tony, who he'd cornered back stage at the theatre. Rehearsals had trudged along for a couple of hours. Sean couldn't focus on anything because of what Dora had found out for him. He had to find out a couple of more things before he sprang the trap.

"What is it, man? We're about to go on."

"It's a delicate question."

Tony shrugged and rolled his eyes. "Since when are they not?" He sat on a props table. "But if it has anything to do with Marie, forget it. Lynn and I have been talking and we've decided that you've got to quit playing detective."

"Oh really?"

"Yes, we have. It's bringing everybody down and making rehearsals a pain," Tony said. "At Cordova we weren't allowed to bring in our baggage during rehearsals. That's how we were taught, to be professionals."

"This isn't college, Tony. This is real life."

Tony laughed hatefully. "Very funny."

"And it does have to do with Marie."

Tony hopped off the table and started to walk away. "Forget it."

Sean jerked him back by the scruff of his neck. "This is important."

"It always is. And get your hands off me, man," Tony threatened. "Nobody pushes me around, Sean."

Sean regretted doing it later, but at the time dramatics were called for. He shoved Tony back against the back wall and shoved his nose just inches from his face. "I am not playing with you Tony. Not one iota."

Tony cursed at him, which he knew Sean despised, so he hissed a string of cuss words at him. "Get off me."

"In a minute. One thing. When was the last time you slept with Marie?"

Tony exploded. Any action that took place on the stage stopped immediately. It sounded like someone had been electrocuted. Sean could hear running footsteps approaching from the stage. He didn't have much time.

"Answer the question, Tony."

"I never did! How dare you suggest...!"

Sean cut him off. "The last time, Tony, when was it?"

"I never did! Get your hands off me! You're about to lose a very good friend!"

"Oh, I don't know about that! You had a fling with Marie, didn't you?"

"No!" Tony yelled.

Lynn ran up to them and jerked them apart. "What is going on?"

Tony ignored Lynn and pointed straight at Sean. "I never did. One night things got out of hand. One night, but nothing happened."

Sean opened his mouth to say something, anything, but nothing came out.

"I'm outta here," Tony said and stormed off, disappearing into the scene shop.

"What are you two doing back here? I don't like fooling around back stage," Darin barked. The others had joined the crowd waiting for some kind of explanation.

"What did you do to him?" Lynn asked, fearing the worst.

"I asked him a question, Lynn. That's all." Sean walked off the stage and out into the auditorium.

"Let's take a break," Darin mumbled, but it didn't mean much. Most of the cast had already meandered outside to see if the argument would escalate.

Tony moped at his car, hoping and waiting for someone to come over and give him some sympathy. *He played the hurt friend all the time*, Sean thought. Everyone there was used to his routine, so they ignored it.

Lynn and Heather, hand in hand Sean noticed, came outside, joining the others. Darin and Sara did the same. All heads turned toward Constance Street when they heard a buzzing sound off in the distance. Dora exited the theatre, walked over to Sean, and slid a hand in his back pocket. She anticipated something big happening and she couldn't calm down because of it. Her breath came in short bursts hard and fast with her heartbeat racing a thousand miles an hour.

"What's she doing here?" Lynn asked, seeing Angie zip into the parking lot on her scooter. She found a spot near the front and shut the scooter off. "Hey, sweetie, is there something wrong?"

"Nope. Just came to say hi."

She, Lynn, and Heather chatted away. Sean walked over. Everyone held their breath. The tension from the fight with Tony hadn't dissipated yet. They all wondered what would happen next.

"Do you ever ride this thing?" Sean asked Lynn. He laughed at the suggestion. Angie got off and he tried to get on it, but couldn't. His legs were too gangly and his back arched forward awkwardly.

"I couldn't ride this thing in a million years," Lynn said.

"That's why I like it," Angie teased. She helped him off and put on its kickstand. Dora waved to her and they started chatting away.

"You're going to have to quit bothering everyone, Sean," Lynn said. He knew to be cautious and kind. Sean smiled at him knowingly. For some strange reason he felt calm and very focused.

"Don't you have to get on home, hon?" Heather asked Angie. "Isn't it close to your bed time?"

"We're out of school tomorrow. Mom said I could come down and say hi to everybody."

"Oh. Okay. I just thought you needed to get back," Heather urged.

"Let's get back on stage in two, people," Darin demanded. He wanted to say something to Sean like everyone else had, but couldn't bring himself to do it. He knew it wouldn't do any good anyway.

Mike's car zoomed into the lot. He flung the door open. He had a folder crammed full of papers. He thrust it into Sean's hands.

"There. That's everything. Have fun."

"That's very good of you, Mike."

"Shove it, Sean. I know what you're trying to do to me," Mike said. "You've suddenly decided you're Sam Spade and we all think it's ridiculous."

Sean held the folder close to him. He would have time to look at it later. His run-in with Mike had produced the desired results. Mike's guilty conscience had finally gotten the best of him. Without looking, Sean knew he had the financial records Marie and some of the others had requested for so long. He gazed around the lonely group.

The killer is standing out here right now.

The thought jolted Sean to a steady alertness. He could play all he wanted to with probing and asking questions, but it all came down to the fact that someone here in his midst had killed twice. First Marie and then his dog.

He saw a familiar car easing down the street. He walked back inside quickly, hoping the others would follow. They did and Darin prepared to direct them back into rehearsal again.

Dora led Angie into the lobby and helped her off with her helmet.

"Maybe you ought to go on and get back," Lynn suggested to her.

"Aw, come on, dad, can't I stay and watch some of it?" she whined.

"All right. Come on."

Heather and Dora fell into line behind them and everyone filed back into the auditorium. Tony came in last. He pouted and expected someone to fix it. It had become such a staple of community theatre life that no one paid him any heed. A shadowy figure followed in behind him, but no one paid any attention.

As the cast made its way back onto the stage and into places, Sean suddenly snapped his fingers. He stood in the light that glared on the downstage area. Darin moaned to himself, as did Lynn. They could see that look in Sean's eyes.

"Hey, I just had a question," he said. He put on the cheerfulness thick, not letting on his own trepidation at doing this. "Do we have the costumes all lined out for this thing?"

"We're working on it, Sean. Lynn and Tony are seeing to it," Darin replied. He made it clear in his tone that he was worn out with delay.

"What about the women? Do we have any dresses for them?" Sean asked.

"We'll find some."

"I'm sure we can have them use their own clothes," Lynn added. "It's a little early, don't you think? We have lines to be worried about, Sean."

"I know, I know. But you know me, I can't help but think ahead about every little thing." He walked back upstage and the directors relaxed. Sean snapped his fingers again. "You know what would work?"

"No; what?" Darin asked, dreading the response.

"That cool dress that Marie wore in the party scene of the musical. That would work great for one of the girls," Sean suggested.

"That was Heather's," Lynn said.

"It was?" Sean found Heather sitting in the dark. "Do you still have that dress?"

Heather stood up from her seat and nodded her head. "I've got it somewhere."

"Yeah. You ought to bring it to rehearsal and try it on for everyone. Marie looked great it in it. You would, too. It would work for your part."

"I think the director can determine that, Sean," Darin growled.

Sean held up his hands. "You're right. The thought just hit me, that's all." He walked back upstage, but then he acted like another thought hit him. He played the drama of the moment for all it was worth. "You do still have it, don't you?" he asked.

"Yeah. I'll bring it. It'll work out fine for the part," Heather said, unbothered by his nagging questions.

"You got it back from Marie? I mean…before, you know," he said.

"Yes. I did. I wish you'd quit reminding everyone about it."

"Me, too," Tony grumbled from the wings, but everyone heard him just the same.

Sean stepped into the light shining on the lip of the stage. "The dress, Heather, is still in Marie's car, which just so happens to be in the police impound."

Not a soul moved in the theatre. Heather tilted her head to one side staring at him.

"How do you know that?" she asked.

"I called and asked." He clapped his hands for emphasis. "That's weird that you'd lie about that, isn't it?"

"What are you getting at, Sean? We're on a schedule here," Darin said. He had come down the aisle to stand at Sean's feet.

Lynn put his arm around Heather for support. "Sean. I think you'd better be very careful what you're doing here."

"No, Lynn, you better be very careful. I think, as a matter of fact, that this involves you, too."

"How?"

"You'll see."

Tony and some of the others from the cast meandered back onto the stage watching the drama unfold. They all knew what this meant. And every one held a collective breath to see the end result.

"Marie died for one reason and one reason only," Sean said.

"Do you have to do this now," Darin demanded, still not getting what was taking place in front of him. "This is my rehearsal time for a very important show."

Sean knelt down. "Would you like to know who killed Marie, Darin?"

Darin stood dumbfounded for a minute and then opened his mouth. "More of your wild interfering."

"I wouldn't say that," Sean retorted. "Marie died for protection."

"Say what?" Tony asked, bewildered by Sean's take on the case.

"She had to go to protect something that was in the process of germinating and growing into the beginning of something good, something sweet." He looked down at Heather. "Right?"

She tried to move her mouth, but nothing came out.

"Let's try and take a look at this," he said. He saw the shadowy figure move further into the auditorium. He felt confident with his presence lurking there in the dark. "Let's look at it as someone who had something to protect. It makes sense when you look at it that way. Run through the facts: no signs of struggle in the house, a spot of blood in the garage, Marie asphyxiated, one of our hammers with a bit of Marie's hair and blood left, and a borrowed dress in the trunk."

"So what? We know this already," Tony said. But like everyone else, he couldn't wait to hear Sean's accusations take shape.

"True. But why no signs of struggle? Obvious. Someone she knew. But this person came over in the middle of the night? Conclusion? A very good friend, possibly. They walk out into the garage. Why? I mean why do that? What was in the garage?"

Darin desperately thought of some retort, but his mind muddled through what Sean said. The others tensed up for more. The figure in the dark eased closer to the group. Sean felt the hot light glare down on his forehead and his face began to break out in a misty sweat.

He repeated: "What was in the garage? What could be there that would get both Marie and the killer into her garage? A midnight drive? Could be. But what about a borrowed dress in the trunk of her car?"

"Give me a break!" Heather yelled. Lynn gripped her tighter to him. She ignored him and advanced toward the stage. "I'll have you know I'm going to have a lawyer on you first thing tomorrow morning!"

"For what? Telling the truth? If it weren't the truth Heather, why get so bent out of shape about it?"

She had nothing to say. Sean could feel the heat of her anger waft up to the foot of the stage. "It isn't true!" she screeched. "Not one bit of it!"

"Then just write it off as me babbling like I usually do," he countered. "You had something to protect, Heather. Something very dear to you and you knew it would be taken away."

"What?"

Sean pointed out into the audience. "Lynn."

"That's crazy!"

"It is. You're absolutely right. With that I agree with you."

"Lynn wasn't interested in Marie," she yelled. The cast feared she might throw a fit with how loud her voice got and how red her face burned. They watched, waiting for the blow up just the same.

"He isn't now, Heather. But one little dalliance, right? It only takes one time, doesn't it?"

Lynn sank into a chair. The tears stung like needles of liquid fire as they rolled down his face and onto the floor.

The truth is coming out. Finally.

"I don't know what you're talking about!" Heather cried out.

"You knew she was pregnant," Sean said. The sentence echoed in the hollow hall of the theatre reverberating through everyone in the cast and crew of the play. Sean let the silence build to a crescendo of suffering. He could see Lynn wailing softly in an aisle seat. Darin stood below him trying to think of something to stop the madness. Dora and young Angie watched in anticipation. Sara and Tony had walked to the lip of the stage to Sean's left. Mike had taken a seat behind Lynn, not wanting to miss a thing. They all collectively held a breath of fear and loathing at the possible truth coming out at last.

"I didn't," Heather replied weakly. "I didn't know."

"But you did. Dora made a phone call for me. She called—what do you call him?—your gyno? She uses the same one and knows the receptionist. Marie went in for a regular checkup a few months back and then returned just a few weeks ago. Why would any woman do that? Trouble?"

"Or, if she thought she was pregnant," Sara said, joining his train of thought.

"Or, if she was pregnant," Sean repeated. "And the receptionist remembers another patient coming with her for moral support. You." He pointed at Heather accusingly. She didn't falter.

"I didn't," she said again, but no one believed it this time.

"But you did, Heather. You did. And what's more, you knew the father of the baby. And that would be the end of it for you. You had something of your own. Something worth keeping. And here Marie was taking it away from you just like she'd always done before."

"It isn't true." Hot tears sprang to life and fell in waves down Heather's cheeks.

Sean ignored her comment this time. He looked down on her without pity or forgiveness. He would find justice out of this somehow.

"It isn't," she repeated.

"Why lie about it anymore? Right Lynn?"

Lynn raised his head not knowing what to say.

"Lynn?" Darin asked. "What is going on here?"

"You've got to be kidding me," Tony yelled. "You're joking, right?"

Lynn shook his head sadly, looking for Heather's support, her love, but they weren't there. All eyes in the theatre accused him.

"They had to see each other on the sly, right, Lynn?" Sean asked. He saw Angie bawling into Dora's blouse. He hated it in the worst way, but she had a part to play in this drama.

"It had to be that way," Lynn said. "She wanted it that way."

"Of course she did. Why? Who knows? Marie's way of making sure none of us down here found out. I really don't know." Sean folded his arms and stepped closer toward Heather. "And she asked you to go down to the doctor with her. And she told you the news. And she had to go. Why, Heather? Why? Because you knew Lynn would do the honorable thing?" He would have and Sean knew it.

Heather refused to speak. Her hands had balled up into tiny fists. Darin backed away from her.

"Is all this true, Lynn?" Sara asked. Lynn could only nod his head. No words came. The tears and self-loathing burned too much. He wanted to reach out for his daughter, for anyone, but he couldn't bring himself to do it.

"So the how was really quite easy. Right, Heather? A hammer from the shop here, a blow to the head, but she must've been heavier than you thought or something because you lost the hammer in the shuffle. It got kicked under a work table. But no matter, right? If it was found, the police would sift through the community theatre folks forever because no one liked Marie. And too many suspects is a whole lot better than one. You stuffed her into the car and started it up. You left without a hint of remorse."

"How dare you!" Heather screamed at him.

"Cut the dramatics, Heather."

"I loved her!"

"So much that you killed her?"

"I didn't!" She backed away from the stage and saw the aisle clear to the lobby. The shadowy figure hidden in the dark sensed it and came forward. Detective Stiles blocked the path. She felt trapped. She couldn't leave either way. She sank to her knees.

"Angie?" Sean asked.

Dora helped Angie to her feet. "Yes, Sean?"

"I'm sorry about this, sweetheart, but there wasn't any other way."

"Okay," she replied weakly. She couldn't bring her eyes to look at her father.

"I have to ask about your scooter."

"What about it?"

"Did Heather ever ride it?"

Angie nodded. "She took it out for a spin one day after school at dad's house. She said she had something like it when she was young."

"Could she ride it okay?"

"Yeah. She asked if she could borrow it sometime, just kidding, you know," Angie said.

"What's her scooter got to do with anything?" Tony asked.

"That's how Heather got to Marie's that night. She couldn't risk taking her own car and she had to get out of there to establish an alibi, I'm sure. So she used Angie's scooter. She tried it out to see how it drove and she used it that night. One of the neighbors swears she heard a chainsaw sound off in the distance that night."

"But she would have had to sneak over there in the middle of the night," Darin said.

"That's right. She did. She had to get over there without being seen. She couldn't risk it. What better ride than Angie's scooter?"

"And Marie didn't know?" Sara asked.

"Would she have noticed or even cared?" Sean looked back out into the audience at Angie. "When did Heather ride it, Angie? Before or after Marie's death?"

Angie thought about it for a minute. "Before. A few days before."

Sean clapped his hands again to keep everyone's attention. It was a futile gesture. Everyone there couldn't wait for the next revelation or fact to appear. "So you rode down there on Angie's scooter, got Marie to go get the dress with you following, and then you bashed her on the back of the head with one of our hammers. You stuffed her into the car and left her to die. Problem solved."

"No," Heather said so quietly no one could hear her.

Sean watched as Lynn crossed the aisle and grabbed his daughter. She reluctantly let him. They cried hard into each other's arms with no words being said. Sean knew the scars would be there, but he had to do it this way. It didn't seem right somehow this all being kept secret from everyone—even Lynn's daughter. It had been a moral decision he'd made with Dora fighting him every step of the way. If he was wrong, he would take the blame.

"Marie's pregnancy meant that Heather wouldn't have what she wanted," Sean continued. She and Lynn were just hooking up quietly where most of us didn't know about it. Marie, I'm sure, didn't care. Not until she found out she was pregnant, though. Then she probably cared a lot and bragged to Heather how she'd have to take Lynn back from her. And that was one thing Heather wouldn't let go of."

"She said…" Heather tried to say. Sean waited for some kind of confession, but Heather could hardly breathe.

"And then I started nosing around and found out a lot of things. Marie had something on everyone here.

She knew things about all of us and used it to her advantage. She knew things about Tony and Sara and Darin that made them all bristle up at the slightest mention of it."

"Shut up, Sean," Tony hissed. "I mean it."

Sean raised his hands as a sign of peace. "No one knows. No one. But I did find it out and a lot of other things about all of us. Financial problems in the theatre, for one." All eyes shot toward Mike, who sat arrogantly in his seat. "Sara had been over at Marie's the night she was killed."

"Sean!" Sara screeched.

"It's all right, Sara. Please. Everyone. Listen to me. Marie used what leverage she could against us. On every one of us. She kept a record of every little thing she thought might give her some sort of advantage. She used it when she thought she needed to. But she had the forethought to keep her own life a secret. Thus, none of knew about her and Lynn. Or, even suspected."

"I had no idea," Darin muttered. "Not a clue."

"And because I got close, I had to be punished somehow. I had been followed. I came here searching for records one night and found someone lurking in the theatre. And then my dog got hit on the head just like Marie had. He got his skull crushed and died because I was close to the truth." He paused to catch his breath. He couldn't chase away the picture of Titan running up to him hoping for a chew toy or bone.

"Heather, is this true?" Sara asked.

Heather looked down at the floor, the heavy sobs racking her body.

"Heather?" Tony asked. "Don't tell us this is how it happened?"

She didn't move or acknowledge that anyone talked to her. The pain filled every part of her body. The ache spread like a disease eating away at her heart. She needed Lynn, someone, to reach out for her to hold her, comfort her somehow. Words were useless. Nothing would make any sense. Her raw emotion had consumed her and devoured the morality of her soul. Sean's accusations rang empty in her ears, but stung inside, clawing away at her, gnawing away at her composure and her life.

"So, in the end, three lives were taken for protection," Sean said finishing his trail of logic. "That's one way of looking at it, anyway. Heather had to protect what she had found in Lynn. They kept it quiet, sure, but we all knew what was coming. Marie and her unborn child had to go. She, for some reason, didn't try to kill me, just sent me a warning by following me and killing my dog. And it isn't so sad as it is pathetic."

"Sean," Sara said with a warning. "Please."

"Please what, Sara? I'm telling the truth about all of us up here, aren't I? In some strange way this whole mess is directly linked to all of us. Don't you think?"

"Don't be so melodramatic, Sean," Tony whispered.

The absurdity of it all crashed in on Sean and he knew his clearer senses were fading fast. "We come up here night after night, month after month, year after year to capture something that we can never have anywhere else. We have to have it here in Lyle where no one really cares. We make a mockery of each other and our patrons every time we take the stage. We get involved with each other, we sleep with each other, we kill each other. You all make me sick."

Sean stalked off the stage without a last glance at Heather or anyone else in the cast. Dora knew better than to try and stop him. He stormed out through the auditorium, passing Stiles without any acknowledgment whatsoever. Every word, every person, everything about the place made him ill. As he opened the front door, a last gasp of guilt melted out of him. If he had to do it again, he would do it the same way.

He started his car and revved the engine. He gunned it hard as he got onto Constance Street and as far away as he could go.

"Good riddance."

Chapter Twenty-Two

A week passed without any rehearsals or anyone, except for Dora, going near Sean. Darin got word to him through her that the show would go on and be re-scheduled, but not until things had quieted down at the theatre. Sean could not have cared less. He had made a vow to never walk across its stage again, but it somehow sounded hollow and false. Dora had nursed his bruised soul back with TLC and home-cooking. She also made it to church with him a couple of times, which endeared her to him.

Darin also sent word that the board would look through what Sean had found and do something about Mike. The paper had been contacted and told not to print anymore reviews from a Ms. Hillway. The accusations had deflated Mike's ego and his supporters on the board were appalled at what had been discovered.

Sara dealt with MoMo's business and secretly hoped Sean would come down for one of their heart-to-hearts, but she wouldn't hold her breath. The words he had said about them that night still stung, but she knew they were true.

Tony continued to tell everyone he knew something was wrong about the Heather/Lynn thing, but he couldn't put a finger on it. He waited patiently night after night watching his growing collection of DVDs for the phone call telling him the play was back on again.

Lynn wanted to stop and see Sean on several occasions, but he knew his anger would get the best of him and cause more trouble. He couldn't bring himself to see Heather at the jailhouse. His loneliness and guilt tore at him every day as he stood in front of his classes trying to recollect his lectures, but couldn't. Darin asked him to stay with him a few days to try and get it back together. He did and was.

"It's getting cold, you old grouch," Dora said, breaking the silence that had been the typical atmosphere as of late. "And I slaved all over it, too. Look at me slaving over a hot stove for you," she teased.

"Okay, okay. You nag just like a wife," Sean said. He blushed after saying it and would regret it later.

"I hope that isn't a proposal."

"It isn't."

Not yet, anyway.

He gave thanks and stuffed the food into his mouth. Dora had come over every day after work, cooked for him, and stayed as late as she thought suitable. It had done little good. The funk that had settled over him and the place had taken root deep. She understood his pain and anger, but didn't know it could go on this long.

"This is good stuff, babe," he said.

"Uh-oh, you just called me *babe*, dear. I think you may be softening up on me."

He bent over and kissed her on the mouth. "I can only say I'm sorry so many times."

"It doesn't matter."

"It does."

"You'll get over it."

If only.

The phone rang. He wearily moped over to it and clicked it to life.

"What's up?" Ric said from the other end.

"Not a thing."

"How's life. Still upset?"

"What do you think?"

"Listen, they've got her. The evidence links her. They found a wrench in the trunk of her car that she used on Titan. It's all sewn up. You did a good thing."

"I suppose so," Sean mumbled.

"You did. The show going up?"

Sean laughed into the phone and refused to answer. His call-waiting beeped at him. "Gotta run, man," he told Ric.

"Come for dinner this weekend. Bring Dora."

"Will do." He clicked over to the other line. "Hello."

Darin's voice whispered something about all of them congregating at the theatre to do some serious talking. He groaned, but Dora stood beside him, shaking her head at him. He reluctantly agreed to come down and see what was up.

The anxiety grew as they approached Constance Street. He knew that he could never drive that street again without thinking evil of the place. He might get over it, but he couldn't forget.

When he and Dora arrived, a crowd of them had gathered in front of the building. They stood in a semi-circle waiting for the last of the "gang" to arrive. The tension between them ran thick and deep and no one knew what to say. In a moment of reflection, Sean thought of forgiveness, the kind that they all deserved and needed. He wrapped his arms around Sara and Dora and the rest of them pulled the group into a tiny knot. Lynn, Tony, and Darin gripped onto each other for dear life. No one said anything for a long time.

"The show must go on," Darin mumbled, knowing it was melodramatic, but not caring. "I know it's trite and cliché, but there it is."

"The show *will* go on," Sara added.

"The show will go on," Tony repeated.

Each in turn did the same until it came around to Sean. Why had he come tonight? Did he really think he would find them all forlorn and humble?

Who am I to talk?

Who are any of us to talk?

Heather had taken her hurt and let it turn into something rotten and evil. She had taken another's life in an attempt to save something in this world for herself. Who in life didn't do that?

But who would kill for it?

Heather had.

His search for Marie's killer had brought him to a place so far away from the others at the theatre. They all grappled and tore at one another all the time. And for some odd reason it had kept them together. In their own way they cared for each other very much.

But a killer had walked among them.

The group hug tightened as they waited patiently, hopefully for Sean. Dora kissed him lightly on the cheek. The words of comfort she whispered made it all worthwhile—and always would.

"The show will go on," he said.

THE END

ABOUT THE AUTHOR

 Bret Jones is the Program Director of Theatre at Wichita State University, Wichita, Kansas. He is a novelist, filmmaker, and director. He lives in Goddard, Kansas, with his wife and children.